Visit us at:
www.gateshead.gov.uk/books

Tel: 0191 433 8410

PRIVATE BERLIN

Mattie Engel is one of the rising stars at Private Berlin, and believes she's seen the worst of people in her previous life with the Berlin police force. That is until Chris, her colleague – and until recently, her fiancé – is found dead, brutally murdered in an old slaughterhouse outside the city. The slaughterhouse is filled with bodies. But just as Private begin their investigations, the building explodes, wiping out all evidence of the crimes, and nearly killing Mattie and her team. Mattie soon realises that a masked killer is picking off Chris's childhood friends. Will Mattie become the killer's next victim?

PRIVATE BERLIN

PRIVATE BERLIN

by

James Patterson and Mark Sullivan

Magna Large Print Books
Long Preston, North Yorkshire,
BD23 4ND, England.

British Library Cataloguing in Publication Data.

Patterson, James and Sullivan, Mark
   Private Berlin.

      A catalogue record of this book is
      available from the British Library

      ISBN   978-0-7505-4003-2

First published in Great Britain by Arrow Books in 2013

Published in Large Print 2015 by arrangement with
Random House Group Ltd.

Magna Large Print is an imprint of Library Magna Books Ltd.

Printed and bound in Great Britain by
T.J. (International) Ltd., Cornwall, PL28 8RW

For the thousands who tried to escape over the wall, and the hundreds that died in the attempt.
                                                    –M.S.

Prologue

THE INVISIBLE MAN

One

At ten o'clock on a moonless September evening, Chris Schneider slipped toward a long-abandoned building on the eastern outskirts of Berlin, his mind whirling with dark images and old vows.

Late thirties, and dressed in dark clothes, Schneider drew out a .40 Glock pistol and eased forward, alert to the dry rustle of the thorn bushes and goldenrod and the vines that engulfed the place.

He hesitated, staring at the silhouette of the building, recalling some of the horror that he'd felt coming here for the first time, and realizing that he'd been waiting almost three decades for this moment.

Indeed, for ten years he'd trained his mind and body.

For ten years after that he'd actively sought revenge, but to no avail.

In the past decade, Schneider had come to believe it might never happen, that his past had not only disappeared, it had died, and with it the chance to exact true payback for himself and the others.

But here was his chance to be the avenging angel they'd all believed in.

Schneider heard voices in his mind, all shrieking at him to go forward and put a just ending to their story.

13

At their calling, Schneider felt himself harden inside. They deserved a just ending. He intended to give it to them.

By now he'd reached the steps of the building. The chain hung from the barn doors, which stood ajar. He stared at the darkness, feeling his gut hollow and his knees weaken.

You've waited a lifetime, Schneider told himself. Finish it. Now.

For all of us.

Schneider toed open the door. He stepped inside, smelling traces of stale urine, burnt copper, and something dead.

His mind flashed with the image of a door swinging shut and locking, and for a moment that alone threatened to cripple him completely.

But then Schneider felt righteous vengeance ignite inside him. He pressed the safety lever on the trigger, readying it to fire. He flicked on the flashlight taped to the gun, giving him a soft red beam with which to dissect the place.

Boot prints marred the dust.

Schneider's heart pounded as he followed them. Cement rooms, more like stalls really, stood to either side of the passage. Even though the footprints went straight ahead, he searched the rooms one by one. In the last, he stopped and stared, seeing a horror film playing behind his eyes.

He tore his attention away, but noticed his gun hand was trembling.

The hallway met a second set of barn doors. The lock hung loose in the hasp. The doors were parted a foot, leading into a cavernous space.

He heard fluttering, stepped inside, and aimed

14

his light and pistol into the rafters, seeing pigeons blinking in their roost.

The smell of death was worse here. Schneider swung his light all around, looking for the source. Large rusted bolts jutted from the floor. Girders and trusses overhead supported a track that ran the length of the space.

Corroded hooks hung on chains from the track.

The footprints cut diagonally left, away from the doorway. He followed, aware of those bolts in the floor and not wanting to trip.

Schneider meant to look into the girders again, but was distracted by something scampering ahead of him. He crouched, aiming the gun and light at the noise.

A line of rats scurried toward a gaping hole in the floor on the far side of the room. The boot prints went straight to the hole and disappeared. He heard rats squealing and hissing as he got closer.

To the left of the hole stood a metal tube of a slightly smaller diameter than the hole. Atop it lay a sewer grate. To the right of the hole was a small gas blower, the kind used to get clippings off walkways.

Schneider stepped to the hole and shined the light into a shaft of corrugated steel. Ten feet down, the shaft ended in space. Four feet below that lay a gravel floor.

A female corpse was sprawled on the gravel. Rats were swarming her.

Schneider knew her nonetheless.

He'd been searching for her all over Berlin and Germany, hoping against hope that she was alive.

15

But he was far, far too late.

The desire for vengeance that had been a low flame inside Schneider fueled and exploded through him now. He wanted to shoot at anything that moved. He wanted to scream into the hole and call out her killer to receive his just due.

But then Schneider's colder, rational side took over.

This was bigger than him now, bigger than all of us. It wasn't about revenge anymore. It was about bringing someone heinous into the harsh light, exposing him for what he was and what he had been.

Go outside, he thought. Call the Kripo. Get them involved. Now.

Schneider turned and, sweeping the room behind him with the light, started back toward the hallway. He had taken six or seven steps when he heard what sounded like a very large bird fluttering.

He tried to react, tried to get his gun moving up toward the sound.

But the dark figure was already dropping from his hiding spot in the deep shadows above the rusted overhead track.

Boots struck Schneider's collarbones. He collapsed backward and landed on one of those bolts sticking up from the floor.

The bolt impaled him, broke his spine, and paralyzed him.

The Glock clattered away.

There was so much fiery pain Schneider could not speak, let alone scream. The silhouette of a man appeared above him. The man aimed his

16

flashlight at his own upper body, revealing a black mask that covered his nose, cheeks, and forehead.

The masked man began to speak, and Schneider knew him instantly, as if three decades had passed in a day.

'You thought you were prepared for this, Chris, hmmm?' the masked man asked, amused. He made a clicking noise in his throat. 'You were never prepared for this, no matter what you may have told yourself all those years ago.'

A knife appeared in the masked man's other hand. He squatted by Schneider, and touched the blade to his throat.

'My friends will come quicker if I bleed you,' he said. 'A few hours in their care, and your mask will be gone, Chris. No one would ever recognize you then, not even your own dear, sweet mother, hmmm?'

Two

At a quarter to four the following Sunday morning, Mathilde 'Mattie' Engel wove through the crowd jammed into Tresor, a legendary underground nightclub set inside an old power plant in the hip Kreuzberg district of Berlin.

In her thirties, strong and attractive, Mattie reached a series of industrial passageways that linked the club's two huge dance floors. She yawned and ran her fingers through her short, spiked blond hair as electronic music throbbed

17

and echoed all around her.

Mattie's roving sapphire eyes took in the graffiti-lined walls, the smoky air, and all the hard-core partiers trying to make their Saturday night last until midmorning at least.

A stocky Eurasian man appeared in the hallway ahead of Mattie. He had a tattoo of a spiderweb beneath his left eye.

'The countess still here, Axel?' Mattie asked, loud enough to be heard.

The man with the spiderweb tattoo jerked his head back in the direction he'd come from. 'She's with the Argentine. They're on something stronger than booze, weed, or blow. I'm guessing ecstasy.'

'Just as long as it's not crystal,' Mattie replied. 'I hate tweakers.'

'You're on your own in any case,' Axel warned. 'I can't have your back on a gig like this.'

'Think it will ruin your image as a creature of the night?' Mattie said.

'That too.'

'Private will send you a finder's fee.'

Axel grinned. 'Even better. Thanks, Mattie.'

She nodded. 'Do I have a clean way out of there?'

'Fire exits at both ends of the floor.'

'High ground?'

Axel thought about that. 'I'll make a call. The bar. You'll have to dance.'

Mattie slapped Axel's big palm and moved by him toward the entrance to the dance floor. She got out her cell phone as she walked, flipped it open, and called up a school picture of a brunette

18

teenager. The Countess Sophia von Mühlen of Austria was seventeen. A week ago she ran off with her father's polo instructor, a thirty-three-year-old Argentine scoundrel and fortune hunter named Raul Montenegro.

In exactly four days, the countess would turn eighteen and of age to wed.

Which is what the countess's family was desperately trying to avoid, and why Private Berlin had been hired to track her down and return her to Vienna.

Sophia's mother had died three years before of a drug overdose. Her grandmother, the formidable Sarah von Mühlen, did not want the family name or fortune tarnished by further scandal, especially when Sophia's father, Peter, a prominent politician in the Tyrol, was preparing to run for higher office.

'Spare no expense,' the grandmother had told Mattie. 'Find her.'

Mattie had done just that, tracking the young countess via credit card charges and GPS data from her cell phone to the nightclub. Luckily she'd known Axel, the head of security at Tresor, since her days as a Kripo investigator with the Berlin Kriminalpolizei.

Mattie put away her cell phone and moved onto a dance floor packed with writhing, sweating bodies dancing to a convulsive mix laid down by a DJ named The Mover.

She angled toward the bar, nodding to the bartender, who was snapping shut his cell phone. She climbed up at the waitress's station and began to dance her way down the bar in time with The

Mover's beat and riffs.

The crowd noticed and began to hoot and cry for her. Mattie smiled, playing the drunken chick. But her eyes moved everywhere until she spotted Sophia von Mühlen and her Latin lover on the other side of the room.

The countess's arms hung around Montenegro's neck. She was kissing his chest. His hands were roaming all over her.

Mattie looked beyond them for the fire escape doors.

But then the countess suddenly pushed away from the polo instructor, and wove unsteadily toward the hallway, a lucky break for Mattie, who jumped off the bar and caught up to her in the tunnel where she'd left Axel.

'Sophia?' she said and flashed her badge. 'My name is Mattie Engel. I'm with Private Berlin. I'm here to take you home.'

Sophia laughed scornfully. 'I'm eighteen. I can do what I want.'

'You're not eighteen for another four days,' Mattie shot back in a no-nonsense voice. 'Let's go. And try not to make a scene.'

Sophia smiled. 'I'm good at making scenes. Big ones. The kind that attract reporters.'

'Not on my watch,' Mattie said, grabbing the countess by the back of her elbow, and applying force to pressure points there.

'Owww,' Sophia whined, 'you're hurting me.'

'You'll hurt more if you don't move,' Mattie replied and began hustling the countess down the hallway, heading toward the main entrance to the club.

'Sophia! Hey! What do you do there?'

Mattie glanced over her shoulder to see the polo instructor, whacked on drugs and booze, angry, and storming after them.

Mattie held on to Sophia and flashed her badge at Montenegro. 'Don't make this more difficult than it has to be, Raul. She's going home.'

Montenegro glowered. 'She consents to be with me. She's eighteen.'

'She might have consented to sex. But she's not eighteen.'

The polo instructor's shoulders dropped as if in submission. But then he rushed right at her.

Mattie let go of the countess and raised her hands to defend herself.

Montenegro tried to bat her hands away.

Mattie snatched his right hand and twisted it sharply toward the floor.

Montenegro grunted in pain and went to his knees, shouting, 'Run, Sophia! Run!'

Three

The Countess Von Mühlen was off like a shot.

She dodged by a girl with shocking pink hair, and started accelerating.

Mattie cursed, released Montenegro, and took off after the countess.

But it was almost impossible to keep up with her. Despite the drugs and alcohol in her system, Sophia proved nimble as she twisted and spun

21

her way through the crowd.

'Stop that girl!' Mattie shouted, holding up her badge.

Instead, one wasted guy in his early twenties tried to block Mattie's way. But she slid her right foot behind his leg, popped him in the chest, and sent him sprawling on his back.

Other people started yelling after Mattie just as she spotted Sophia running past Axel, who stood at the doors to the side exit.

The countess disappeared outside.

Somebody grabbed Mattie's jean jacket from behind.

She twisted. It was Montenegro. She let her arms go limp and let the jacket slip off her. Then she kicked the polo player in the shin.

He screamed and fell.

Mattie scrambled after the countess, snapping at Axel, who watched in amusement, 'You could have grabbed her or something.'

'And miss this fun?'

'Stop the crazy lover for me at least!' Mattie shouted over her shoulder.

She ran out onto the street without listening for the bouncer's reply.

The sidewalk was lined with people still waiting to get into the club.

Mattie flashed her badge at them. 'A girl just came out a minute ago. Where'd she go?'

The guy closest to her was sucking on a joint. He shrugged.

The girl behind him said, 'I didn't see her.'

Oh, for Christ's sake, I lost her, Mattie groaned to herself. Damn it! She could just hear Sophia's

22

imperious grandmother ripping her apart for the blunder.

But then Mattie heard a groan and violent retching coming from behind a large Dumpster parked across the street.

'There goes the hundred euros she promised us,' the joint smoker said, sighing.

Mattie flipped him the finger and crossed the street. She looked behind the Dumpster, finding the Countess von Mühlen hunched over, and vomiting everything she'd churned up making her escape.

'C'mon now, Sophia,' Mattie said, helping her to stand after she'd finished and was just panting. 'Let's get you somewhere I can wash you up.'

For a moment the countess seemed not to know where she was, or who Mattie was, but then she started crying, 'Where's Raul?'

'He's going to be lying low for a while,' Mattie said, taking gentler hold of her arm and steering her away from the club toward her car.

'I'll get away,' Sophia vowed. 'I'll find him. We'll be married.'

'When you're eighteen you can do what you want. Until then there is someone who wants to talk some sense into you.'

'My father?' the countess replied with open contempt. 'All he cares about is himself and his career.'

'Actually, it's your grandmother who hired us.'

Mattie saw fear surface in Sophia, who said, 'But I want to see my father.'

'I bet you do, but Oma's calling the shots now.'

Something seemed to go out of the countess

23

right then, all the hostility and fight certainly. She trudged along in a submissive posture until they reached the car, a BMW 335i from the Private Berlin pool.

When Mattie went to open the passenger side door, Sophia fell into her arms, blubbering, 'I just wanted someone for myself. What's so wrong with that?'

Mattie's heart melted. 'Nothing, Sophia, but...'

Mattie's cell phone rang. She couldn't do a thing about it. She held on to the young countess and let her sob her heart out.

Four

Twenty minutes later, Mattie was driving the young countess through the streets of Berlin toward Tegel Airport. She checked her phone at last, seeing that the call had come from Katharina Doruk, her best friend as well as the managing investigator at Private Berlin.

At four in the morning?

She got Katharina's voice mail and left a message: 'Kat, it's Mattie. Don't worry. Got the package. Heading to the jet. Get some sleep.'

When Mattie hung up she heard snoring. Sophia was lights-out, face against the window, drooling from the corner of her mouth. Mattie prayed she wouldn't get sick in the brand-new car. It still had that sweet leather smell.

Fortunately she reached the private air terminal

at Tegel International without another accident. She roused Sophia, who looked around blearily, got out, and followed her as if in a trance.

The pilot was inside, filing his flight plan, and told Mattie to get Sophia aboard the jet.

They were entering the jet's cabin when Mattie's cell phone rang again.

'Mattie Engel,' she answered.

'It's Kat.'

Mattie heard weight in her friend's voice. 'What's wrong?' she asked.

There was a long hesitation before Katharina replied, 'Chris is missing.'

Sophia went to a high-backed leather chair and plopped into it. 'I need a Coke or something,' she said. 'Maybe some rum in it.'

But Mattie ignored her and listened intently to her phone.

'He took personal leave early last week,' Katharina was saying. 'He was supposed to be back the day before yesterday, but he never checked in. He still hasn't. I've tried his cell, the house, e-mail, text. Nothing.'

This wasn't like Chris Schneider at all, Mattie agreed. He was a careful, methodical detective, and a stickler for following the agency's rules and procedures, which included checking in when you were supposed to.

'You try the chip?' Mattie asked at last.

The year before, Private employees around the world had been offered a small locator chip that could be embedded under the skin of the upper back so they could be found in case of emergencies. Mattie had balked at the idea, thinking

25

that if it was misused it could turn totalitarian in nature.

But to her surprise, Schneider had agreed to the procedure.

'That's why I was calling,' Katharina replied before hesitating again. 'I'm lying in bed, couldn't sleep after some voodoo tea my mother made me drink. And I was thinking that you could authorize it.'

'I don't have that authority, Kat,' Mattie said.

'You're the closest to it, Mattie.'

'Not anymore I'm not. Are you ready to report Chris missing to Kripo?'

'I don't know. I'm confused. You know ... he could be off with someone.'

Mattie hesitated, and then sighed. 'I can't control that.'

'I'd hate to send in a rescue team in that sort of situation.'

'I can see your dilemma, but I can't help you. Look, you're going to have to call Jack Morgan to get authorization.'

Morgan owned Private and ran its famous Los Angeles office.

'I put in a call to him an hour ago. He hasn't gotten back to me.'

Mattie chewed on her lip, then said, 'I'm sure he's okay. But if he hasn't checked in by noon, say, or if Jack hasn't called in, we'll activate the chip.'

'Unless you hear from me, I'll be at the office at noon,' Katharina said.

'I'll be there too,' Mattie promised, and hung up.

Outside, thunder boomed and through a port-hole window she saw lightning split the sky. Rain began to drum on the roof of the aircraft. Mattie looked over at Sophia, who was watching her with genuine concern.

'Who's Chris?' Sophia asked softly.

Mattie swallowed at a sick taste seeping into her throat, and then replied, 'Until six weeks ago, countess, he was my fiancé.'

Five

As dawn approaches, I find myself standing in a room with mirrors for walls and ceiling, and a big round bed with red sheets.

I am naked in this room of mirrors, stripped of all disguises save one – the reconstructed face a surgeon in the Ivory Coast gave me twenty-three years ago.

I look at my face, this ultimate mask, and smile because no one would ever know that behind it is me, and because a rare beauty has agreed to join me here in this room of reflection and pleasure.

Except for the snakeskin stiletto heels, the stunning brown woman shutting the door is naked too. She's from Guadeloupe, or so she says. Her name is Genevieve. Or so she says.

Whoever she *really* is, she smiles weakly as I set the canvas bag I carry on the bed.

'I have seen you around before,' she says in an uncertain French accent.

27

I don't even blink. 'Have you now?'

'I think.' She looks at my case and tenses. 'What's in there?'

'Don't worry,' I say. 'It's something rare and beautiful.'

She nods, but there's no conviction in the gesture.

'You seem concerned,' I say.

She rubs her hands together. 'Just nerves. One of my friends here, Ilse? She disappeared last week. You might have seen her. A spinner? German?'

I wave my hand dismissively. 'I don't remember names, my dear. They're artificial. Made up. I mean, do you use your real name here, Genevieve?'

She hesitates, but then shakes her head.

'There you go now,' I say in a teasing, friendly manner. 'It's all a fantasy. You can be whatever person you want to be. Or anything you want to be. I am comfortable with that. Are you?'

Her eyes shift, pause, and then she nods the tiniest of nods.

'Good,' I say, but part of me feels a twinge of anxiety. Did she see me with Ilse? No. That's impossible. I'm certain we were alone at all times.

And so I open the bag, revealing a primitive ivory and black leather mask crafted as a leering monster. The stain and lacquer finish is cracked with time, and burnished in places. But the lips have retained their deep henna color. So have the areas around the slits cut for the wearer's eyes.

'A Chokwe tribesman in the Congo made it a hundred years ago,' I tell Genevieve. 'It's very rare. It cost me a small fortune.'

I put the mask on, hooking the hemp straps that hold it to my face so I can see clearly through the eye slits.

The mask smells of Africa, of moldering wood and nutmeg and roasting peppers. My breath echoes inside the mask, slow and languid, like a leopard contemplating prey.

I gesture for Genevieve to lie down on her back on the bed. She's staring at me, and at my mask, and there's enough fear in her eyes that I feel myself stir and harden.

That, my friends, is just perfect. Her mind is playing games, inventing scenarios far worse than what I have in mind for a late, late-night delight.

Isn't it interesting how that works, that the mere suggestion of threat stirs the darkest regions of the mind?

Sensing her fear, indeed feeding on it, I kneel next to Genevieve, caressing her soft cocoa breasts, and then slide my fingers into her bare mystery, all the time glancing around at the mirrors that surround me, admiring my newest mask from an array of perspectives.

I am not a young man, but I tell you one and all that my manhood stands like a spear when Genevieve begins to writhe under my insistent touch. It's an anxious writhing, and that only fuels me more until it's simply impossible to keep my desires at bay any longer.

Pulling her around and throwing back her legs, I poise to enter her, my hips cocked. The breath of the beast I'm becoming rasps from my throat in sharp, cutting bursts.

Genevieve looks up, clearly frightened by the

monster crouched above her, which only excites me more.

'What is your name, *chéri?*' she asks in a quivering voice. 'What should I call you while we have sex?'

'Me?' I say, and then thrust savagely into her. 'I am the Invisible Man.'

Book One

THE SLAUGHTERHOUSE

Chapter 1

Private Berlin occupied the penthouse suite atop a green glass and exposed-steel Bauhaus-style building on the south side of Potsdamer Platz in Berlin's Mitte district.

Clutching a cup of strong coffee, increasingly worried about her ex-fiancé, and still groggy after less than five hours of sleep, Mattie Engel stepped out of the elevator into the agency's lobby at a little before noon.

Three days late was not like Chris at all, she thought for what seemed the hundredth time.

Unless he went off with someone.

To Greece. Or to Portugal.

Like we did when we first fell in love.

Private Berlin's lobby featured polished steel sculptures that depicted milestones in the history of cryptography. She passed one of an Enigma machine, and another that included the death mask of Blaise de Vigenère, the sixteenth-century French secret code genius, whose blank eyes seemed to follow her as she crossed to a retina scan on a black pedestal next to pneumatic doors made of bulletproof glass.

Before she could look into the scanner, Katharina Doruk appeared on the screen above the doors. Olive-skinned with long, wild ringlets of hair, Katharina was one of the most exotically beautiful women Mattie had ever known. She

33

was also one of the toughest – a second-generation Turkish-German who'd grown up in Wedding, a rugged immigrant neighborhood, and the only daughter among six sons.

Katharina peered through her reading glasses. 'We're in the briefing room.'

'Any word?' Mattie asked.

'No, but we've got a video conference with Jack in five minutes.'

Mattie tried to suppress the anxiety that firmly took root in her after the screen went dark. She pressed her right eye to the scan, seeing a soft blue light pass left to right. The glass doors opened with a hydraulic sigh.

Mattie trudged down a hallway that overlooked a long, linear park where the ground had been shaped into two huge triangles, one facing west and the other east.

Until the fall of the communist German Democratic Republic, or GDR, the park had been an infamous stretch of the Berlin Wall's no-man's-land, a garishly lit, wide, and sandy stretch between the inner and outer cement barriers and the barbed wire and gun towers that had divided the city in two back in 1961.

Ordinarily, Mattie would have paused to look down at the park because, no matter what her mood, it usually made her feel better. The park represented a terrible time in her family's life, and in her city's life.

But it was also a powerful symbol of new beginnings, and she believed in new beginnings. New beginnings were the only way to survive.

That morning, however, Mattie could not get

34

herself to look at the park. Deep in her gut, no matter how much she tried to quash it, she feared that Chris's disappearance hinted at the end of something.

But I wanted us to stop, didn't I? Didn't I?

Before Mattie could drown in those questions she ducked into an amphitheater with rising tiers of desks that faced a curved wall of screens glowing flat blue, waiting for a feed.

Katharina sat at a desk on the highest tier beside a man who looked like an aging hippie, with long silver hair, round wire-rimmed glasses, a scruffy beard, and a Grateful Dead tie-dye sweatshirt.

His name was Ernst Gabriel, Dr. Ernst Gabriel, and he was the smartest person Mattie had ever known, a polymath with five advanced degrees, including an MD, a PhD in computer science, and master's degrees in physics and cultural anthropology.

Gabriel was also a forensics expert and ran Private Berlin's investigative support system. He'd be the one turning on the tracking system and operating it.

Mattie was climbing the stairs toward Gabriel and Katharina when a tall, muscular, bald man in his late thirties appeared behind them. Tom Burkhart was Private Berlin's newest hire. Until recently he'd been a top operator with GSG 9, Germany's elite counterterror unit. He usually ran security details.

Mattie frowned, wondering why Katharina had called him in.

'Hi, Burkhart, Doc,' Mattie said, before kissing Katharina on both cheeks.

She took a seat between Burkhart and Gabriel just as the big screen at the front of the amphitheater blinked and then lit up with the handsome and very tanned face of Jack Morgan, owner and president of Private.

Morgan peered at them and said, 'I just got in. I was sailing over from Catalina and don't have coverage out there. Is he still missing?'

'He is, Jack, going on three days now,' Katharina replied in English. 'I'd like permission to activate his chip.'

Morgan winced slightly. 'The chip? You're sure? I wouldn't want to invade his privacy unnecessarily.' His eyes shifted. 'Mattie? What do you think? Shouldn't this be your call?'

Mattie flushed. 'Jack, uh, I don't know if you heard, but we broke off the engagement.'

Morgan looked greatly surprised. 'I didn't. I'm sorry. When?'

'Six weeks ago,' she said. 'So it's entirely your call, Jack.'

Morgan digested that, and then said, 'Gabriel, have you had a chance to look at his credit card receipts? His cell phone records?'

'I just got in, myself, but I did manage a quick search,' Gabriel replied. 'I've got a steady trail of purchases in and around Berlin and Frankfurt, all on his Private card, until this past Thursday evening. And then nothing. And I've got a long list of phone calls that ended about the same time. Nothing since. I haven't dug into the particulars yet.'

Morgan put his hands in a prayer pose. 'What was he working on?'

Chapter 2

Katharina gave her laptop several commands. Morgan's face shrunk and shifted left on the big screen. A photograph of a soccer player performing a dramatic scissors kick appeared beside him.

'This is Cassiano, the top striker for the Hertha Berlin Sports Club, and the top goal scorer in the German second league,' Katharina said. 'Manchester United hired us to look into him because they are thinking of acquiring him.'

Even though Cassiano had proven himself a prolific scorer, the British team was concerned about the Brazilian's erratic play in a handful of games. They'd wanted him vetted before offering him a contract.

Katharina said, 'But as of two Fridays ago, Chris told me he had just a few loose ends to look into, but he was leaning heavily toward clearing Cassiano.'

'And Chris's other case?' Morgan asked.

Katharina typed on her laptop again. A video clip played showing a man wearing a wide-brimmed hat and dark sunglasses that shielded much of his face. He exited a black Porsche Cayenne and walked away from the camera. A beautiful, elegant woman climbed out the other side and followed him.

'That's Hermann Krüger,' Katharina informed them. 'Billionaire. Early fifties. Big art and car collector. Very secretive. Doesn't like his name in the media. Grew up in the GDR, but took to capitalism quickly after the wall came down. He built a fortune in real estate here in Berlin and big public works projects in Africa.'

Mattie said, 'Didn't we do some work for his company?'

'Two years ago,' Dr. Gabriel confirmed as he reworked the band that held his ponytail. 'A comprehensive review of their security system. But we didn't deal directly with Krüger himself.'

'But Chris was dealing with him?'

'No,' Katharina said. 'Krüger's wife, Agnes, is the client. She believed he was seeing other women and asked us to look into it. As of the last update I got, Chris had located at least three mistresses. He'd also discovered that Krüger visited prostitutes, lots of them, sometimes twice a day.'

Burkhart snorted. 'Twice a day? An older guy like that must be taking testosterone supplements to be able to get it up that often. And Viagra.'

Mattie cringed. She'd had limited interaction with Burkhart since he'd joined Private. But overall she'd found him to be headstrong, crude, and abrasive, perhaps good traits for a counter-terrorism expert and bodyguard but not, in Mattie's opinion, for the kind of delicate investigative work Private Berlin often performed.

'Chris didn't mention testosterone or Viagra,' Katharina sniffed. 'But I know he had an appointment set for tomorrow to update Frau Krüger.'

'How much would Hermann Krüger stand to lose if his philandering went public in a nasty divorce case?' Morgan asked.

38

'A billion,' Gabriel replied. 'Maybe two.'

Private's owner thought about that. 'Why did Chris take time off?'

'I don't know,' Katharina said. 'He texted me last Monday that he needed a few days' personal time and that he would call me on Thursday at the latest. He's such a hardworking guy, I gave him the time without questioning it.'

'Of course,' Morgan said. 'That's it. No other cases?'

'Not that I–'

'Not true,' Gabriel interrupted. 'He was working on something else, Jack.'

Chapter 3

My mother was the first to show me the power of masks.

She was a makeup artist with the German State Opera and Ballet. She was also a traitor to her country, to her husband, and to me.

But those are stories for another time.

The masks.

As a child I lived with my mother and father in a prefabricated apartment building that the state erected in the far eastern reaches of Berlin, out where the city met farms where livestock was raised for milk and slaughter.

I note this, my friends, only because in addition to being a raging alcoholic, my father was a professional butcher.

The day I learned about the power of masks, my father was at work, and the opera house was dark for the season. I must have been about seven and had been sick with chicken pox.

Trying to cheer me up, my mother climbed into the attic and brought down a large trunk. She opened it, and I swore I could smell old people in there – you know, the scent of slow, inevitable decay?

She pulled out a *Papierkrattler* mask, which featured smirking, cartoon features: ruby lips, a gargantuan nose, wild eyes, and a raccoon tail for hair. She said it was last used fifty years before during a parade in Ravensburg, down near the Swiss border.

My mother said that the mask had once belonged to her mother, who had died in the bombing that reduced Berlin and my father to smoking rubble and desperation in the last year of Hitler's war. The mask had somehow survived.

'This mask is a miracle,' my mother told me. 'A miracle.'

She set it aside and brought out another mask, this one black, narrower, and fitted across the bridge of the nose like a criminal's disguise.

'It's from *Don Giovanni*, the opera,' she said as she slipped it on me.

'Who's Don Giovanni?' I asked.

'A bad man who dies badly. That is how an evil person dies. The death of a sinner always reflects their life. Remember that.'

Of course I would later learn that this was complete and utter nonsense.

Death is never a form of retribution.

40

Death is a thing of beauty, something to behold, a moment to celebrate.

But good son that I was, I agreed earnestly. My mother brought out her makeup kit and showed me how to paint my face. She gave me surly lips, sunken eyes, and wicked brows that made me laugh.

After she'd added a wig and glasses, I remember looking in the mirror and thinking I really was someone else, most certainly not me anymore.

'Do you know why they use masks and makeup in the theater?' my mother asked.

I shook my head.

'A mask changes you. So does makeup. With the right mask you can be anyone you want to be. With a mask you can hide in plain sight. You can do what you want, act the way you want. With a mask, it's almost like you're invisible and free to be anyone or anything you desire. Like a prince. Or a tiger.'

I nodded, feeling possibility swelling inside me. 'Or a monster?'

'Even a monster,' my mother said and kissed me on the head.

Chapter 4

A new video appeared on the screens to the right of Jack Morgan's head.

It showed a woman wearing a shabby black dress over black denim jeans. Mattie's initial thought was that at one time she must have been attractive.

But the woman's hair was dry and mussed. Her skin was sallow. And her eyes were sunken and dark. She looked like she'd lived a very, very hard life.

'This is from our lobby camera, early morning, two Fridays ago,' Gabriel told them. 'Here, Chris comes out to meet her.'

Mattie frowned, feeling strange and then hollow when Chris went to the woman and embraced her, pressing his cheek to hers and rubbing her back.

'Who is she?' Mattie managed.

'I don't know,' Gabriel replied, taking off his glasses and rubbing his eyes. 'But I did see her come out of his office about an hour after these images were taken. I also heard him say that he would look into something for her and there would be no charge. They hugged again. She left.'

Morgan said, 'Can you go into Chris's files, find out who she is?'

'With your permission, Jack,' Gabriel replied.

'Granted,' Morgan said.

Gabriel typed again. He paused, seemed puzzled, and typed again. 'That's odd,' he muttered.

'What?' Mattie asked, leaning over to see the scientist's screen.

The old hippie was typing again. 'This should do it.'

But instead of Schneider's digital file folders, Gabriel's screen was filled with bright pink, emerald, and black pixels that seemed to shift and move and crawl over one another, as if they were alive.

'What the hell is that?' Gabriel said, shocked and staring at the screen.

'What's going on, Doc?' Morgan demanded.

Gabriel mumbled in disbelief, 'I think we've been hacked.'

Up on the big screen, Morgan looked perplexed and then angered. 'That's impossible,' he sputtered. 'I just spent millions upgrading the security system. Gabriel, you were part of that effort.'

The computer scientist held up his hands in surrender. 'I was, Jack. But I've never seen anything like this before. It's like someone dumped thousands of termites into Chris's work area. They've eaten all the data...'

Katharina Doruk interrupted, 'I thought you once told me that you can always bring back echoes of files, Doc.'

'Not this time,' he replied. 'Whoever did this was good, Kat. Scary good.'

Morgan looked furious, but said: 'We'll deal

43

with this breach later. Between the hacking and the cases he was working on, I think we've got cause enough to activate Chris's chip. Do it, Doc.'

Mattie nodded her agreement with Morgan's decision, but she felt agitated by questions that suddenly shot at her from all sides.

Who hacked the system? Why? What if it's a coincidence? What if this is separate and Chris is off on a vacation he decided to extend? What if we find him there with another woman? Should I care?

I do.

But should I?

'Give me a minute, Jack,' Gabriel said, entering a command that stripped his screen of the brilliant termites.

He typed in a second command and his screen filled with a long list of names. He scrolled down to Chris Schneider's, and then highlighted a corresponding series of numbers and letters.

After making a copy of that code, Gabriel called up an application called Sky Eye. He entered the code into a blinking box and hit Enter.

Half of the amphitheater's screen jumped to a Google Earth view of Berlin. Mattie was first to spot the blinking orange icon out on the far eastern outskirts of the city, several kilometers south of the neighborhood of...

'Ahrensfelde?' Mattie said, puzzled. 'Can you bring us in, Doc?'

Gabriel was already ahead of her. He highlighted the blinking icon and hit Enter. The picture zoomed down and in, revealing the blurry image of a building in the shape of an L. It had an arched roof that looked broken in places.

Dense vegetation pressed in around the place, which abutted a large undeveloped space choked with trees and brush.

'Cross-reference it with the city plan,' Mattie said.

A moment later, an address popped up on the screen along with a file. Gabriel clicked on the file and it opened, revealing a PDF of the building's handwritten property records.

Blown up on the screen that way, the words Mattie read sent an involuntary shudder through her for reasons she could not fully explain.

'What's it say?' Morgan demanded.

Mattie looked at her boss and replied with a slight tremor in her voice: 'It says the building is abandoned now. Has been for twenty-five years. But back in the communist era, it was a state-run *Schlachthaus*. A slaughterhouse.'

Chapter 5

A few minutes later, Mattie rode in the passenger seat of an agency BMW while Tom Burkhart drove them across the Spree River and then east through the city toward the neighborhood, or *Kiez*, of Ahrensfelde.

Jack Morgan had ordered them out to the slaughterhouse, and demanded that Dr. Gabriel start figuring out how in the hell someone had

45

managed to breach Private's state-of-the-art firewall. Katharina was supposed to go to Chris's apartment to see if his personal computer contained any notes on the cases he was working.

Burkhart said nothing as he drove. Mattie was glad for it. She was in no mood to talk. Apprehension had enveloped her, and she tried to fend off the sense of being trapped by studying the giant television tower with its revolving ball and spire looming high above Berlin, getting closer with every moment.

The communists built the tower in 1965 as a way of showing the West that they were modern enough to accomplish such a feat. At more than three hundred meters high, it was visible from virtually everywhere in Berlin on a sunny day.

But it was gray now. The clouds hung low in the sky. Drizzle had begun to fall on the tower and on the S-Bahn, the elevated train station at Alexanderplatz, a bustling part of the city day and night.

The tower loomed over it all as did the Park Inn Hotel, a communist-era building that had been spruced up. The Park is where Westerners would stay when visiting East Berlin before the wall came down. It was said that there were more electronic bugs in the Park Hotel than anywhere else on earth.

Mattie tried to imagine Chris at eighteen. In her mind, she saw her ex-fiancé standing out there on the plaza between the tower and the Park Hotel, one of half a million protesters gathered in early November 1989.

She saw Chris and the others acting and speak-

46

ing in defiance of the scores of Stasi – the dreaded and oppressive East German secret police – who surrounded Alexanderplatz that night, filming the crowd, trying to intimidate the protesters into disbanding.

During their two-year romance, Chris had told Mattie very little about his childhood and adolescence. She knew that his parents died in an auto accident when he was eight, and that he'd grown up in an orphanage out in the countryside somewhere southeast of Berlin.

But Chris also told her that shortly after the uprising began in earnest, he left the orphanage with some friends and went to Berlin, ending up on Alexanderplatz the night of the largest protest, the one that showed the world how much the East Germans wanted freedom.

Chris said that he'd felt like his life really began that night as the wall began to crack and crumble, falling not five days later.

'I was free for the first time in my life,' Chris said. 'We were all free. Everyone. Do you remember, Mattie? What it felt like?'

Sitting next to Burkhart as they drove east, hearing Chris's words echo in her mind, Mattie did remember.

She saw herself at sixteen on the west side of Checkpoint Charlie, cheering and singing and dancing with her mother when East Berliners broke through the wall there and came freely into the West for the first time in more than twenty-eight years.

Mattie remembered seeing her mother's face when her sister came through the wall that night.

They had all wept for joy.

Then, in Mattie's mind, her mother's teary face blurred and became Chris's the morning he'd asked her to marry him.

She felt a ball in her throat and had to fight not to cry in front of Burkhart.

Mattie's cell phone rang. It was Dr. Gabriel. 'Good news,' he said. 'He's moving. Not much, a couple of meters this way and that, but he's moving.'

'Oh, thank God!' Mattie cried. Then she looked at Burkhart. 'He's alive!'

'Well, all right then,' the counterterrorism expert said, downshifting and accelerating east on Karl-Marx-Allee.

Mattie's mind spun as the prefabricated, Soviet-style architecture that surrounded them became a blur out the window.

Was Chris injured? What was he doing in an old slaughterhouse?

Was I wrong to have ended it? Was I? Do I still love him?

'Don't beat yourself up,' Burkhart said, breaking her from her thoughts.

Mattie looked over at him. 'About what?'

'Ending your engagement with him,' Burkhart said.

'Easier said than done given the circumstances,' Mattie shot back, annoyed that she was evidently so transparent.

'You break it off?' Burkhart pressed. 'Or did he?'

'That's none of your business,' she said hotly.

'I take it you did, then. Mind telling me why?'

'I do mind. Just get me there, okay?'

Burkhart shrugged. 'Helps to talk about stuff with an impartial observer.'

'Not always,' she said, and turned to look out the window again.

Chapter 6

The skies had taken on a coal and ash color by the time they reached that wooded area they'd seen on the satellite imagery. They circled the woods, seeing only bike trails before finding the vine-choked drive that led to the old slaughterhouse.

The rain was squalling now, blown by gusts from the east.

Burkhart parked just as Mattie's cell phone rang. It was Katharina.

'We're just getting here, Kat,' Mattie said.

'The super at Chris's building won't let me in,' she complained. 'He says he'll let you in but not me.'

'I don't think it's going to be necessary,' Mattie replied. 'Gabriel said he's moving around inside.'

'Oh,' Katharina said, sighing. 'Oh, thank God, Mattie.'

'I'll let you know when we've got him,' Mattie said, and hung up.

She tugged up her hood and got out, heading straight into the vines, which she pushed and hacked through until she'd reached a clearing of sorts.

49

The walls of the slaughterhouse were cement block and rose to a line of blown-out windows below the eaves of an arched roof. The place was covered in old graffiti, including a skull stamped with a dripping bloodred X.

Mattie felt unnerved, which was completely unlike her. She'd been a full-fledged Kripo investigator for the Berlin criminal police for ten years, five of them in homicide, and had another two years working high-profile cases for Private.

She'd seen the worst one man could do to another, and Mattie always handled these incidents like the professional she was.

But now, seeing that graffiti, she felt like ignoring years of training and yelling out to him.

Out of the corner of her eye, she caught Burkhart drawing his Glock. She drew her own pistol, whispering, 'Bluetooth. I'm going to call Doc.'

Burkhart fished in his pocket and came up with an earpiece. Then he donned latex gloves. Mattie did the same. The wind gusted, amplifying the drumming of the rain on the leaves and causing a chain to clank somewhere.

'I think that door's open,' Burkhart muttered.

Mattie moved toward it through the sopping-wet grass and weeds, redialing Dr. Gabriel's number. He answered immediately.

'Give us a patch, Doc.'

She saw Burkhart pause, then touch his Bluetooth and nod.

'You reading our position?' Mattie murmured.

'Great signal,' Gabriel replied. 'You're a hundred meters from him.'

'Guide us,' Burkhart said. 'We're going in an

open door on the southeast face of the longer, thinner section of the building.'

'You're looking to go down through that long arm to the north,' Gabriel said. 'He's in the wider part. Looks like he's up against the east wall.'

Mattie followed Burkhart's lead when he got out a penlight that he held tight to his Glock. He pushed at the barn door with his foot. It creaked open, revealing a cement-floored hallway with drains set at intervals down its center and partitions every four meters or so.

Mattie peered closer at the floor. It was covered in old trash and dust.

'No footprints,' she muttered to Burkhart, who'd stepped inside.

'Probably came in from the other end.'

Mattie stepped into the hallway after Burkhart, who moved forward like a cat while flashing his light into the side rooms. Trash. Rat shit. Graffiti. Grime. And bolts sticking out of the wall about knee high and again about shoulder height.

Seeing the bolts, Mattie felt a distinct sense of menace around her.

'What did they do in here?' she whispered to Burkhart.

He twisted his head quickly. His neck made a cracking sound. 'Look like animal stalls to me. They probably kept the livestock in here awaiting slaughter.'

It made sense. But Mattie could not shake that sense of threat. Indeed, the closer they got to the barn doors at the end of the hallway, the more pronounced the feeling became.

She could barely breathe when Burkhart slid

back one of the double doors.

Pigeons spooked and flapped toward the empty windows.

'East wall,' Mattie said.

She and Burkhart both swung their beams in that direction, hearing Gabriel say: 'He should be right there at thirty meters.'

Mattie felt her heart sink as their beams played over garbage, rusted bolts jutting from the floor, and old pipes sticking out of the wall. 'No one here, Doc.'

'What? That's impossi–' Gabriel paused. 'There, he's moving.'

'Moving?' Burkhart said. 'He's not moving. He's not here.'

'I'm telling you he's moving north along that east wall.'

But they saw nothing but cobwebs, dirt, and old bottles and trash.

Then Mattie caught a flicker of movement and heard glass rolling on cement. She swung her light, the powerful beam finding an enormous rat that froze, blinded, sitting up on its haunches, staring into the light, eyes blinking, and nose twitching.

There was something shiny between its teeth.

Boom!

The gunshot surprised Mattie so much she jumped hard left, landing and then tripping on one of the bolts on the floor. She sprawled in the dirt.

She glared up at Burkhart. 'What the hell did you do that for?'

'It had something in its mouth,' Burkhart said,

crossing to the east wall, light trained on the dead rat. As Mattie struggled to her feet, he crouched over the rodent a moment, then stood and turned to face her. 'We need to call in Kripo now.'

She felt her heart break. 'Why?'

Burkhart held up what looked like a thin hearing aid battery partially wrapped in a chunk of gnawed and livid flesh.

Chapter 7

Have you ever seen that old movie *The Invisible Man?*

Claude Rains, the same guy who played the enigmatic French captain in *Casablanca,* stars as a mad scientist who turns homicidal after he figures out how to erase his visible body.

Not surprisingly, it's one of my absolute favorite films of all time.

One scene in particular never fails to leave me howling with laughter. In it, Rains is covered in bandages and has taken refuge at an inn run by the Irish actress Una O'Connor. She happens to enter Rains's room when he's removed the bandages on his head.

He looks decapitated, but alive.

O'Connor's eyes bulge. She goes over-the-top insane. She starts to shriek bloody murder.

It's my special moment. One I wish I could recreate in my own life.

But alas, attaining invisibility is an art more

53

than a science.

For instance, I have found over the past twenty-five years that the best thing you can do to remain unseen is to relax and inhabit your mask so thoroughly that people come to think nothing of you, especially in Berlin, my beautiful city of scars.

I'm not being poetic here. I'm telling you the truth. Pay attention now.

My friends, let me state unequivocally that if you are relaxed in Berlin, comfortable in your own scarred skin, and not causing outward trouble, the millions of scarred Berliners around you will just go on about their silly days, unaware of beings like me.

Or at least not believing in their wildest nightmares that someone like me could still live among them.

Unexposed.

Unrecorded.

Still hunting.

With all that in mind, I am very, very cool as I drive an unmarked white panel van – one of a small fleet of vehicles I've collected over the years – through the rainy Berlin streets, past the scars of Hitler, and the Russians, and the Wall, way out to a forest north of Ahrensfelde, and down a wet wooded lane to a children's camp on Liepnitz Lake not far from the sleepy village of Ützdorf.

Do you know Ützdorf?

It doesn't matter.

Just understand that there is no one at that camp today. At least that's how it appears at first glance. Then again, why would there be? It's pouring out and cold and there's dense fog building out on the water around the island.

I park near the dock. No sooner do I shut off the engine than my young genius friend appears on the porch of the boathouse.

He's bearded, midtwenties, and his soaking-wet hair hangs on his fogged glasses. He takes them off and tries to dry them on a wet sweatshirt that features the emblem of the Berlin Technical University.

I take a gym bag from the passenger seat of my van and climb out, leaving the engine running.

'How did you get here?' I ask, climbing up onto the porch, out of the rain.

'Bus and walked, like you said. I got fucking soaked.'

'Ever heard of a raincoat?' I ask.

'Wasn't raining when I started,' he says, irritated. 'You have the money?'

I hold up the bag. 'Twenty-five thousand euros, as agreed.'

'Let me see,' my friend says, reaching for the bag.

I keep it just out of his reach. 'Not before I see what I'm buying.'

He looks pissed off, but he goes to a hiker's pack against the boathouse wall. He retrieves a disk and hands it to me, saying, 'All of Schneider's work files.'

'Did you look at them?' I ask in a super relaxed manner.

'That would be against my ethics,' he replies.

But his body language says otherwise.

55

Once he hands me the disk, I play along and give him the bag of money.

He opens it and checks several packets of fifty-euro notes.

'Nice doing business with you,' he says, zipping the bag up.

'Yes,' I say, pocketing the disk and finding the handle end of a flat-head screwdriver. 'Need a lift to the bus stop?'

'That would be great,' he says, turning back toward his knapsack.

I take two quick steps behind him, grab his hair, and drive the sharpened blade of the screwdriver up under the nape of his skull.

Chapter 8

My young genius friend never has the chance to scream.

But as the blade finds the soft spot where spinal column becomes brain, his entire body goes electric and herky-jerky.

When at last he drops my money and sags against me, I'm panting, spent and rubber-legged, as if I've just had the most explosive sex imaginable.

What a thrill! What an amazing, amazing thrill!

Even after all these years that rush never gets old.

I stand there for several moments in the aftermath of a great death, calm, drained, sated, and yet hyperaware of everything around me: the rain, the clouds, the forest, and the whistling of ducks out there in the fog.

With his body in my hands, with the sense of his life force still vibrating in me, it's like I'm here and not, hovering on the edge of the afterlife, you know?

At last I roll him over on his belly and draw out the screwdriver. I get out a tube of superglue and use it to seal the entry wound at the back of his neck. No more blood. It's done in seconds.

I chuckle as I drag my young genius friend toward my van, thinking how strange it is that there are people out there in the world, people far deeper and more philosophical than me, who spend their lives wondering if a tree falling in woods like this makes a crashing sound if there's no one around to hear it.

What a stupid goddamn thing to spend your life thinking about.

Don't they know they would be better off pondering whether a man like me can exist when he's never been truly seen?

Chapter 9

Hauptkommissar Hans Dietrich was a living legend inside Berlin Kripo, an investigator with low-key, unorthodox tactics that nevertheless resulted in the highest solve rate of any detective in the department's eight divisions.

The high commissar was a tall crane of a man, early fifties, quiet, moody, and extremely private, rarely fraternizing with other cops. He was even said to resent the fact that he had to work with a second detective on homicide cases.

Mattie had heard about Dietrich during her many years with Berlin Kripo, of course, but she'd never had the chance to work with him directly.

Still, an hour after their initial call to Kripo she was more than relieved when she saw him walking toward her beneath a black umbrella in a gray suit, his somber face revealing nothing.

If anyone could find out what had happened to Chris, it was this man.

Mattie and Burkhart moved around the uniformed officer now guarding the front of the slaughterhouse and went to meet Dietrich. They showed him their Private badges and identified themselves.

'I know who you are, Frau Engel,' Dietrich said, his eyes flickering toward the abattoir. 'Your reputation precedes you.'

Mattie felt Burkhart looking at her, puzzled. Her cheeks started to burn.

A blue Kripo bus appeared, splashing toward the slaughterhouse.

Mattie knew what that meant. Every time a body is found in Berlin, Kripo sends out one of these specially equipped buses. They contain all the equipment and supplies needed to fully document a murder scene.

Seeing the bus, Mattie became angry. 'With all due respect, High Commissar, we don't know that this is a homicide yet. Someone could have taken Chris, discovered the chip, then cut it out of him so we couldn't find him.'

Dietrich blinked, took his attention off the slaughterhouse, and replied in a chilly tone, 'That's what *I* am here to find–'

'High Commissar!' came a woman's shrill voice.

Dietrich grimaced and looked over his shoulder at the stout little woman in her mid-twenties marching earnestly up the driveway toward them. He sighed heavily. 'Inspector Sandra Weigel. My trainee.'

Inspector Weigel beamed at Mattie and Burkhart as they introduced themselves before turning to Dietrich. 'What shall I do, High Commissar?' Weigel asked.

'Stay out of my way and listen,' Dietrich growled at her. Then he looked back at Mattie and Burkhart. 'Now, take me inside, show me where you found the chip, and tell me everything I need to know.'

Chapter 10

As they donned blue surgical booties and latex gloves under an awning that had been set up outside the slaughterhouse, Mattie and Burkhart brought Dietrich up to speed on Chris Schneider's cases and activities during the prior two weeks, finishing with the decision to activate the GPS chip and its discovery in the main hall of the slaughterhouse two hours before.

Inspector Weigel took copious notes. Dietrich took none. He just stood there, listening intently, expressionless. He asked only one question. 'No footprints?'

Burkhart shook his head. 'None, but the dust in there is rippled. Like someone used one of those blowers that gardeners use to erase all tracks.'

Mattie frowned. Burkhart had not mentioned that before.

Dietrich gave Burkhart a glance of reappraisal, and then went inside the slaughterhouse. The hallway was lit now with klieg lights. The high commissar walked toward the main slaughterhouse slowly, methodically, his eyes going everywhere, saying nothing.

Mattie said, 'The room where we found the chip – it's big. Private could bring in its forensics team to help. We have state and federal certification.'

Dietrich shook his head and continued on with his inspection as if the idea were completely out of the question.

A team of criminalists was setting up lights and gathering samples at the east end of the main slaughterhouse where the chip had been found.

Dietrich examined the dead rat and then looked up at Burkhart. 'Remind me not to anger you, Herr Burkhart.'

Burkhart shrugged. 'Just a lot of practice.'

'You have the chip?' Dietrich asked.

Mattie dug in her pants pocket and came up with a plastic evidence sleeve with the chip and the flesh inside.

Dietrich took it from her and studied it closely.

'High Commissar?' one of the evidence specialists called. He was crouched over a bolt protruding from the floor beneath the rusty overhead track. 'I've got something here.'

Dietrich stiffened and hesitated before looking at Mattie and Burkhart. 'I'm sorry, but I'll have to ask you to leave now.'

'What?' Mattie said. 'Why?'

'This is a crime scene. I can't have any more contamination.'

'Contamination?' Mattie said. 'We did everything by the book in here. We backed out the second we found the chip, and we waited for Kripo.'

'So you did,' Dietrich replied calmly. 'It does not change things. You'll have to leave. You should know, Frau Engel. It's department policy.'

Mattie shook her head, unable to contain her anger. 'High Commissar, until six weeks ago, Chris was my fiancé. I have every right to be here.'

Dietrich softened but still shook his head. 'I'm sorry for you,' he replied quietly. 'But you have no right to be here. So leave, or I'll have you taken out.'

Mattie was gathering herself to protest one more time when she felt Burkhart's massive hand on her shoulder. 'We should go now, Mattie. Give Kripo some space. We've got other things to take care of.'

Mattie's shoulders sagged and she felt like crying, but she nodded.

'Good,' Dietrich said. 'And if you'll be so kind as to come to my office tomorrow morning at

61

nine I will tell you what we've found.'

'We will too,' Burkhart offered. 'Private wants to help.'

'I'd prefer you don't launch a shadow investigation,' Dietrich said.

Mattie hardened. 'As long as Chris is missing, we'll keep searching.'

Dietrich shrugged. 'Fair enough. Negotiated cooperation then.'

'Deal,' Burkhart said and led Mattie away.

The high commissar followed them to the south entry to the slaughterhouse, and watched them walk down the driveway in the pelting rain.

Inspector Weigel came up beside him. 'Excuse me, sir, but I thought you told me before they came that we wouldn't be cooperating with Private in any way.'

Dietrich did not look at his young trainee. 'What's that old saying, Weigel? Keep your friends close, and your enemies closer?'

'Private's investigators are enemies?' Weigel asked.

'There's a man missing, their man, Weigel,' Dietrich said. 'We certainly can't treat them as friends.'

Chapter 11

I take a left turn onto the lane that runs past the old slaughterhouse and see the police barrier immediately. A uniformed police officer is letting two people leave, a tall man, imposing and bald, and a blond woman wearing a navy-blue rain slicker with the hood up.

They walk toward me and a BMW parked on the shoulder.

For a second I can't breathe. Dots dance before my eyes. I feel like they're a pack of snarling dogs suddenly biting at my ankles.

What have they found?

My young genius is wrapped in a blue tarp behind me on the van floor, but I'm not thinking of him. I'm being strangled by that question.

What have they found?

Then old training kicks in. I get a hold of myself and quickly lower the sun visor. The passenger windows of my van are slightly tinted. All the man and the woman will see is a silhouette of me as I pass them and the police barrier.

I take my first breath, then another, and by the fifth I have to fight not to hyperventilate. But I get the van turned into an alley that runs between the two old apartment buildings up the hill from the slaughterhouse.

In seconds I'm out on a main drag, heading back toward the neighborhood of Mehrow. My stomach churns. The first chance I get, I pull over, park, and put my head on the steering wheel.

What have they found? And who was that big bald guy with the woman?

The air around me suddenly seems negatively charged, and that sets off true panic in me. Sweat boils on my forehead and trickles down my spine.

I force myself to go through everything that occurred inside the slaughterhouse three days ago. Everything.

What could be left? Blood stains on the bolt, perhaps. Or spinal fluid? Maybe some bone fragments, I decide at last.

But they won't know whose blood or bone it is, now will they? Unless dear Chris left behind DNA samples. But those tests take days. Weeks. Right?

There's nothing else. I've seen to it all. I'm sure of it.

Unless Chris told someone where he was going?

No. It was personal. He came for me alone.

Given the lack of other evidence, I tell myself the police will soon let it go. A blood stain in an old slaughterhouse? They'll think someone tripped and gouged their leg or something. Right?

I almost convince myself before doubt takes a stroll through my mind.

What if they were to keep looking?

This possibility agitates me so much I twist around to look into the rear of the van at the shape of the corpse in the tarp.

Every cell in my body wants to drive by the slaughterhouse to get another look, try to get a

64

sense of the scope of the police action, but I know I can't. Smart cops look for that kind of thing.

In the end, I tell myself to return home, or better to call and meet the woman who thinks I love her.

Put a sense of normality in my visible life, rebuild the mask once more.

I'll come by tomorrow in a different vehicle.

If the police are gone, then I'll dispose of the young genius's body in the normal way and things will go on as they always have.

But if they're still there, I'll have no choice but to erase the slaughterhouse and all its dirty little secrets forever.

Chapter 12

'I should be in there,' Mattie complained as Burkhart clicked open the doors of the BMW. The white panel van passing by barely registered in her brain.

Burkhart shook his head and climbed in.

Mattie got in angrily beside him. 'I should.'

'No. Dietrich's right. They need impartial people in there.'

'You're saying I'm not impartial?' Mattie demanded.

'Yes, that's what I'm saying,' Burkhart said, starting the car. 'You couldn't be. If you were impartial in this situation, I'd wonder about you as a human.'

Mattie did not know what to say. Burkhart turned on the windshield wipers, which slapped away the wet leaves.

Mattie threw up her hands. 'I've got to do something. I can't just–'

'We're going to Chris's apartment.'

Berlin is a huge city geographically, almost 341 square miles. And Chris Schneider lived far from Ahrensfelde, west of Tiergarten Park and the zoo.

It took them forty minutes to get there in the late-afternoon traffic. Mattie had gone quiet again, looking out at the cityscape as they crossed back from the old east into the west.

Mattie had lived in Berlin her entire life. She was a Berliner through and through. She loved the city, its architecture, people, art, laid-back attitude, and entrepreneurial spirit.

But now, in light of the mystery surrounding Chris's disappearance, Berlin seemed suddenly to her to be an alien place inhabited by creatures who might cut a tracking chip out of a man's back and feed it to rats.

They passed the ruins of the Kaiser Wilhelm Memorial, the roofless grand entry hall and wounded spire of a church that somehow survived a bombing raid in 1943. The scorched ruins sat on a grand plaza beside an ultramodern belfry.

The ruins were among Chris's favorite places in the city. He liked to sit and contemplate the spire, which looked like it had been cleaved in two by the bomb. One side collapsed and fell. The other still stood, jagged against the sky.

'Left on Goethe, yes?' Burkhart asked, shaking Mattie from her thoughts.

She startled, looked around, and then said, 'Correct.'

Chris lived in a second-floor apartment on Gutenbergstrasse in the Charlottenburg district of the city. It was a slightly frumpy address for a man of Schneider's age, but he'd loved the place because it gave him close access to the zoo and to Tiergarten Park, where he liked to run.

Mattie had not been to Chris's place in more than six weeks. Her last visit weighed heavily on her mind as they used her key to open the door to the building. There was a courtyard with grass and raised garden beds. The one below Chris's apartment had been freshly tilled. There were bags of tulip bulbs sitting near a hoe and shovel. A BMW motorcycle was parked on the grass.

Mattie frowned. She knew the superintendent of the building, a cantankerous man named Krauss. She'd never known him to allow motor-cycles in his courtyard, or bikes for that matter.

She put that aside and led Burkhart up an interior staircase to a second-floor landing. She hesitated. At some level, she felt like this place was forbidden to her now, no matter what might have happened to Chris.

'That key doesn't work on this door?' Burkhart asked. 'Or are you worried Dietrich is going to have a shit fit if he finds out we've been in here?'

'Screw Dietrich,' Mattie said and rammed the key into the lock.

She turned the knob and pushed the door open.

Chapter 13

The leather couch and chairs had been over-turned, the upholstery slashed, the stuffing torn out. Books littered the floor. The closets had been opened, their contents strewn all about.

Mattie smelled trash rotting and heard a cat mewing.

'Socrates?' she called, walking inside. 'Here kitty.'

'This is a crime scene now,' Burkhart said. 'We can't go in.'

'It's a tossed apartment,' she shot back. 'Let's figure out what they took.'

Mattie stopped and donned the same latex gloves she'd worn at the slaughterhouse. The cat had stopped crying.

Burkhart grimaced, but then followed her lead. She walked gingerly through the debris, including shattered glass from picture frames. Several of the pictures showed Chris and Mattie, arms around each other, smiling as if they were the happiest couple on earth.

How had it all gone so wrong?

How had this happened? The chip. The hacking. And now his apartment is tossed. And why? What was Chris on to?

Mattie reached the alcove where Chris often worked at home. She spotted the smashed laptop on the floor and went to it. She crouched and used a pen to push aside the pieces, barely aware of Burkhart picking up a photograph of Chris and a young boy.

'Engel, is this–?' Burkhart began.

'Fuck!' Mattie cried, cutting him off. 'They got his hard drive. Fuck!'

'All right, we know what they were after then,' Burkhart said, setting the picture down. 'We're out of here. We call Kripo.'

Mattie stood and pushed by him. 'I'm finding his cat. You wait at the car.'

She did not wait for an answer, but instead walked down the hallway past the kitchen, where dirty dishes and takeout Thai food boxes contributed to a foul reek. She stopped breathing in through her mouth and went into the bedroom, which was painted bright white.

The comforter was bright white too. So were the drapes, which billowed with the gusts of wind and rain blowing in through the open French windows that overlooked the courtyard. Rain soaked the rug below the windows.

There was a wastebasket by the bed filled to the brim with papers, one of the few containers that had not been emptied in the entire apartment. Mattie crossed to it and saw several crumpled pieces of paper on top.

She was picking one up when she heard a meow. She looked over and saw Socrates, Chris's charcoal and gray tabby, coming out of the bathroom.

Mattie took a step toward him, grinning. 'There you are.'

Then she spotted the imprint of soles on the

wet rug.

She followed the tracks with her eyes to the closet door at her immediate right, then slipped the crumpled paper into her pocket, took a step toward the cat, and started to reach for her pistol, saying, 'Good Socrates. You hungry?'

The closet door exploded outward.

Chapter 14

A burly man in black leathers and a motorcycle helmet smashed into Mattie's left side and blew her off her feet.

She crashed to the rug next to Socrates. The man tried to kick her in the stomach, but she saw it coming and curled up so her thigh took the impact.

He took two steps to the window and jumped out.

Mattie fought to get to her feet, drawing her pistol. She heard the motorcycle engine growl to life and staggered to the window just as he popped the clutch, throwing up grass as he wove toward the entry to the building.

Without thinking, Mattie jumped.

She landed in the soggy, freshly tilled bed and then rolled out of it as a parachutist might. She saw Krauss coming into the courtyard from the opposite side, horror on his face.

'Mattie!' he cried.

She had no time to explain. The motorcyclist

was getting away. She sprinted through the building's main door, hoping to catch the license plate.

The motorcyclist was accelerating west. She could see his back and helmet but no license plate.

'Shit!' she cried.

The BMW screeched up beside her, Burkhart at the wheel. 'Get in.'

She jumped in the passenger seat and they went squealing after the motorcyclist, who braked and turned onto Englische Strasse, heading south.

By the time they reached the corner he was turning west again, paralleling the canal and the campus of the Technical University. Burkhart downshifted and almost caught him before he crossed the March Bridge onto campus.

Students were diving out of the way of the motorcycle and Burkhart's car as they raced through campus.

At a roundabout the rider curled left onto Hardenbergstrasse and then crossed under the Zoologischer S-Bahn station, where he wove hard to his right onto Joachimstaler, then sharply left onto Kantstrasse, heading east toward the ruins of the belfry tower.

Despite the serpentine course they ran through the city, Burkhart had somehow managed to close the gap again when the man who'd trashed Chris's apartment dodged without warning across traffic and up onto the plaza that surrounded the ruins.

'Don't you dare!' Mattie cried at Burkhart. 'There are people all over that plaza. Take the next right at Budapester instead.'

71

Burkhart gritted his teeth but did as he was told, lucking out that the light was in his favor. The street ran parallel to the plaza. Mattie could see the motorcyclist weaving through pedestrians, who scattered ahead of him.

'There's got to be a cop there somewhere,' Mattie said.

'They're never around when you need them,' Burkhart said, barreling down Budapester Strasse.

The motorcyclist veered off the plaza and out onto Budapester.

But Burkhart was right behind him.

'He's got no license plate,' Mattie said.

'I imagine not,' Burkhart said as they shot off-road through the busy Palme-Platz.

Burkhart was a genius behind the wheel. He made every move the motorcyclist did, until they crossed the canal again east of the zoo.

On the immediate north side, the motorcycle suddenly braked hard, as if trying to avoid something in the road ahead.

'Bastard, gonna knock you down,' Burkhart said, hammering the gas.

The BMW's front left fender just missed the rear wheel of the motorcycle as it veered hard left onto Corneliusstrasse.

Burkhart slammed on his brakes, threw the car in reverse, and then squealed after the motorcyclist. But Mattie already had a sinking feeling in her stomach.

She knew this part of Berlin well. She and Chris had run here often.

Straight ahead two blocks, the way west was blocked, except for pedestrians and bicyclists who

72

could access a trail that ran along the canal inside Tiergarten Park and between the zoo and Neuer Lake.

The last Mattie saw of the motorcyclist, he was accelerating west on the canal path, and then he disappeared behind the falling leaves, the pouring rain, and the waning light of day.

Chapter 15

'Hauptkommissar?'

Hans Dietrich turned to his trainee. He towered over her, looking exasperated. 'What is it, Weigel?'

Standing in the eastern end of the slaughterhouse, Inspector Weigel's cheeks reddened, but then she stammered, 'The technicians have found blood samples. Many of them.'

Dietrich stiffened, hesitated, and then sputtered,

'Well, I imagine so. It was a slaughterhouse.'

'Sir, they want to know what you want them to do.'

He hesitated again, and then said, 'Take twenty random samples.'

The inspector paused, then nodded uncertainly. 'Hauptkommissar, are you not feeling well?'

Dietrich stared at her a moment, and then he looked at his watch. Four ten.

He did his best to appear stricken. 'No, as a matter of fact, I feel like I'm coming down with something. I... I think I shall have to go home.'

'Sir?' Weigel said.

'A twelve-hour bug,' Dietrich said. 'If you find something of significance, call me.'

Twenty minutes later, the high commissar was driving his old Opel down a corridor of horse-chestnut trees that lined both sides of Pusch-kinallee, heading toward Treptower Park in southeast Berlin.

Dietrich glanced in his rearview mirror, seeing the television tower at Alexanderplatz framed in the road behind him. His lip curled. He hated the tower. He hated everything it stood for.

He'd heard lately that real estate speculators were going to tear it down as part of the re-development of Alexanderplatz. Dietrich thought the tower was a good thing to be rid of, a very good thing.

As an investigator he had learned well that the past is always eventually buried, especially in a city. It may take centuries, it may take mass de-struction, but the past is always eventually reduced to rubble, dust, and rumor.

As far as the high commissar was concerned, the sooner the burial happened in certain parts of Berlin the better.

Which is why, as he approached Treptower Park, Dietrich felt like he'd been forced to pick up a shovel and dig into a mound of radioactive material; he knew he had to do it, but he feared he might be destroyed in the process.

He parked the Opel and checked his watch.

It was 4:40 p.m. He had twenty minutes.

He swallowed hard, grabbed his umbrella, and

struggled from the car.

In a long, ungainly gait that caused his head to bob forward with every step, the high commissar hurried south on a lane that ran through sopping autumn woods until he reached a vast rectangular opening in the forest.

He passed a statue of a mother crying, Mother Russia crying. He walked up a long promenade lined with weeping silver birches toward two massive red monuments facing each other. The red granite had been taken from Hitler's Chancellery and then carved into giant stylized flags adorned with the Soviet Union's hammer and sickle.

Below the flags, bronze statues of war-weary Russian soldiers knelt facing each other. In the distance, framed between the two soldiers, stood a third statue. This warrior was ten times the size of the others. The noble Soviet carried a German child. At his feet lay a broken Nazi swastika.

The high commissar climbed the stairs and walked between the kneeling statues. He looked out over a graveyard of five thousand of Stalin's soldiers who died in the battle for Berlin at the end of World War II.

But Dietrich was not looking at the sixteen crypts that held the bodies, nor was he thinking about Stalin, or the particulars of the Soviet War Memorial. He was peering beyond all of it through the lightly falling rain to a path that ran parallel to the cemetery through a grove of trees.

In the dull pewter light and the rain, a lone figure appeared from the trees in a black raincoat, jogging pants, and shoes. He strode briskly down the path, arms pumping and his head up like a dog on alert.

The high commissar checked his watch.

Five pm. on the dot.

He shook his head in mild disbelief. 'Like fucking clockwork.'

Chapter 16

Dietrich watched the figure move away from him toward the rear of the war memorial and calculated his speed. When he thought he had it right, he headed off at a slant to the walker, weaving through the sarcophagi and losing sight of his quarry for several minutes.

The high commissar stopped on the north side of the statue of the victorious Soviet and the German child. The rain had slowed, so he could hear the slap of the man's feet coming long before he spotted him.

'Oberst?' Dietrich said. 'Colonel? Can I have a moment of your time?'

The colonel was old, in his eighties at least, but his bearing was autocratic, a man used to giving orders and having them carried out. And he had a steel-blue penetrating stare that slashed all over the high commissar before a look of disgust curled his lip. He did not slow his pace, and tried to get by him.

Dietrich reached out and grabbed the older man by the elbow. 'I need to talk. I need your help. Your advice.'

'You need my help?' the colonel laughed spitefully and wrenched his arm free with surprising strength. 'For years you want nothing to do with your own father, and now, out of nowhere, after what, ten years, you need?'

For a moment, Dietrich felt as sick as he'd claimed to be earlier in the afternoon. His stomach ached and he was bombarded by a sense of claustrophobia that he had not felt since the last time he'd spoken with his father.

'I'm on a case,' Dietrich said.

'Yes,' the colonel said with mild contempt. 'You are a police officer.'

'Hauptkommissar,' Dietrich said, feeling old anger stirring in him. 'I just need to rule a few things out.'

'About what, *Hauptkommissar?*'

It had begun to rain again in earnest. His father's hood was down, but the old man showed no bother.

Dietrich hesitated, and then said, 'I need you to tell me what you know about certain ancient rumors.'

The colonel turned suspicious. 'What kind of ancient rumors?'

'About the old auxiliary slaughterhouse near Ahrensfelde.'

Something cracked in the old man's expression. But it sealed tight a moment later. 'I don't know anything about it. And neither should you.'

Dietrich said, 'I have reason to believe someone might have been murdered in there. Assaulted certainly.'

'Blood but no body then?'

'A piece of skin but no body. And animal blood. Lots of it. We're searching the place now. Are we going to find anything?'

The colonel blinked at raindrops that hung from his lashes, and then said, 'It could be squatters fighting.'

'No evidence of that yet.'

'Then I can't tell you.'

Dietrich did not believe him. He'd understood at a relatively young age that the more in control his father seemed, the more likely he was to be lying through his teeth.

'I've got a life, Colonel. A position. A reputation. People who count on me.'

'People who don't know who you really are.' His father snorted in derision, and then soured further. 'In all honesty, Hans, I don't care about your life, your position, your reputation, or your people.

'And in case I did not tell you this the last time I saw you, when I think of you – and that is admittedly a rare occurrence – I think of you as an utter disappointment. Your actions today have not changed my assessment.'

With that, the colonel turned and took up his brisk evening walk as if he'd never paused.

Dietrich's throat flamed with anger.

But his stomach churned with fear.

Chapter 17

The apartment building where Mattie Engel lived on Schliemannstrasse south of Prenzlauer Allee was painted bright green and red and white. The building stood next to a preschool painted with images of kids on tricycles and others playing with dump trucks.

Tom Burkhart slowed to a stop on wet cobblestones in front of the school. Mattie had Socrates on her lap. They'd gone back to Chris's apartment, found the cat, secured the place, and tried to call Dietrich with the news.

But the high commissar had not answered his cell phone, and Mattie had not left a message. He'd find out soon enough. She reached for the door handle.

'You going to be okay?' Burkhart asked.

'As long as I never get in a car with you again, I'll be fine.'

'What?'

'We're lucky we're not in jail.'

'Nonsense,' Burkhart said. 'I had total control. But do you?'

Mattie hesitated and said, 'I've got to sleep. Chris could be out there somewhere alive and I'm going to sleep.'

Burkhart's tone softened. 'You'll function better if you do. I'll meet you at Dietrich's office first thing in the morning.'

Mattie nodded, climbed from the BMW, and hurried to her front door with the cat in her arms. Burkhart waited until she was inside and then drove off. She took the elevator to the third floor and walked to her door. She paused, hearing a television blaring inside and smelling onions frying.

She looked at the cat. How am I going to do this? What do I say?

Socrates just stared at her, blinking. Then he meowed.

Mattie stuck her key in the lock and went in to an open area with a couch, two chairs, and a coffee table. There was a counter at the back that looked into the kitchen where Mattie's aunt Cäcilia, a stout woman in her seventies, bustled about cooking Sunday dinner.

Aunt Cäcilia had lived on and off with Mattie since the Berlin Wall fell. She had watched Mattie grow into womanhood, and she'd cared for Mattie's mother as she died. Mattie did not know what she'd do without her.

From a room opposite the kitchen, the television got louder with the roar of a crowd and an announcer screaming, *'Goal Cassiano! Goal Cassiano!'*

A boy's voice pitched in, screaming: 'Goal Cassiano! Goal Berlin!'

Socrates leaped from Mattie's arms and scampered toward the commotion. Mattie followed the cat, worming her arms from her rain jacket and calling, 'Niklas? I'm home.'

'Hello, dear,' her aunt called from the kitchen. 'I'll have your dinner ready in a second.'

'Thanks,' Mattie said, and looked around the corner into the small room opposite the kitchen. Her nine-year-old son bounced on the couch, watching the replay and yelling, 'Goal Cassiano!' when the striker drove the ball into the upper-right corner of the net.

The cat leaped into Niklas's lap.

A whippet-lean boy with large, welcoming eyes, Niklas looked shocked and then even more over-joyed than he'd been celebrating Cassiano's goal.

'Socrates!' he cried, and then hugged the cat. 'Where'd you come from?'

'I brought him,' Mattie said. 'I wish you'd get that excited to see me.'

Niklas finally seemed to notice her. He grinned. 'My mommy!'

Mattie went to him. She hugged him close to her and petted Socrates's head. 'Missed you,' she said.

Niklas pressed his head into her belly. 'Missed you too. But you should have seen it, Mommy – Cassiano. He's ... like no one on Berlin ever.'

Mattie looked over at the television, studying the Brazilian who was being shown in close-up. Did *he* have something to do with Chris's disappearance?

Niklas's smile disappeared. He looked down at the cat. 'Why is Socrates here?' His smile returned before she could answer. 'Is Chris here?'

Mattie was amazed sometimes at how intuitive Niklas was, one of those people who seemed to sense hidden emotion. Then again, that's how you grow up when you don't have a father.

'I've got some troubling news,' Mattie said at last.

Niklas's face tightened. 'You're working next weekend again?'

Mattie hesitated, still unsure of what to say and how to say it.

Niklas got up, dropping the cat and barging by his mother. 'You promised we could go to the lake and canoe again. It'll be too cold soon!'

'Niklas!' Mattie said sharply. 'It's Chris. That's why Socrates is here.'

Her son stopped and looked back at her, his face suddenly pale and puzzled as the cat arched and rubbed against his ankles. 'What?'

'He's missing, Niklas. Chris is missing.'

Niklas appeared even more confused. 'What does that mean?'

'No one knows where he is,' Mattie said, deciding not to tell him about the chip that was found. 'And he's been gone a long time without anyone hearing from him. Too long.'

Niklas picked up Socrates, held him tight to his chest, and asked, 'Who was he with? What was he working on?'

'I don't know.'

'You used to know everything. You always knew what he was doing.'

'Niklas, I...'

Niklas's expression turned bitter. 'If you hadn't said you weren't going to marry him, you might know where Chris is. He'd probably be right here watching the game with me!'

Mattie's son burst into tears and stormed off down the hall toward his bedroom, holding on to Socrates like he was his last friend on earth.

Chapter 18

Mattie's aunt Cäcilia witnessed the entire epi-
sode. Upset, rubbing her hands on her apron, she
shouted, 'Niklas, come back here. You come back
here and apologize to your mother right now!'

But Niklas slammed the door to his bedroom
shut behind him.

Mattie put her hand on her aunt's shoulder.
'Let him go. He's right. Chris and I used to share
everything. I would have known.'

Her aunt looked ready to argue, but then
caught the tension in Mattie. 'But he's just
missing, right? Couldn't he have gone on a vacation?'

'No. Definitely not a vacation.'

'Then...'

'I need to go talk to Niklas.'

Her aunt nodded. 'And then you come eat.
Schnitzel with lemon zest.'

Mattie kissed Cäcilia on her cheek and went
down the hall to her son's room. She knocked.
He didn't answer. She twisted the knob. Locked.

'Nicky? Can I come in?'

Several moments later she heard the lock
freed. She went into the bedroom of her soccer-
mad son. A big poster of Cassiano hung above
his bed.

Niklas climbed back onto his bed and curled
himself around Socrates, who purred. Mattie sat

on the bed next to them and rubbed her son's back.

'You have the right to be upset,' she said.

For several moments, Niklas showed no reaction, but then he asked, 'Is Chris alive, Mom?'

'We have to believe so.'

'And if he's not?'

Mattie did not answer.

'Why don't you still love him, Mom?'

Mattie's lower lip trembled. 'I do love Chris. And I love you, and we're going to get through this.'

'And get him back?'

'If it's in my power. Now it's time for pajamas and toothbrushes.'

'No book?'

'Aunt C will read to you,' she promised. 'I'm starving.'

The cat meowed, squirmed from Niklas's hold, and pranced to the door.

'Looks like he's hungry too,' Mattie said.

'There's still some dry food that Chris left.'

'I know where it is.'

She left her son's room, returned to the kitchen, and saw that her aunt had already found the cat food. It was in a bowl next to another filled with water. Socrates went to the food and ate hungrily.

'And your supper is on the table,' Cäcilia said.

Mattie kissed the old woman's cheek again. 'Niklas's almost ready for you to read a little *Harry Potter* to him.'

'I'll need to find my glasses then,' Cäcilia said, pulling off her apron.

Mattie went to the table and had her aunt's incomparable schnitzel with lemon zest and twice-baked potatoes, a salad, and a cold Berliner Weisse. After she'd finished, cleared the table, and washed the dishes, she went into the refrigerator in search of a second beer. She needed it.

She popped the top. Her cell rang. It was Katharina Doruk.

'Burkhart called in and told me what happened,' Katharina said.

'We're all right,' Mattie replied.

'So he said,' Katharina answered snippily. 'I would have rather heard that from you, Mattie. You're lucky the two of you weren't arrested. A high-speed chase? You're not cops.'

Mattie sighed. 'I know. It was the heat of the moment, and then I was too exhausted to call. I needed to take Socrates home and tell Niklas what happened.'

'How's he taking it?'

'He's got Socrates.'

'And you?'

Mattie shook inside. She'd not allowed herself to reflect at all since arriving at the slaughterhouse.

Now it threatened to spill out of her in a torrent.

'You want me to come over?' Katharina asked.

'I'll be okay.'

'Burkhart said the guy on the motorcycle got the hard drive from Chris's laptop,' Katharina said.

'Looked that way.'

'Nothing else?'

'The place was wrecked,' Mattie replied. 'It was a little hard to figure–'

She remembered the crumpled paper she'd retrieved from Chris's wastebasket just before the burglar attacked her. 'Hold on a second.'

Mattie put the phone on speaker, dug out the paper, and unfolded it. She scanned the list in Chris's distinctive scrawl. She smiled, but with little joy.

'Looks like the burglar missed something,' she said.

Chapter 19

'What?' Katharina asked.

'A to-do list that Chris wrote,' Mattie said, picking up her phone, the paper, and the beer and heading toward her bedroom. 'It's dated last Tuesday and says he had an appointment with Hermann Krüger at eleven in the morning that day.'

'Not the wife?'

'No, it says H. Krüger, and it has an address on Potsdamer Platz, the Sony building, I think.'

'So, what, he meets with Hermann, tells him he knows he has multiple mistresses and consorts with prostitutes and...'

'You're assuming too much, Kat,' Mattie snapped. 'Krüger's name's just here on a list. So is Cassiano's. He was to meet with him at three that afternoon. And he has a third name here, Pavel.'

'Maxim Pavel?' Katharina asked, suddenly excited.

'Doesn't say,' Mattie replied. 'Why?'

'Because Gabriel was able to trace a series of phone calls Chris made last Monday and Tuesday to a Maxim Pavel. He's a Russian expat. Owns two or three nightclubs, including Cabaret.'

'The drag-queen show?' Mattie asked.

'Very successful business according to Gabriel. But there's more. He evidently has ties to Russian organized crime.'

Mattie checked her watch. 'It's only eight o'clock; we could–'

'We already checked,' Katharina said. 'Pavel's away in Italy. Won't be back until tomorrow morning.'

Mattie thought about that. 'We're going to need reinforcements.'

'Way ahead of you again,' Katharina said. 'I've called in Brecht from Amsterdam, and Jack Morgan's on his way from Los Angeles in the Private jet.'

'I'll be at work by seven,' Mattie promised and hung up.

She put the beer, the list, and her phone on her nightstand, and then went in to kiss Niklas good night.

'I'm praying for Chris,' Niklas said after she'd shut off the light.

'I am too, sweetheart,' Mattie said.

She closed the door, told her aunt good night, and went into her bedroom. After showering and putting on her nightgown, she got in bed with the beer. She almost turned on the television, but then got out her laptop.

She signed in to her Private e-mail account, and found a note from the Countess von Mühlen's grandmother, thanking her for her prompt, efficient work. Mattie replied that she thought Sophia was just a sweet, mixed-up kid and wished her well.

Mattie quit out of the mailbox before she thought to sign in to her personal account. She hadn't looked at that e-mail account in well over a week, but then again the only person to use it regularly was...

Amid the spam, Mattie spotted an e-mail from Chris with a date stamp of the prior Wednesday evening at approximately 10 p.m. She opened it and saw only an MPEG attachment. She clicked on it.

Chris's face appeared on her screen. He was in his apartment, in the alcove, looking weary, and sounding partially drunk, with Socrates in his lap.

'Hi, Mattie. I've tried to respect your wishes and not contact you, but...' He stopped, looking away from the camera.

He cleared his throat, gazed at the lens again, and said, 'Mattie, I've gotten on to something, and I feel that if I can see this through, then it'll be better, better for me, and better for you, and for Niklas.'

Chris's eyes glistened, watering with tears. 'These past few weeks have been the worst I can remember since I was a kid. I miss you, Mattie. I miss Niklas, too. And Aunt Cäcilia. Call me? Or send me a message back? However you want to contact me, I'll be waiting. I love you both. I always will.'

The clip ended and went dark.

Mattie collapsed into sobs so loud that Aunt Cäcilia came running.

Chapter 20

It's just after dawn, my friends, and the rain pours as I drive south out of Berlin in the Mercedes Benz ML500 I picked up last year. Do you know the ML500? It's like a tank in wet conditions, my power vehicle, my go-anywhere car.

Normally I'm the picture of confidence behind the 500's wheel. But I'm nervous as I drive, thinking about the police at the slaughterhouse last night. When I awoke, I desperately wanted to pass by again this morning, but I had such a long way to drive and so little time before I needed to be back at work.

Southeast of Halle, I find a two-track lane that goes down by the river, a secluded spot. Especially in this foul weather.

I park and wait, thoughtless except for the pleasant task before me.

Twenty minutes later, a motorcyclist rides up wearing rain slickers and a black helmet. The deluge has ebbed to a light drizzle. I get out wearing a rain jacket with deep pockets and my gloved hands shoved into them.

My friend pulls off the helmet, revealing a swarthy man in his late thirties, a Turk who is also a thief. And as a thief would, my friend says, 'I want more money. I almost got caught. I almost got killed.'

'So you said on the phone last evening,' I reply agreeably. 'Fifty thousand euros instead of the twenty-five. Will that cover it?'

I could see the thief had expected an argument, but now he nods.

'You show me yours,' I say. 'I'll show you mine.'

My friend goes to dig in his saddlebags. I open the rear of the Mercedes. Next to the tarp that contains the body of the computer hacker, I find a leather satchel. I open it and draw out a little something to help speed things along. Then I pick up the bag as if I were serving it at a fine restaurant, the jaws gaped so the cash inside is visible.

I walk to the thief. He's holding the hard drive.

I make as if to hand him the moneybag and then stumble. The bag pitches from my hands.

My friend instinctively reaches out to catch it.

I stick him with a stun gun and jam the trigger.

He jerks violently and collapses.

I stun him again, then drop the device and ram the screwdriver up under the nape of his skull.

Now the thief quivers on his own, but I hold him tight, feeling the mystery drain from him and fill me once more.

But on this occasion I cannot pause to savor the moment or the sweet stillness that follows death. I'm in the open. It is raining. But I could be seen if I remain too long.

Instead, I superglue the wound, and drag the thief's body to the riverbank. I wade out and push him into the main current, hoping that the cold rushing waters will take him deep and far away.

I get out, chilled but not caring.

I get the satchel and fling it in the back of the Mercedes. Then I drag the tarp and the carcass of my friend the computer genius to the river. I roll the bundle into the river, pull the tarp, and roll his body into the water.

The thief's body is already out of sight.

I quickly fold the tarp and put it beside the satchel in the ML500.

I hurl the helmet into the river. I start the motorcycle, put it in gear, hold the brake, gun the throttle, pop the clutch, and let go.

The bike roars forward, flies off the bank, and disappears.

I have to hurry back to Berlin now. I can't take it any longer. I have to check the slaughterhouse.

I have to make decisions about its future, my friends.

Terrible decisions.

Chapter 21

Mattie put her right eye to Private Berlin's retina scan at six forty-five on Monday morning. She'd slept fitfully. Her eyes were bloodshot and puffy. She wondered if it would affect the scan, but it did not, and the bulletproof doors hissed open.

Dawn was just breaking when she walked through the glass hallway above the park. No lights had been turned on yet. She was the first to arrive.

Or so she thought. When she entered the lounge area, meaning to start coffee brewing, she flipped on the light. Someone groaned loudly.

Mattie jumped and looked at the couch. 'Who's there?' she demanded in German.

Jack Morgan sat up from the other side and looked at her blearily. 'I don't speak German, Mattie. What time is it?'

Like many Germans, Mattie spoke fluent English. 'Ten of seven,' she replied. 'Jack, I'm sorry I didn't...'

Private's owner waved a hand at her and got to his feet. He wore a pilot's leather jacket, jeans, and low-heel cowboy boots. A tall, lean man who always seemed in a hurry, Morgan pushed back his dark sandy hair and said, 'Don't worry about it. They say you're better off staying up, right?'

Mattie smiled. She liked Jack Morgan. He was smart without being overbearing, and he owned the company but didn't act like God.

He came over to her. 'How are you?'

Mattie shrugged and started making coffee. 'As well as you can be when you find out that your ... uh, colleague and friend is missing except for a tracking chip dug out of his back.'

'It's why I came,' Morgan said sympathetically. 'The moment I heard.'

'When did you get in?'

'About an hour ago,' Morgan said. 'Thirteen-

92

hour flight.'

'You must be beat,' Mattie said, flipping on the coffeemaker. 'I can bring you up to speed on what's happened while you've been in transit. Do you want to go have a real breakfast some-where?'

'Coffee's fine for right now,' Morgan said, taking a seat at the lounge table. 'And I would appreciate a briefing, but first, because it was bugging me the entire flight, why did you and Chris break off your engagement?'

Mattie made a puffing noise and looked away from him. She rarely talked about her personal life except with Katharina and her aunt. But her boss had just flown thirteen hours to help her find Chris. She figured an honest answer was the least she could offer.

In a strained voice Mattie said, 'We had a whirl-wind romance shortly after you hired me. We were engaged in six months. But I eventually found out that Chris was a troubled man, Jack. There was a part of him that I could not reach, that I could not know. He never talked about his childhood. But there was something from that time that haunted him. The longer I was with him, the more I could feel how large a space it occupied in his soul. I pleaded with him to tell me, but he refused. Finally I decided I couldn't marry a man with so much unknown inside him, no matter how much I loved him. It wouldn't have been fair to me. And it would not have been fair to my son, Niklas.'

'So you ended it?'

Mattie nodded. 'One of the most difficult

things I've ever done.'

'How'd Chris take it?'

'Like he'd been expecting it. He said he didn't blame me, and that he still loved me.'

'No idea what this secret was that he carried?'

'I just know that he used to have these nightmares. They'd come in waves. And he'd start crying in his sleep, calling for his mother. Sometimes screaming for her.'

'You ever ask about the nightmares?'

'Only if I didn't want him speaking to me for a few days,' Mattie replied, pouring coffee into a mug and offering it to Morgan.

He took it. 'I knew he grew up in East Berlin and that his parents died when he was eight or nine. And he grew up in an orphanage out in the countryside, right?'

Mattie nodded. 'That's about all he ever tells anyone. He once told me that the past is best forgotten, but I don't think he's ever forgotten. He just won't tell anyone about it.'

Chapter 22

Katharina Doruk arrived at seven fifteen. Dr. Ernst Gabriel checked in at half past the hour. So did Tom Burkhart.

Together they and Mattie briefed Morgan on what they'd found so far, including the slaughterhouse, Chris's scheduled meetings with soccer star Cassiano and billionaire Hermann Krüger in

94

the days before he disappeared, and the various phone calls he'd made to the nightclub owner Maxim Pavel and others.

For a man operating on just a few hours' sleep, Mattie thought Morgan acted soundly when he decided to split the investigation three ways.

Katharina would take the lead on Hermann Krüger.

After he arrived from Amsterdam later in the morning, Daniel Brecht would begin working the Cassiano angle with Morgan helping. Private's owner had conducted several major sports investigations in the past. Brecht spoke six languages, including Portuguese, the Brazilian striker's only tongue.

Gabriel would track Chris's movements in more detail while Mattie and Burkhart continued shadowing the official police investigation and pitching in on the other veins of inquiry as needed.

But when Mattie and Burkhart were preparing to leave for their scheduled meeting with Dietrich, her cell phone rang. It was the high commissar himself.

'I'm calling you under orders from my supervisor,' Dietrich said, the annoyance evident in his voice. 'Our meeting at my office is canceled.'

'What?' Mattie said, growing angry. 'You said–'

Dietrich cut her off. 'What I am about to tell you is not, I repeat, not for public dissemination. Are we clear?'

That took Mattie aback. 'Yes.'

Dietrich cleared his throat. 'As you might imagine, because of the nature of the building we found a great deal of blood evidence, so much that I decided to take twenty random samples and have them run overnight. Of the twenty, twelve were animal – four swine and eight bovine. The remaining eight were human. I'm sorry to say that four small spatters have been identified as Chris Schneider's. The other four were completely unlike one another.'

Mattie froze, blinking, trying to understand what he was telling her. 'You found blood from four other people besides Chris?'

Dietrich hesitated, coughed, and then replied, 'That is correct, which is why we are returning to the slaughterhouse this morning. And it turns out our forensics teams are under heavy demand at the moment. Though I am opposed to this, my supervisor would be pleased if Private Berlin's forensics team could help us examine that slaughterhouse in more detail.'

'We'll be there in an hour,' Mattie promised, and hung up.

Chapter 23

At ten fifteen, Mattie, Burkhart, Dr. Gabriel, and three Private forensics techs entered the slaughterhouse carrying equipment, including blue lights, cameras, thermal imaging systems, and a pressurized tank attached to a hose and nozzle.

Hauptkommissar Dietrich was already on site, waiting for them along with Inspector Sandra

Weigel and a Kripo forensics team.

'We'll assign you a piece of the floor and wall,' Dietrich told Gabriel, whom he eyed with open distrust after the hippie scientist removed his jacket to reveal a bright orange sweatshirt featuring Bob Marley's image.

Gabriel smiled agreeably. 'I'm calling this place eighty meters by forty.'

'Roughly,' the high commissar replied. 'So?'

'So let's reduce the space,' Private's forensics expert replied. 'Or at least let's understand the full-dimensions of what we're dealing with.'

Dietrich looked at him suspiciously. 'How?'

'Superpressurized luminol fog, my own invention,' Gabriel said as he retied his gray ponytail and tucked it up under a surgeon's cap. Then he put on goggles, picked up the pressurized tank, and twisted the valve.

'Shut down the kliegs, please,' he called.

Dietrich nodded to his assistants. They killed the lights, leaving the place dim and shadowed. Rain pattered on the roof.

'Start recording,' Gabriel told two of his technicians who waited with video cameras mounted on tripods.

Private Berlin's chief scientist aimed the spray wand toward the western end of the building, then squeezed a lever trigger. With a burst and hissing, a fine aerosol fog of luminol, hydrogen peroxide, and hydroxide salt shot from the wand, widened into a cloud that drifted into the rafters, crept down the walls, and settled on the floor.

'Sonofabitch,' Burkhart said.

97

Awed and horrified, Mattie nodded.

It was like looking at depictions of galaxies – tens of thousands of stars in clusters, splashes and pinpoints, a chemiluminescent, glowing-blue constellation of blood.

Chapter 24

The chemical reaction ended in less than thirty seconds. The blue glow died and the slaughterhouse returned to its ruined self. The sheer scope of the blood evidence revealed by Dr. Gabriel's device stunned everyone into silence.

Except for Weigel, who whined, 'It's everywhere, High Commissar!'

Dietrich scowled at her. 'As I said last evening, Weigel, this *was* a slaughterhouse. Luminol only gives us an indication of the presence of iron in blood hemoglobin. It says nothing about that blood's source.'

Dr. Gabriel cut in. 'In any case, we'll have to microgrid the place, sample every three inches, say.'

Dietrich looked annoyed. He hesitated and then nodded with little certainty before saying, 'I think six inches will do.'

Mattie closed her eyes, seeing the glowing-blue galaxy of blood traces in her mind, and noticing that one area seemed more saturated than others. She went to the video camera and replayed it just to be sure.

'What's up?' Burkhart said.

Dietrich was off talking to one of his forensics men.

Mattie gestured to the glowing-blue pattern on the camera screen. 'See where it's more concentrated?'

Burkhart looked and nodded. 'Over in that corner.'

They walked through the trash and filth to the corner and an iron sewer grate. They shined flashlights into a steel-lined well, seeing that at the bottom, some three feet down, there was a second grate of sorts where the metal had been perforated with pencil-sized holes.

'Why isn't there stuff on the bottom down there?' Mattie asked.

Burkhart said, 'I don't follow.'

'It's like a drain catch in a kitchen sink, right?' she asked. 'But in this trashed place, except for a few leaves, it's clean.'

Burkhart thought about that, and then said, 'Well, maybe it is a catch, which means there's something underneath it. Let's take a look.'

He squatted down, got his fingers entwined in the sewer grate, and with a grunt lifted.

Mattie had expected to see the grate come free of the floor.

But to her astonishment, the grate and the steel tube welded beneath it came up, leaving a gaping hole that gave off a horrible stench.

Chapter 25

The hole in the slaughterhouse floor stank of urine and something fouler.

As Burkhart set the false well aside, Mattie held her arm across her nose and shined her light into a metal-walled shaft that dropped eight feet before giving way to four feet of space and then a gravel floor.

'Probably a secondary drain field system,' said Dietrich, who'd come over, and looked somewhat rattled by their discovery.

'Someone needs to go down, but it's too tight for me,' Burkhart said.

'Me too,' the high commissar said.

Inspector Weigel peered down the shaft and shook her head. 'There are rats down there. I can smell them. I hate rats. My brother had one. Used to taunt me with it. I hate them.'

'Then I guess it's me,' Mattie said.

'You know I can't let you–' Dietrich began.

Mattie cut him off. 'If I find anything, Hauptkommissar, I'll back out. Besides, you'll see what I see. I'll be wearing a camera.'

After hearing what Mattie proposed, Gabriel went out to his equipment van and returned with a white disposable coverall, a hard hat, goggles, knee pads, and a headlamp attached to a fiber-optic camera, as well as a radio headset with a supersensitive mic that he taped to the side of her neck, and a respirator to keep her lungs protected from any diseases that might be airborne because of all the rat feces.

They put her in a climbing harness and attached her to a rope.

'Sure you want to do this?' Burkhart asked.

'No,' Mattie said before kneeling and backing slowly into the shaft.

Burkhart and Dietrich lowered her while Gabriel watched a laptop receiving the signal from Mattie's camera.

The shaft was barely bigger than Mattie's shoulders. For a moment she felt a growing claustrophobia, but then the shaft gave way to open space and her feet touched ground.

She released the rope from her harness. Crouching down and swinging her headlamp, she saw that the gravel surface went out in all directions in a black space that swallowed her beam.

'It's like a huge drain field or something,' she said.

'We can't see very well,' Gabriel said in her ear. 'Use your SureFire, too.'

Mattie got out her flashlight and flicked it on, instantly happy for the powerful beam that shot through the space.

She spotted something dull white about ten yards ahead behind a load-bearing steel column. Then she heard chattering to her left. She swung the beam and spotted dozens of rats watching her, and sniffing her presence, some of them scolding her angrily while others worked their chops.

It was creepy, and she heard Niklas's voice telling her to get out of there.

Instead, Mattie crouched and duckwalked toward that white object behind the column. Three feet from it, she saw what it was, and froze.

A bone stuck up out of the gravel.

'That's a human femur,' Gabriel said in her ear.

Mattie swallowed hard and swung her lights deeper into the subbasement, seeing more bones.

And then a human skull. And then two more.

And then more bones and skulls, scattered like seashells everywhere.

Chapter 26

'It's a boneyard,' Mattie whispered.

'We see them,' Burkhart said in her ear. 'Dietrich wants you out of there.'

Mattie had no argument. She'd never been in a more frightening place in her life, and she wanted out before everything went claustrophobic.

But as she pivoted to leave, her beams played across something twenty meters away. Mattie rocked back on her heels as if hit on the chin.

Two fresher corpses lay there, both almost devoid of skin.

A woman. A man.

Clothes hung in tatters from them.

Though she absolutely did not want to, she moved to within several feet of the bodies. She recognized a black ribbed turtleneck that hung off the larger of the two, and felt her whole world cave in.

Mattie fell to her knees and stared, her breath coming hard and fast, echoing in the respirator and making her feel like a zombie, the living dead.

'Mattie?' Gabriel's voice came in her ear.

'Do you see them?' she asked numbly.

'Mattie, we do. Please, come up out of there.'

'The bigger one is Chris,' she said.

'My God, no,' Gabriel said.

Mattie swooned and thought she was fainting.

She rocked her head back, gasping and feeling drunk, when through the spots dancing before her eyes she spotted the first package. It was strapped to the ceiling support about four feet in front of her.

It was about the size of a paperback book and wrapped in green wax paper that had Russian Cyrillic writing on it, and a fuzzy stamp in German.

For several seconds nothing about the situation seemed real, and what she was seeing did not compute.

But then she lolled her head over, seeing similar green paper packages strapped to the ceiling supports, scores of them.

They were all connected with electrical wire.

'Engel!' Burkhart yelled 'Those are bombs! Get the hell out of there!'

103

Chapter 27

All things must pass. Isn't that what they say, my friends?

It's certainly what my mother said the last time I saw her, traitorous bitch.

All things must pass. As if that explains anything to a boy of eight. As if that justified what she'd done to herself, to my father, and to me.

But this time, the old saw is true. All things must pass. I know it as sure as I know myself despite the masks I'm forced to wear.

I'm musing this way in the driver's seat of the ML500 because I've just driven by the entrance to the slaughterhouse at an insistent speed, as if eager to be somewhere else.

There are more vehicles there than yesterday, twice as many, police cars and forensics wagons, and unmarked sedans, and the whole place roped off with yellow crime scene tape.

But instead of feeling on the edge of panic as I did the day before, I go cold, almost reptilian inside. Pulling past the apartment buildings west of the slaughterhouse, I swiftly come to a difficult decision.

A long time ago, very early in my life as a matter of fact, I learned that survival means acting in the moment with the best information you've got. With that many people inside, they were bound to find the secrets of the slaughterhouse eventually. It's just logical.

So I pull over several hundred yards away at the top of a slight rise where I have more or less a direct line of sight to the roof of the abattoir.

For a moment, I feel stricken by nostalgia. The slaughterhouse has been part of my life for so long, I'm conflicted about what I must do.

But there's no way around it, is there?

I open a paper bag on the passenger-side floor, and come up with an old, bulky Soviet-era military two-way radio with a whip antenna. I find the battery and snap it into the housing.

I turn on the power switch. For a moment, the little bulb by the switch is dark and I feel concerned.

But then it glows green.

The air tastes bittersweet as I adjust the radio to a channel with a frequency I set almost twenty-five years ago.

My fingers find the transmit button. My throat clicks with pleasure.

Well then, my friends, I guess it's about time we raised a little hell in Berlin, hmmm?

Chapter 28

'Mattie!' Burkhart roared. 'Get out!'

Down in the basement of the slaughterhouse, Mattie snapped out of the haze of shock. She reached up, grabbed at the green wax paper, and tore off the area with writing on it.

She took one last look at Chris's body, and started going as fast as she could to the shaft, all the while fighting the urge to stop, lie down, and sob her heart out.

When she reached the bottom of the shaft, she looked up and saw Burkhart looking down at her with great concern. 'Clip in,' he ordered.

Mattie stuffed the green paper in the pocket of the coverall, attached the line to her harness, and yelled, 'I'm on.'

She rose instantly. She guided herself into the narrow tube and closed her eyes at the tightness of the passage until Burkhart snagged her by the back of the harness, lifted her, and set her firmly on the slaughterhouse floor.

Mattie trembled as if she'd just been blasted by cold air. 'Did you see?'

She addressed the question to High Commissar Dietrich, who appeared stunned. 'How many bodies are in there?'

'Twenty? Thirty? Like I said, it's a boneyard.'

'I don't care what it is, we are getting out of here, now,' Burkhart said. He looked at Dietrich. 'The place looks booby-trapped. Get your people out now, and call in a federal bomb squad.'

Dietrich hesitated, clearly upended by the scope of what lay before him.

Burkhart got more insistent. 'Hauptkommissar, I worked for GSG 9 in an old life, and I'm telling you to get your people out until the experts can get in there.'

Dietrich's face contorted and then paled. He looked over at Inspector Weigel and the rest of his team watching him.

'Out!' the high commissar finally barked. 'Everyone. Take only the essentials. Now!'

The ten people inside the slaughterhouse went into gear, grabbing computers, cameras, and the evidence samples they'd already gathered. In under a minute they were all hustling through the barn and out the front doors.

The rain had settled to a mist as they came out and trotted back toward the road to Ahrensfelde. Mattie followed Burkhart mutely, feeling battered by what she'd seen underground.

Chris was gone. He would always be gone.

When she was almost to the police barrier the first bomb detonated.

Mattie spun around.

Smoke and dust billowed out the windows and doors before a giant, deafening eruption hurled Mattie off her feet and blew the slaughterhouse to smithereens.

Book Two

WAISENHAUS 44

Chapter 29

Jack Morgan walked down a hallway in a large two-story apartment north of Monbijou Park in central Berlin.

He was following a slim, pale man in his late twenties with ice-blue eyes, pierced eyebrows, a long black trench coat, bleached white hair, and leather half gloves with studs, all of which made him look like he belonged in a vampire movie.

But Daniel Brecht was one of Private's best detectives in Europe, a fascinating character who slipped easily through cultures and languages.

Brecht shifted a black book bag to his left shoulder, rapped his studs on the door, and turned the handle. They entered a dark room that smelled of sex.

Brecht flicked a switch. Light flooded the bedroom.

An angry, fit, caramel-colored man shot up in bed and began shouting at them in Portuguese. Morgan didn't understand a word Cassiano was saying.

Brecht did. He flashed his badge, which cooled the soccer player. That's when Morgan noticed the woman, a blonde with enormous breasts, who lay passed out next to Cassiano.

It surprised Morgan. Earlier he'd seen Internet photos of the striker's wife, Perfecta, a Brazilian model with stunning, exotic looks and an incredible body. The woman in the bed looked plain in comparison.

Over the next five minutes, Brecht interrogated Cassiano and translated for Morgan.

'You know Christoph Schneider?' Brecht asked. 'He works for Private.'

The striker shook his head. 'Never heard of him.'

'Where's your wife?' Brecht asked, nodding at the passed-out woman.

Cassiano shrugged and smiled. 'Perfecta's on a photo shoot in Africa. Be back the day after tomorrow.'

'Be tough if she found out you had a sleepover,' Morgan said.

The athlete sobered. 'Okay. So I met with Schneider for ten minutes last Monday. He asked me about games where I played poorly earlier in the season.'

'You mean these?' Brecht asked, removing an iPad from his carryall. He gave it a command and a clip played of Cassiano missing a great pass.

'We looked at all the videos this morning,' Morgan said. 'You don't look anything like the scoring machine you are in other games.'

'I was sick, nauseated all those times, the shits,' Cassiano said indignantly. 'I went to doctor. He says I am having problem with German food. It came and went, but I still played. Sick. Hurt. I play. I'm known for that.'

'Sure you weren't taking a dive?' Morgan asked.

Cassiano turned furious after Brecht translated, and started shouting at him in Portuguese. 'No way. There is World Cup in three years. Do you honestly think I'd screw that up?'

Brecht gestured at the woman, who had stirred and groaned at the shouting. 'You look like you're trying to screw up a marriage with a supermodel, so what do we know?'

'This is recreation,' Cassiano said, indignant once again. 'And my answer is still no. I was not taking a dive. I never take a dive. It is a matter of honor.'

'You know Maxim Pavel? He owns that drag-queen club, Cabaret.'

Cassiano looked insulted. 'Do I look like fan of female impersonators?'

'Doesn't answer the question,' Morgan shot back. 'Do you know Pavel?'

Cassiano sighed. 'Like I told Schneider, I met him once at another of his clubs, not Cabaret, Dance, I think.'

'Did you know he's associated with Russian mafia?' Brecht asked.

'Not until Schneider asked me the same question,' he replied evenly. 'Like I said, I met him once. We talk for maybe five minutes.'

'About what?'

'He says he is a big fan. Gets my autograph.'

'Can anyone corroborate this? Your wife?'

'Perfecta wasn't with me when I went to the dance club. But Cabaret's a ten-minute walk from here, so do the same thing I told Schneider to do. Go there and ask Pavel.'

Chapter 30

Firemen trained hoses on the smoking ruins of the slaughterhouse.

Her ears still ringing from the blast, her mind flashing with images of Chris's corpse, Mattie sat on the bumper of an ambulance, wincing as an EMT used a butterfly bandage to close the scalp wound she'd gotten during the blast.

Burkhart sat next to her getting his arm wrapped with gauze. Next to him, High Commissar Dietrich was being treated for a cheek contusion.

They were facing Dr. Gabriel and Risi Baumgarten, a German federal agent who'd seized control of the investigation.

Dr. Gabriel said, 'I just spoke with Jack Morgan. He's given the okay for me to call in forensics teams from our offices in Amsterdam, Zurich, Paris, and London. Anything you want from Private is yours.'

'I think Private's already been involved too much,' snapped Baumgarten, who stood a full six inches taller than the hippie scientist.

Mattie heard that through the ringing in her ears and said, 'What is that supposed to mean?'

'It means perhaps this explosion would not have happened had you not gone down there, Frau Engel.'

'Someone had to go,' said Dietrich. 'She was the right size, and we had no idea there was a bomb

114

down there.'

Dietrich had seemed much less tightly wound and adversarial since the explosion. Mattie smiled grimly at him, thankful for the backup.

But Baumgarten was having none of it. 'You sent in an amateur.'

'I am not an amateur,' Mattie cried.

'You set off a booby trap,' Baumgarten said.

'I did not set off anything. I did not trip anything.'

'So it's simply a coincidence that the place blew right after you'd been down there?'

Burkhart shook his head. 'If it was a booby trap and she tripped something, it would have gone off right away. I figure this was done remotely, by radio. We just got lucky getting out before it blew.'

Baumgarten eyed them all, and then looked at Gabriel. 'You said there was a video of what Frau Engel saw in the subbasement.'

Gabriel nodded and cued it up on his computer. Baumgarten was sobered by the images from the boneyard. Mattie could not watch when the camera picked up Chris's corpse. But she did see herself reaching up to tear green paper from one of the bomb packets. She dug it from her pocket and handed it to the federal agent.

Baumgarten examined it for several moments before saying, 'Czech-made Semtex, similar to C-4. Soviet era. Got to be twenty-five or thirty years old.'

'Who put it down there and when?' Mattie said. 'I mean, if Burkhart's right, whoever set those bombs off had to have been watching us, or at least had to have known there were police at the site. He didn't know we were rushing to get out. He was willing to kill all of us to keep that bone-yard buried.'

While Baumgarten considered that, Dietrich said, 'I agree. And more, I think what Frau Engel discovered could be a dumping ground for a serial killer. How else do you explain thirty skulls in the same place?'

'Maybe he's an assassin,' Burkhart said. 'Maybe when people hire him to make their enemies disappear, this is where he dumps them.'

Dietrich nodded. 'I could see that too.'

Baumgarten did not comment on any of it. Another agent called to her and she left them just as Inspector Weigel reappeared. 'Where does this leave us, High Commissar?'

'Blocked, at least as far as this place is concerned,' Dietrich said. 'We really have no other course of action except to wait for the forensics teams to find us some evidence.'

'That could be a week or more!' Mattie protested.

'It could,' the high commissar said.

'So you're going to put this investigation down?'

'Not at all,' Dietrich said. 'But I know what my supervisor is going to say. We've got a backlog of homicide cases and the federal agencies have taken the lead now. Until we get more physical evidence, I'm sure I'll be spending my time working cases with more short-term promise.'

Mattie looked at the Kripo investigator in disbelief and then anger. 'Well, you can be damn sure of one thing, Hauptkommissar – Private Berlin will be spending every waking moment working

116

on this case. We are not resting until we nail the bastard who killed Chris and the other people buried under that debris.'

Chapter 31

The nightclub Cabaret was empty and dark except for a few workers and a man in a leotard on stage practicing a dance routine in time to an amplified tune that Jack Morgan could not place.

Cabaret's décor was over-the-top lavish with velvet booths and crystal chandeliers and a booming sound system.

Morgan took one look and wanted to leave for Ahrensfelde. He'd just heard from Burkhart about Mattie's discovery of Chris's body, the mass grave, and the destruction of the slaughterhouse.

But Burkhart had assured him they were fine, and there was little Morgan could do there because the federal police had taken over the investigation. He'd reluctantly decided to continue pursuing the Cassiano angle.

A burly, big-necked man stocking the bar regarded Morgan and Brecht suspiciously and asked them what they wanted. Brecht showed him his Private badge, introduced Morgan, and asked for Maxim Pavel.

The bartender, a Russian, seemed amused and switched to stilted English, addressing Morgan: 'You have office in Moscow, Mr. Private?'

'We do,' Morgan replied.

The bartender grinned, revealing a missing tooth. He nodded at Brecht. 'Good think you put this bloodsucker in Berlin. He wouldn't last ten minutes in Russia. They'd put a stake through his heart.'

Without a change in expression, Brecht showed his canine teeth, and said, 'I bite guys like you in the neck.'

The bartender snarled at Brecht, 'Get out of here before I call police or throw you in the sun.'

'Not before we talk with Pavel,' Brecht said.

'He's not–'

'I am Pavel,' said a voice behind them.

Morgan turned to find a man coming at him from the main entrance, removing a raincoat and setting it on a chair. Pavel was a fit, handsome man whose age was hard to peg; his skin was so taut Morgan believed he'd had plastic surgery at some point.

'What do you want?' Pavel demanded.

'We're with Private,' Morgan said.

'Getting to be a regular thing with you guys.'

'Chris Schneider came to visit you last week?'

'That's right,' Pavel said. 'Why?'

Morgan said, 'Soon after he came to see you, he was murdered and dumped in a rat-infested slaughterhouse that blew up about two hours ago, almost killing two more of my agents.'

That threw Pavel and he shrank a little. 'Blown up? Schneider's dead?'

'Uh-huh,' Brecht said. 'Where you been this morning?'

'Driving in the countryside,' Pavel said. 'It calms me.'

'Anyone able to vouch for that?'

'I'm sure if a real police officer asked I could find someone.'

Morgan said, 'Did Schneider ask you about Cassiano?'

'I told him that I met Cassiano once at Dance, another of my clubs.'

'No other contact?' Morgan asked.

'Other than what I see on television, no,' Pavel replied.

'What about his wife, Perfecta?' Morgan asked. 'You ever met her?'

The nightclub owner hesitated, but then said, 'Once. That same night.'

'So they were together?' Brecht asked.

'That's right,' Pavel said. 'A handsome couple. But now I have to oversee rehearsal and attend to other business before tonight's show.'

Brecht made to protest, but Morgan stopped him. 'We appreciate your time, Herr Pavel.'

Pavel studied Morgan before smiling broadly. 'You come back and see the show, Mr. Morgan. It's on me.'

Morgan smiled coldly. 'Drag queens aren't my thing.'

'Cabaret is so much more than that,' Pavel said, not missing a beat. 'The costumes, the makeup, the talent. It's a great art form.'

'I'll be in touch if I have a change of heart.'

Outside the club, the rain had slowed to a drizzle.

Brecht said, 'Somebody's lying to us, Jack.'

Morgan nodded. 'I know.'

Chapter 32

An hour later, Agnes Krüger exuded an almost regal bearing as she sat in the drawing room of her lavish townhome on Fasanenstrasse in the elite Wilmersdorf district of Berlin, and listened to Mattie Engel and Katharina Doruk give an account of her husband's extracurricular activities.

'Three mistresses?' the billionaire's wife said at last in a voice like an ill-tuned piano string. 'And two prostitutes a day, you say?'

'Yes, ma'am,' Katharina said. 'I'm sorry.'

There was a long silence. Mattie sat numbly on a plush couch, wanting to feel sorry for the woman, but all she could think of was how she was ever going to tell Niklas that the only man who'd ever been solidly in his life was gone.

She and Burkhart had left the explosion scene while journalists and federal agents swarmed the area. They returned to the office where she'd met Katharina, who had told her to go home, but Mattie refused, saying she could not face Niklas yet.

Katharina had decided to keep Chris's appointment with Krüger's wife. Mattie could not bear sitting still, so she'd showered and changed in Private Berlin's locker room, and gone along.

But now she just wanted to go home, hold Niklas, and Socrates, and cry.

'It is hard,' Agnes Krüger said, breaking the silence, and then coughing. 'It is hard to learn

120

that you do not satisfy your husband in any way, shape, or form. Do you have names? The mistresses? Their phone numbers, addresses?'

Katharina looked pained. 'We do, but–'

'What're you gonna do, Mother?' a snide male voice said, cutting her off. 'Buy them off? Cover up for him again?'

The billionaire's wife reacted as if she'd been slapped.

Mattie startled and looked over to see a gaunt young man with grungy clothes and a scruffy beard. He was peering into the drawing room from the hallway.

Agnes Krüger's chin rose as if in defiance. 'My son, Rudy.'

'The name's Rude, Mother.'

'This is not the time.'

'Sounds like it is,' her son said, strolling in and taking a seat. He nodded to Mattie and Katharina. 'Go on. I'd like to hear just what old stepdad's been up to.'

The billionaire's wife sat even more erect in her chair.

Mattie and Katharina said nothing.

Rudy Krüger snorted. 'You know what? I don't need to know the details. I know all about Hermann. Except for his money, and his business, his art collection and the cars, he only has one other dimension. Stepdad's a goat, driven by his prick and balls. And those women? They're just holes. Even mother is a hole, a hole who completed Hermann's façade of respectability.'

Agnes Krüger's façade broke into rage. 'Enough!' she shouted at him. 'Go back to that

121

hell *hole* you prefer to my house! Get out!'

Her son smiled and stood. 'I know what you're going to do, Mother. You're going to figure out a way to sweep it under the rug, and you know why?'

Agnes Krüger said nothing. She just glared at Rudy.

'Because of the money,' he told Mattie and Katharina. 'With my mother and stepfather it's always about the money.'

Chapter 33

Jack Morgan and Daniel Brecht sat at the window table in a café diagonally across the street from Cabaret, debating why Cassiano would claim he met Pavel alone when Pavel said they met with his wife.

'Perhaps a memory lapse,' Brecht allowed. 'Or it's a flaw in a cover story.'

Morgan had been looking out the window. He threw down his napkin and got up fast. 'So much for rehearsal and other business. Pavel's on the move.'

Brecht tossed money on the table and rushed after him into the street.

Out in front of Cabaret, the nightclub owner climbed into a taxicab.

Morgan was already hailing another cab. They jumped in and told the driver to follow the cab ahead.

As they drove, Morgan began to feel the effects of jet lag. His head nodded and his brain buzzed with thoughts, wondering if Pavel had actually had something to do with Chris's death, wondering how Mattie Engel was taking it all.

Burkhart had said she was acting like a professional.

Morgan's last thought before he dozed was: But how long can that last?

Several minutes later, Brecht nudged him and he jerked awake.

'Pavel's getting out at the Hotel de Rome,' Brecht said.

Even in his groggy state, Morgan recognized the hotel. It was the most luxurious in Berlin as far as he was concerned. He usually stayed there during his visits.

'Know anyone in security?' Morgan asked as they climbed from their taxi down the street from the hotel.

'Definitely,' Brecht said. 'I helped them out last year. The American movie star. Did you see that report?'

Morgan came fully awake. 'I'm so tired I forgot that happened here. Jesus, what a mess that must have been to clean up.'

'Crazy mess,' Brecht said. 'Crazy, crazy mess.'

They entered a lobby with soaring ceilings and marble columns, and went to the concierge. Brecht asked to see the hotel's head of security.

Exactly nine minutes later, Brecht and Morgan were inside the room directly across the hall from one Pavel had reserved. They also knew that the nightclub owner had just ordered champagne and caviar.

He was expecting someone.

Brecht unscrewed the peephole and inserted a tiny fiber-optic camera and microphone, which he connected to a transmitter linked to his iPad.

'I pay for all that?' Morgan asked after he flopped on the king-size bed, feeling depressed again about Chris Schneider's death.

'Private Berlin issued,' Brecht said. 'Here comes room service.'

Morgan watched the cart with the champagne and caviar arrive and then Pavel open the door to let the waiter in. He left moments later.

'Why don't I have one of those mini surveillance kits?' Morgan asked.

'Euro technology,' Brecht said. 'Hasn't made it to LA yet.'

'I forgot I live at the end of the universe,' Morgan said, throwing his arm over his eyes. 'I'm going to snooze. Wake me up if...'

Private's owner drifted off. Right on the edge of sleep, just before falling, Brecht tapped him on the shoulder. 'Pavel's got a visitor.'

Morgan groaned and opened his eyes blearily to see Brecht showing him the iPad. A woman in a long, dark trench coat and a floppy rain hat stood with her back to the camera outside the door across the hall.

They heard Pavel's muffled voice through the door. 'Who is it?'

'I have delivery for you,' the woman replied in a soft Portuguese accent as she fumbled with the belt of her raincoat.

They heard the dead bolt thrown.

124

The woman looked both ways, and then shrugged the raincoat off.

Morgan sat upright. She was magnificently naked when the door opened.

Pavel's eyes went wide with delight. 'Delivery accepted.'

She stepped into his arms. The door closed behind them.

'Who is that goddess?' Brecht asked. 'I didn't see her face.'

Morgan shook his head in disbelief. 'I didn't see it either, but I'd recognize that teardrop Brazilian rear anywhere. That, my friend, was Perfecta.'

Chapter 34

When the front door to Agnes Krüger's town house in Wilmersdorf slammed shut, the billionaire's wife regained her composure and bearing.

'My son fancies himself an anarchist and an artist,' she said. 'He despises my husband for his money.' She smiled sourly. 'But he doesn't refuse the ten thousand euros Hermann deposits in his account every month.'

She laughed caustically and then looked at Mattie. 'You have children?'

'One,' Mattie said. 'A son.'

'Rudy is an only child as well,' she began. She hesitated and then said, 'But he's not why you are here.'

'No,' Katharina said. 'We're here because Chris

Schneider is dead.'

That shocked the billionaire's wife. 'Dead? How? He was such a young man!'

Katharina gave her the bare bones of the circumstances. Mattie listened to her report as if it were arriving from outer space, incomprehensible even to her.

'In a slaughterhouse?' the billionaire's wife said. 'Why?'

'We don't know,' Mattie replied. 'We're hoping you might help.'

'Where has Hermann been the last few weeks?' Katharina asked.

Agnes Krüger fidgeted in her chair. 'He was here in Berlin for the most part, I believe. Ask his secretary.'

'I did,' Katharina said. 'She said he's off on business.'

'Or tending to his mistresses.'

'Doesn't he live here with you?' Mattie asked.

Her face flickered painfully. 'Hermann has a bed here. He uses it from time to time. Comes and goes as he pleases. Doesn't give a damn if I'm in it or not.' Agnes Krüger looked closely at Mattie, who'd somehow won her trust. 'You know, he wasn't always like this. At least I don't think so. This belief that anything goes came with the money.'

'Where did you meet?' Mattie asked.

'Here in Berlin shortly after the wall fell. He was making his first fortune bringing textiles into the newly liberated east as fast as he could. I worked for him as his secretary. Rudy was just a baby. My first husband had deserted me, and,

126

well, Hermann is a good talker.'

'Who knows how to make money,' Katharina said.

'He came to capitalism naturally. It suited him.'

'I don't understand,' Mattie said.

'He grew up in East Berlin, but as soon as the wall fell he was in motion.'

'Same thing with Chris.'

She studied Mattie again. 'He was more than a colleague to you.'

For the second time in twenty-four hours, Mattie wondered if she was that transparent, but she said, 'My ex-fiancé.'

'Oh, dear,' the billionaire's wife said, her hand traveling to her lips. 'I'm so sorry for you, Frau Engel.'

Mattie nodded, swallowing hard at the loss pulsing in her.

There was a pause and another painful flicker in her skin before Agnes Krüger said, 'And you think my husband might have been involved in his death?'

'What do you think?' Katharina asked. 'Is he capable of it? Would he have reason? Would Chris's knowing about all the women, and being ready to reveal them to you, drive him to murder?'

The billionaire's wife was still for several moments, and then she turned, disgusted. 'On this my son is correct: Hermann's soul is black.' She hardened. 'You should know that there have been rumors about Hermann.'

'What kind of rumors?' Mattie asked.

Agnes Krüger gazed at Katharina and Mattie in turn before saying, 'You'd have to talk with Rudy for any particulars, but evidently people who cross my husband have a way of disappearing or dying in convenient accidents.'

Chapter 35

The rain lifted just before five that afternoon, casting the grounds of the Soviet War Memorial in Treptower Park in a light that looked nickel-plated to Hauptkommissar Hans Dietrich.

The homicide detective stood at the base of the dripping statue of the Soviet soldier carrying the German child. His cheek ached and felt swollen.

With an air of victory surrounding him, the colonel strode into view at precisely 5:07 p.m.

Again his eyes slashed all over his son, lingering on the bandage on his cheek before his lips twisted in contempt.

'Leave me alone, Hans,' he commanded.

'I will after tonight, Colonel,' the high commissar promised. 'That slaughterhouse in Ahrens-felde—'

'I told you to leave *that* alone,' the colonel said and kept walking.

This night Dietrich did not reach out to grab his father. To his back, he said, 'Someone blew it up this morning with GDR-era Semtex.'

The colonel stopped and turned, incredulous, but then said, 'I thought I heard something like cannon fire.'

The high commissar nodded. 'Before it went

128

off, we found decomposing bodies and skeletons in a subbasement. Thirty of them.'

Dietrich always thought his father was unshakable, but that news rattled him. 'No,' the colonel said in a voice that sounded suddenly old. 'That's not—'

'They were there,' Dietrich insisted. 'What do you know?'

The colonel rubbed his left arm as if to soothe an ache. 'I honestly don't *know* anything.'

'But there were rumors,' Dietrich pressed. 'I heard you one night—'

His father's face twisted and he held his arm tighter as he hissed back, 'There were rumors everywhere about everything and everybody. No one knew what was true and what was fiction. No one. And I still don't.'

'Don't you want to know?'

'No,' his father croaked, then turned, now clutching his left arm.

The colonel made three steps in the direction of the closest sarcophagus. He stopped, weaving unsteadily. Then he reeled to his right and pitched over on his side in a puddle on the gravel path.

For an instant Dietrich was too stunned to move. He did not think it possible that... 'Papi!' he cried, rushing to his father's side.

The colonel was choking and looking at him bug-eyed. Dietrich threw himself on his knees to perform CPR.

But his father's right hand shot up and grabbed him by the collar of his jacket. 'I know I wasn't a good father,' he rasped. 'But was I a good man?'

For once in his life, the high commissar did not

know how to answer a question. His silence was a response that the colonel understood. The old man's cheeks tightened. He turned his gaze away from his son to the statue of the triumphant Soviet warrior and the German child towering above them.

'I was a good citizen,' the colonel gasped. 'You know I was.'

And then in a harsh sigh, the life went out of Dietrich's father and his eyes took on the dull and glazed stare of fate.

Chapter 36

It's 8 p.m when I enter the Diana FKK, a high-class mega-brothel in a luxurious spa setting on the outskirts of West Berlin.

Indoor pools. Jacuzzis. Saunas. Masseuses. And beautiful women of every race and color parading around completely nude.

One would think that my thirst for flesh would have been satisfied by my late-afternoon interlude with my friend, the woman who honestly believes I love her. But the lethal events of the past two days seem to have filled me with an unquenchable desire for all things carnal.

I pay my entrance fee, and go down to the locker room where I strip and put on a robe and rubber slippers. I take the canvas bag with my latest mask acquisition and head upstairs, hearing the sound of women laughing.

Is there anything like it? The sound of women laughing? I feel alive here among these laughing women. I can be anyone I want to be. They can be anyone I want them to be.

And that's a relief after such a long and difficult day.

But as I wander, evaluating the women against my criteria, my mind keeps flashing to the expression on my friend the thief's face when I hit him with the stun gun.

Even with the music blaring from the brothel bar I can honestly hear the crunch and squish of the screwdriver entering his brain.

And behind it all, like a shimmering backdrop, the memory of that unbelievable fireball that rose above the slaughterhouse, scorching and pulverizing that part of my past into dust.

As I walk through the brothel's spa, admiring the women soaking in the whirlpools, these pleasant memories bow to pressing concerns. I have much to do to finish burying my past for good, and it will take every bit of my skill to get it done swiftly and without a trace of my participation.

But I'll wait until tomorrow to address those crucial tasks.

For now, I'm seeking to cleanse myself, a sensual reduction to the primal, a release from all that I appear to be to the ignorant outside world.

I spot my prey on an elevated platform in the middle of one of the pools.

She's exotic. Black hair. Dark, flashing eyes. A copper stain to her skin.

She's naked except for a gold chain about her

waist, and she's writhing in a slow-motion belly dance to the appreciation of several men lounging in the water below her.

I stand there, watching until our eyes meet. I smile and crook a finger at her. She smiles and keeps dancing.

We keep this up and a nice little tension builds between us before she finally leaves, crosses the pool, and comes up to me. Her brown eyes are dazzling. Her hips to die for.

She says her name is Bettina and asks if I want company. I smile warmly. She comes into my arms as if she belongs beneath me. Which she does.

I tell her I've got a little surprise for her in my bag.

'What kind of surprise?' Bettina asks.

'The kind that surprises, silly girl,' I tease.

Moments later in a mirrored room, I have her get on her knees and elbows, her legs open so I can see every little bit of her mystery.

I unlock the case and draw out the mask: a black jaguar with golden eyes and ruby mouth, baring golden teeth.

Bettina's looking back over her shoulder, uneasy at the mask.

I can already feel myself rising.

I put the mask on and prepare to enter her.

Bettina's clearly unnerved now, and I don't think I could be more excited if I'd planned to throttle the life out of her or stick a screwdriver in her brain.

'What's with the mask?' she asks in a tremulous voice.

'It's an ancient Mayan relic, Bettina,' I say as I crouch over her and drive myself into her as a panther might, thrilled at her grunt of disbelief and fear. 'It depicts their Jaguar God, the ruler of the night and the lord of the fucking underworld.'

Chapter 37

At eight thirty that evening Mattie stood unsteadily outside the door to her apartment. She smelled fresh cookies baking. She could hear a radio announcer giving the news, and caught something about the slaughterhouse explosion.

She leaned her head against the door. She was more than a little drunk.

The 6 p.m. strategy meeting Jack Morgan called in order to better manage the various threads of the investigation had eventually devolved into an impromptu wake for Chris.

Drinks were poured. Toasts were given. Stories were told. Tears were shed. They'd even laughed a few times at old memories.

Now standing outside her apartment door, digging for her keys, she realized that memories were all she had of Chris.

It was all he would ever be.

But Niklas was alive. Niklas had a future. She had to make him see that.

Mattie opened the door to see her aunt Cäcilia coming out of the kitchen.

'Where is he?' Mattie asked, unable to hide the sadness.

'He just went to his room,' Aunt Cäcilia replied, her face twisting with concern. 'Chris?'

Mattie bit her lip and shook her head. 'He's dead, Aunt C.'

'No!' Aunt Cäcilia cried as she hurried over. 'No! What happened?'

Mattie fell into her arms, tears brimming in her eyes. 'I'll explain it to you later after I explain it to Niklas. But how am I supposed to do that when I can't explain it to myself?'

Her aunt hugged her tightly and the dam burst. Mattie sobbed in her arms.

'Life can be so cruel sometimes, child,' Cäcilia said, rubbing her back.

'Why is that?' Mattie cried. 'Why is that?'

'That's a question beyond my qualifications, dear, one better addressed to God.'

'Mommy?'

Mattie raised her head and saw Niklas watching her from the hallway. He was already in his pajamas and looked so frightened that she almost collapsed with grief. But she got hold of herself, left her aunt, and went toward him, saying, 'I'm sorry, Nicky.'

Her son's chin trembled and for a moment she thought he was going to blame her and run away. But, dissolving into tears, he ran into her arms and cried in a hiccupping voice, 'But I thought... I prayed... Aunt C said...'

Mattie picked him up and carried him to the rocking chair in the television room. 'I know. I know.'

Niklas curled up in his mother's lap. Socrates appeared and jumped into Niklas's lap.

Mattie held on to them and watched her aunt sit down crying on the couch, realizing that these three beings were among the very few anchors left in her life.

Chapter 38

The next morning, after a near-sleepless night, Mattie resisted the urge to go to work early. She stayed with Niklas, cooked him his breakfast, and walked him through the streets to the John Lennon Gymnasium, where he attended elementary school.

When they neared the school, Niklas stopped and looked up at her, asking, 'Are you going to be all right, Mommy?'

She had been about to ask him the same thing. She hugged him. 'As long as I've got you, little man, I'll always be all right.'

'Me too,' Niklas said.

She kissed him and said, 'Go on, or you'll be late. Aunt C will be here to pick you up.'

'I know the way home.'

'I know you do,' Mattie said. 'But she'll be waiting just the same.'

She waited until he'd disappeared up the steps inside the school. Her cell phone rang. It was Katharina Doruk. 'Meet me at Tacheles.'

'I was heading to the office.'

'I found out that Rudy Krüger lives and works in Tacheles. It might be a nice time for a chat. I hear early is always good when you're dealing with artists and anarchists.'

Mattie had her sights set on Chris's past, but she could see the value in talking to the billionaire's son.

'When?'

'I'll be there in twenty minutes.'

Mattie headed toward the underground at Rosenthaler Platz. It was a cool, blustery day, with dark puffy clouds racing across a deep-blue sky, and Mattie found herself wondering if life was nothing more than that, a cloud racing across a blue sky, and then, simply, gone on the wind.

That thought consumed her until she entered the underground station and noticed the *Berliner Zeitung* and *Berliner Morgenpost* newspaper headlines at one of the kiosks. She snapped up both, paid, and read the articles about the slaughterhouse on the train to Oranienburger Strasse.

Both stories noted the explosion, the fact that police vehicles had been seen in the area the day before, and the rumor that High Commissar Hans Dietrich had been working the case. Federal agent Risi Baumgarten was the only official quoted in either story, however, and she had revealed very little, refusing to say what police had been doing inside the old abattoir before it blew up.

The *Morgenpost* article went further, noting that the GDR government built the slaughterhouse as an auxiliary to East Berlin's main stockyard and slaughterhouse in the late 1950s. As the communist economy slowly crumbled the building had been used less often, and then abandoned. It had stood that way until yesterday's blast.

'That place was never fully abandoned,' Mattie muttered to herself as she got off the underground train. 'Someone knew about that sub-basement and that fake drain going way, way back.'

Chapter 39

Tacheles was the epitome of cool in Berlin, a bullet-ridden, bomb-scarred, and graffiti-clad building in Mitte that the East Germans never tore down after Hitler's war.

When the wall fell, squatters moved in to the former department store on Oranienburger Strasse and formed an artists' collective. Twenty years later, more than one hundred artists lived and worked in the building and on the grounds, which over the years had evolved to include studios, an avant-garde cinema, restaurants, a squatters' village, a giant sculpture garden, and an outdoor performance area and stage.

It was eight fifteen in the morning, but the lower building was nearly dead quiet. They climbed upstairs. Rudy Krüger's rented squat was on the third floor. Katharina's smartphone dinged. She looked at it.

'Interesting,' she said. 'Olle Larsson, the Swedish financier, just announced that he's taken a five percent interest in Krüger Industries.'

'Which means what?' Mattie asked.

'Possible target of a take-over bid, and according to this report, there's been no comment by Krüger – who is said to be out of the country on business.'

'I bet a hostile takeover would put a lot of pressure on Hermann.'

'Keep him away from his women, certainly,' Katharina said.

'Maybe enough to make him homicidal?'

'I don't know. Let's ask.'

They found the door to Rudy Krüger's studio. Electronic music played inside. Katharina pounded on the door.

'I'm working!' Rudy Krüger yelled back immediately.

Katharina identified herself and a moment later the music lowered and the door opened on a chain. The billionaire's stepson wore a white coverall spattered in black and blue paint. 'I'm busy. I've got an exhibition opening in three days, and a meeting to be at in an hour.'

'We just want to talk to you about your stepfather, the alleged murderer,' Mattie said.

He gave them a calculating stare and then opened the door.

They entered a loft area with north light beaming into a large, high-ceilinged studio. There were canvases up on easels and others stacked against the walls. They were all abstracts in blues and blacks and featured the words *Rude, Rot,* and *Riot* splashed somewhere in brilliant yellows or reds.

'Selling any?' Katharina asked.

Rudy looked at her contemptuously. 'Buying

and selling have little to do with art. I'm more about the doing than the marketing.'

'Uh-huh,' Mattie said. 'Tell us about your stepfather. Your mother said he's had people killed, but she had no particulars.'

His lips curled as if he'd tasted something sour. 'Those are the rumors.'

'From?'

'The rumor mill,' he said.

'Any particulars?' Mattie demanded.

'Just look at his projects,' Rudy said. 'It's there if you really want to dig. Check Africa.'

'We plan to,' Katharina said. 'Is that what Chris Schneider called you about last Monday?'

Mattie frowned. She knew nothing about any call to Rudy. The billionaire's son looked surprised as well. 'How did you...?'

'We ran Schneider's phone records,' Katharina said. 'Yours came up.'

'Why'd you look?'

'He's dead,' Mattie said. 'Murdered.'

Rudy appeared shocked but then said, 'Yes, Schneider called me. He was about to meet with my stepfather and wanted to know if Hermann really is the ruthless corporate bastard he's made out to be in the press.'

'What did you say?' Katharina asked.

Rudy's smile resembled a hyena's. 'I said that my stepfather in person is much, much worse, someone who'd cut his mother's throat if he thought it would fetch him a euro.'

Chapter 40

'We get it – you don't like your stepfather,' Katharina said. 'Why?'

Rudy Krüger picked up one of his paintbrushes from the palette and considered one of his masterpieces before responding. 'Because Hermann is a pure corporate capitalist pig, emphasis on pig.'

'Example?' Katharina pressed.

He tossed the paintbrush back on the palette. 'How about the way he treats my mother? Twenty years ago he made her sign a prenuptial agreement that limits what she'd get in a divorce. It's what keeps her tied to him. She'll never give up the money no matter what he does. Plus, she honestly believes he loves her deep down.'

He snorted and shook his head.

'How much does she get in a divorce?' Mattie asked.

'Ten million euros.'

'Not terrible,' Katharina observed.

'If your husband is worth three and a half billion, and you were married to him when he made most of it?'

Mattie said, 'I see your point, but what can she do?'

'What can she do?' Rudy Kruger laughed caustically. 'She can show some backbone and character and leave him.'

'That's your advice?'

140

'It's either that or she learns to live with three mistresses and a house full of whores.'

'What do you know about Olle Larsson?' Katharina asked.

The billionaire's son's head pulled back like a turtle's toward its shell. 'Who?'

'Swedish financier,' Katharina said. 'He launched a hostile take-over bid of your stepfather's company an hour ago.'

Rudy's breath came partly out in a rush. 'Never heard of him.'

'Rude?' a woman's voice called.

She was tiny, no more than one hundred pounds, with a pretty face and a haircut that made her look waifish. She wore a kaffiyeh scarf around her neck.

'This is Tanya,' Rudy said. 'My ... uh, student.'

'Right,' Katharina said.

'We're due at the rally, Rude,' Tanya said.

Unzipping the painter's coverall, revealing jeans and a dark sweater, Rudy told Mattie and Katharina, 'If you're here to ask me if my stepfather had something to do with Schneider's death, I honestly don't know.

'But if you're here to ask whether I think he's capable of it, my answer is that Hermann Krüger is capable of anything.'

141

Chapter 41

It's nine on the dot when I park the Audi A5 well down the street from the German Federal Archives in West Berlin.

Call it the German in me, call it how I was raised as a child, but I do so like to be punctual for an opening.

I check myself in the mirror. The makeup, gray hair color, and clothes I wear make me look elderly. I put on a Bavarian alpine hat that is too large for me, so the brim sits just above my eyebrows. I climb from the car with a satchel briefcase, and a cane.

As I approach the gatehouse to the archives I make myself shake every so often, as if I've had some kind of stroke and it's left me palsied.

At the gate, I present an expertly forged identification card from Heidelberg University and portray myself as absentminded history professor emeritus Karl Groening, who has failed to bring his driver's license after coming all the way to Berlin by train to do research into nineteenth-century agricultural policy.

The guards give me a blue researcher's badge, and let me in.

The grounds of the archives look like a decaying college campus with huge spreading chestnuts and long empty lawns. I find the building I need on the far side of the complex.

When I enter the public reading room, like many of the other researchers, I don cotton gloves. Then I go to the archivist's desk and request all documentation associated with East German orphanages in and around Berlin.

'It may take an hour or so for the files to come up,' the clerk says.

'This is okay, my dear,' I say. 'I booked the late train to Heidelberg.'

Chapter 42

Jack Morgan was sitting at the break table nursing a coffee and looking very hungover when Katharina and Mattie arrived at Private Berlin.

'You didn't sleep here, did you, Jack?' Mattie asked, pouring herself a cup.

'No. I kept the room at the Hotel de Rome,' he said. 'How's your son taking all this?'

'As well as could be expected, thank you.'

Morgan nodded. 'I liked Chris. He was a good person, and when good people die, it reminds you of everybody else you've lost.'

'I saw my mother in my dreams last night,' Mattie said. 'She was right there with Chris.'

'Your dad, he lives in the US, a cop, right?'

'Chicago,' she replied.

Katharina asked, 'Who have you lost, Jack?'

The owner of Private thought about that. 'Comrades in arms, dear friends, and an old and dear lover.'

'How did she die?' Mattie asked.

'Justine's alive. What's dead is what we had between us.'

'How long ago did that end?'

'A few years. Long enough I should have moved on.'

'You're still not over her?'

'My relationship with Justine is like waves on a beach, coming and going, but always coming back. Especially because she works at Private in LA.'

'You have a complicated life, Jack,' Katharina said.

'Uh-huh.'

'No other love interests?' Mattie asked.

He laughed with little enthusiasm. 'I'm always looking for love. I'm just not too good at creating it.'

'And I'm not good at holding on to it.'

'Seems to me like it was taken from you by forces beyond your control,' Katharina said. 'I'm going after Hermann Krüger.'

Mattie nodded, her eyes watering. But she refused to cry again, and she got up from the table. 'I'm going to find Gabriel. It's time I figured out Chris's terrible childhood secret once and for all.'

Chapter 43

When Mattie found Dr. Gabriel in his lab on the second floor of Private Berlin, he was wearing black jeans, a red bandana, and a Jimi Hendrix 'Live at the Monterey Pop Festival' sweatshirt that featured a burning red guitar.

She told him what she was after and he graciously put down what he'd been doing to help her. They used a giant translucent screen that allowed them to call up documents, pictures, and video and study them all at once, as if they were looking at them on a corkboard.

They mined Private's records first and found Chris's personnel file, including a digital scan of his birth certificate, which said that Christoph Rolf Schneider was born in Dresden in 1975 to Alfred and Maria Schneider.

They tried to match the birth certificate and found no Christoph Rolf Schneider registered in the Dresden files. They searched for Alfred and Maria Schneider in the marriage records and again came up empty-handed.

They expanded the search to include all of what had been East Germany, and found several men named Christoph Schneider, but none were remotely Chris's age. And nowhere did they find a record of a marriage between an Alfred Schneider and a woman with the first name Maria.

They dug deeper, trying school databases.

Again nothing.

'I'm beginning to think nothing about Chris was real,' Dr. Gabriel said.

'I know,' Mattie said, now seriously confused. 'But he was real. Let's go back. Do we have his army records in his personnel file?'

'I'm sure,' Gabriel said. He searched a minute and then called them up.

The picture of Chris made her smile. He looked so young. The base information was all in line with what he'd listed on his Private application after leaving the German military police: Same parental names, same bogus birth certificate from Dresden, and the same bogus address.

Mattie thought they had hit an impenetrable wall until she noticed something on the sheet in the army file that listed Chris's educational history. Listed under his place of primary and secondary education was 'Waisenhaus 44,' an orphanage out in the countryside south of Berlin and east of the city of Halle.

'Ernst, where would they keep records of GDR-era orphanages?'

Dr. Gabriel thought about that. 'I don't know, the Federal Archives?'

Chapter 44

At ten o'clock exactly, I hear: 'Professor Groening?'

German precision, my friends!

Is there anything more reassuring?

I smile and shuffle from my seat in the back left corner of the reading room, mindful of the cameras mounted to the ceiling.

At the desk, I find sixteen boxes of files and am told that there are more waiting for me in the microfilm room down the hall.

The kind clerk lady helps me roll the cart back to my spot.

I start with the paper archive first, scanning rapidly. In the fourth box I find the records of Waisenhaus 44, an orphanage outside of Halle, about an hour south of Berlin. There are hundreds of names and they're not listed alphabetically. They seem all jumbled and out of order.

But then I study several closely and discover that they've been filed by date of admission.

That brings a smile to my lips.

In takes less than ten minutes to find the documents of six children, including snapshots taken on the day they were brought to Waisenhaus 44.

For a moment, I linger on a picture of Christoph as a boy.

Scrawny. Dark, sunken eyes showing fear and hatred.

He's exactly as I remember him as a boy.

But I can't afford to relive the good old days. I've got business to attend to.

I count the pages in the six files. Fifty-six.

I leave the files on the table, pick up my briefcase, and go to the toilet. From a secret side pocket in the interior of the briefcase, I retrieve a sheaf of white antique-finish paper covered in typed gibberish. I count out fifty-six pieces and slip them into several gray, well-worn legal-size files.

I set them in the briefcase, and shut it. I return to the archive reading room and my spot, noting the position of other researchers. I set the satchel down, open wide to my right on the floor next to my chair.

Then I wait. Five minutes pass.

At the stroke of eleven, clerks wheel in fresh documents.

Researchers who've been waiting charge toward the counter. All eyes rise and follow the rush of activity.

In a series of fluid motions, I slip the six files off my desk into my briefcase, and return the phony files to the tabletop, immediately reaching past them to the box that held the real documents.

They're packed in less than a minute.

I put those boxes on the cart, get up, and take my briefcase to the men's room, where I slide the files into the interior side pocket of the valise.

Then I go down the hall to the microfilm section, pick up the boxes I ordered, and retreat to the rear of the room behind a machine that faces

148

the counter. I spin rapidly through the microfilm reels until I find more documents on the children, laid out one after another on almost twenty feet of film.

I check. The clerks are busy.

I reach into my pocket and pull out a razor-sharp folding knife. With no hesitation I cut the microfilm. I take the free end and wind it on my fingers until I get to the other end of the documentation and make a second cut. Then I put a rubber band around the microfilm and stick the tiny roll inside my jacket pocket.

When I withdraw my hand, I'm holding my trusty tube of superglue.

My friends, you can do so much with that stuff, can't you?

I scan the room for activity, and then run a bead of the glue on one end of the cut reel and press it to the other with a quarter-inch overlap.

I hold it one minute, then take up the slack on the film reel and gingerly rewind. It holds. I set the reel back in the box and put the box neatly in the middle of the other microfilm boxes I have stacked beside it.

I get up, take my briefcase, and head toward the door.

'Are you returning today, professor?' the clerk asks.

'Of course,' I reply. 'A quick supper, and then back.'

I can't help it. I make that clicking noise in my throat, and smile.

I make another clicking noise as I go out the door to the archives, flashing on that picture of

149

Christoph as a boy.

You didn't have a chance, I think. And none of the others do either.

Chapter 45

Mattie walked to the front gate of the German Federal Archives. Inside the gatehouse, the guards were checking the briefcase of an elderly man in a long raincoat and a Bavarian hat whose hands shook as if he had a neurological disorder, like Parkinson's disease, but not.

Mattie knew what Parkinson's looked like. Her mother had died of it. This rhythm of tic and tremor was different, however, and for some reason it made her feel odd. Still, Mattie could not help pitying the old man as he took back his briefcase and returned his researcher pass.

Mattie never got a good look at his face, but for reasons she could not explain, she watched him shuffle down the sidewalk before showing the guards her badge and ID and turning over her weapon.

She walked across the campus and found the archival reading room, where she asked one of the clerks how best to track down the files of an East German orphanage called Waisenhaus 44.

The clerk frowned, and then went over to another archivist and had an intense conversation.

She returned and said, 'Those files are out with a researcher already.'

That surprised Mattie and she instantly scanned the room. 'Which one?'

Flustered, the clerk said, 'It's not our policy to...'

Mattie leaned over the counter, flashing her Private badge.

'This is a murder investigation,' she said softly. 'Which one?'

The archivist's brow knitted and she pointed over at a desk in the far left corner. 'He was sitting over there, but then he went down to the microfilm room.'

'What does he look like?' Mattie demanded.

'An older man. A professor at Heidelberg, I think. He's got Parkinson's. You can't miss him.'

'I just did,' Mattie groaned. 'Did you touch those boxes after he left?'

'He wore cotton gloves, if that's what you're thinking,' the clerk said. 'You don't think he killed someone, do you? He couldn't. He's got Parkinson's. He told me so himself. I don't think that old man could hurt a fly.'

Chapter 46

Trying not to hyperventilate, I drive until I am well east of the archives before I tear off the wig.

My friends, I recognized the woman at the archives gate. She was the same woman I saw with the big bald guy outside the slaughterhouse. There are dozens of pictures of her on Christoph's hard drive.

Her name is Mattie Engel. She and Christoph had been lovers, engaged I believe. She and Chris worked for Private. She has a son, Niklas.

She's looking for me, and that makes me agitated. But there's more. Her face – it's true, she resembles my mother, and that makes me infuriated.

For an instant I fight the urge to clean out all my money and flee Berlin and all of Germany for that matter.

South America?

No, I decide, growing angrier, the bitch will find nothing.

With no documents left in the archives, it's as if Christoph and the others never existed. No masks, but they're as invisible to the wide world as I am.

And soon, very soon, they will cease to exist at all, while I will go on.

Ten minutes later, I pull into my garage. I park between the white work van and the Mercedes, make sure I'm alone, and then leave the Audi coupe. I climb in the back of the van and start removing the makeup with wipes I keep there.

I have several hours of real work to do. Clients and business associates to meet. I must be presentable for the time being.

But as I stare into the rearview mirror, I flash once more on Mattie Engel, and get a nervous feeling that has served me well over the years. Christoph was her lover once. Even if their official relationship had ended, she must have feelings for him, which means she has a strong motivation to find me, which means she's dangerous – very, very dangerous.

Right there, my friends, I decide that if it comes to it, I'll have to make Mattie Engel permanently invisible too.

But until then, I've got other people to take care of, people who could identify me, people who could tear off my masks.

Chapter 47

The midget rolled an unlit cigar between his lips as he squinted at Daniel Brecht and Jack Morgan before saying in a raspy voice, 'You think a fix was in?'

Tiny Heine Wagner was a black-market bookie, someone Brecht had used as an informer for years. Around noon that day, Tiny Heine, Brecht, and Morgan were sitting at a table overlooking the Spree River inside the Georgebräu beer hall in central Berlin.

'We're asking you if you think a fix was in,' Brecht said.

The bookie shrugged and put the cigar down. 'Hertha Berlin is second league. I haven't seen deep action on any one of their games. Certainly not compared to what you'd see in the premier league.'

'We wouldn't expect so,' Morgan said after Brecht translated. 'But maybe that helps. Do you know of any big payoffs on any of those games?'

Tiny Heine shrugged again. 'Not on my book,

anyway. But you know, sports betting is changing in Germany. Every day.'

'Explain that,' said Jack.

'The government passed a gambling treaty a few years back that says they're the only ones who can handle sports betting,' the bookie said, and then started chortling. 'It's supposed to limit gambling addiction.'

'Not working?' Jack asked.

'Doing the exact opposite,' the midget replied. 'My business is up twenty-five percent this year. Online, it's even bigger. Thirty percent.'

'Online brokers in other countries?' Brecht asked.

'It's officially against the law, but there you go,' Tiny Heine said and started laughing again. 'Stupid government bastards. They think because it's a law that people will pay attention to it, especially addicts!'

Brecht turned to Morgan. 'I wonder just how many of these online betting ops there are.'

'Thousands,' Morgan said. 'All over the world. Maybe tens of thousands.'

The bookie nodded after Brecht translated. 'Who do you figure for the fix?'

'What should I tell him?' Brecht asked in English.

Morgan replied, 'Ask him what he knows about Maxim Pavel.'

That name seemed to impress Tiny Heine. 'Oooh, that's heavy. He plays the cool nightclub owner, but the way I hear it, that's one mean, twisted motherfucker. Word on the street is he'll kill you as soon as look at you. He'll like killing

154

you too.'

'Russian mafia?' Morgan asked.

'I have it on authority that he's ex-KGB. And you think he was in on a fix?'

'We don't know for sure,' Brecht said.

'Any way for us to find out what kind of betting volume was on the Hertha Berlin games?' Morgan asked.

Tiny Heine thought about that. 'I dunno. You got any contacts in Vegas?'

Morgan brightened. 'As a matter of fact, I do.'

Chapter 48

At half past noon, Agnes Krüger was already late for a luncheon date at Restaurant Quarré with Ingrid Dahl, an old friend. The billionaire's wife wanted to talk to someone she could trust, someone outside her immediate family, and Ingrid Dahl, who was both discrete and wise, fit her needs perfectly.

She had a driver at her beck and call, but that day she felt the strong need to make a visible show of independence. She'd drive herself. She took the elevator to the garage and found her black Porsche Cayenne among the myriad of other cars her husband stored there.

Agnes Krüger hit the button that raised the garage gate and then pulled out, heading south toward Fasanenplatz, which was empty due to the heavy rain that was falling again.

She pulled up to the intersection of Fasanen and Schaperstrasse. Before she could take a left onto Schaper, a figure in a black rain jacket with the hood up ran to her and knocked sharply on the window.

The billionaire's wife startled and then rolled down the window angrily.

'What do you want?' she demanded. 'I already told...'

Agnes Krüger was suddenly staring at the empty bottom of a plastic Coke bottle that had been taped to the barrel of a pistol.

'No, please—' she began.

The shot hit her above the right eye at point-blank range, spraying her life across the passenger seat and window.

Her foot came off the brake.

The Porsche rolled across the street and crashed into a parked Fiat.

Alarms began to wail as the killer walked off into the storm.

Chapter 49

In the amphitheater inside Private Berlin, Dr. Gabriel loaded a copy of the German Federal Archives surveillance tape featuring Dr. Groening.

Mattie snapped shut her cell phone. 'Surprise, no Professor Groening at Heidelberg. Not even close.'

'I didn't expect there would be,' Gabriel replied.

Katharina Doruk shut her own phone. 'That was Brecht. They went back to the nightclub and were told that Pavel hasn't been seen since yesterday.'

'So Hermann Krüger's and Pavel's whereabouts are now both unknown?'

'Apparently,' Katharina said.

The surveillance tapes appeared on the screen. Gabriel enlarged them.

In the reading room, the professor did a remarkable job of keeping his hat tucked down over his eyes, but they saw how he managed to steal six files from the archives of Waisenhaus 44.

'He's very clever, whoever he is, and his hands are as fast as a close-up magician's' said Gabriel.

Mattie nodded. 'Zoom in on that briefcase.'

Dr. Gabriel did. 'Looks like old crocodile skin.'

Mattie was positive there would be a better look at Dr. Groening at the front gate. But both entering and exiting, his body shook and quivered so much it was hard to get an image of him that wasn't blurred. And even then, it was at a steep downward angle, from the upper-right corner of the guard's shack.

'Look at me watching him walk away,' Mattie cried after seeing herself step to the guard's window. 'I had this feeling about him, but I let him walk away because he reminded me of my mother and I pitied him!'

'You couldn't have known,' Katharina said.

Mattie knew she was right, but it sure didn't make her feel any better.

157

Was that the man who killed Chris? Was that Kruger or Pavel in disguise?

Pavel owned a nightclub for female impersonators. He'd know all about makeup, wouldn't he? What about Krüger? A billionaire could hire someone to disguise him, right? Or he could have paid someone to steal the documents.

She was lost in these thoughts when Katharina's phone rang again.

'What?' Katharina cried. She stabbed at her phone and the speaker came on.

'He's done it!' Rudy Krüger shouted over a background din of voices. 'He's killed my mother!'

'Slow down, Rudy,' Katharina said.

'She's dead,' he said in a quivering voice. 'I just got a call from Berlin Kripo. Someone shot her in her car near the house. It had to be Hermann. I know it. He did it or he had her killed. That fucking capitalist pig! He–'

Rudy was choking. 'Oh, God. He– I told her–'

'Rudy, I know this is tough. Take a deep breath. Where are you?'

'Leaving the rally. We were protesting corporate pigs like my stepfather who are trying to tear down Tacheles and turn it into another high-rise. The police want me to identify her.'

'We'll meet you there in ten minutes.'

Chapter 50

Hauptkommissar Hans Dietrich was already on the scene when Mattie and Katharina arrived. He was standing in the rain by the open door to the black Porsche Cayenne, grim, drawn, and gray, and even more hunched over.

From behind the yellow crime scene tape, Mattie spotted Inspector Weigel and called to her. Weigel came over, puzzled.

'What are you doing here?' the inspector asked.

'Agnes Krüger was Chris Schneider's client,' Mattie said. 'Dietrich knows about it.'

Suddenly annoyed, the young inspector glanced at the high commissar. 'The man tells me nothing. It's like I don't exist. But he has a lot on his mind. His father died of a heart attack last night in Treptower Park. He found him.'

'That's awful,' Mattie said.

'And he's here at work?' Katharina asked.

'The way I understand it, work is all Dietrich has,' the inspector replied.

Mattie had heard the same thing and was about to say so when she heard Rudy Krüger cry, 'Where is she?'

The billionaire's stepson had just left a taxi and was rushing to them. He slowed when he saw the crashed Porsche on the other side of the street. He moaned, 'Oh, God. What's he done to her?'

To Mattie, Rudy Krüger no longer looked the

part of the arrogant artist and anarchist. He was just a boy who'd lost his mother.

Tears came to his eyes and he rubbed fiercely at his cheeks. 'What's he done? What's he done to her?'

'Are you Rudy Krüger?' High Commissar Dietrich asked.

He'd come over to Weigel and seen Rudy crying.

'He is,' Mattie said.

Dietrich ignored her. 'Herr Krüger, I know this is hard, but I need you to identify your mother. Your stepfather is apparently nowhere to be found.'

Sounding dazed, Rudy Krüger said, 'It's her.'

'You can't see her from here.'

'It's her car.'

'Please, sir, I need you to look at her face. We'll drape the wound.'

Rudy looked at Katharina and Mattie. 'Would you go with me?'

Dietrich appeared displeased, but Mattie said, 'Of course we will.'

The billionaire's stepson was shaking like a leaf. His lower lip trembled as he walked up beside his mother's car. Mattie could see her in there. Her body was rocked to the right. A stream of drying blood ran out of her mouth.

Tears rolling down his cheeks, Rudy Krüger nodded. 'It's her. My mother.'

Then he spun around, doubled over, and vomited.

160

Chapter 51

When Rudy Krüger's spasms subsided, Mattie and Katharina led him away.

'I need some water,' he said dully.

'I'll get you some,' Inspector Weigel answered and hurried off.

The rain had stopped and the wind had picked up, blowing leaves from the trees in front of Agnes Kruger's home. Rudy Krüger sat on the wet front steps looking wounded and alone.

'Herr Krüger...' Dietrich began.

Mattie stepped in front of the high commissar and in a low voice said, 'Remember what you felt like last night? Give him a minute.'

Dietrich was a man not used to taking orders and not used to other people knowing his affairs. But in a measured tone, he replied, 'Just so, Frau Engel.'

Weigel came up and handed the billionaire's stepson a bottle of water. 'Thank you,' Rudy Krüger said. 'You're very kind.'

Dietrich waited until he'd drunk it before informing him that no witnesses to his mother's murder had come forward yet. There had been a driving rain at the time and none of the neighbors seemed to have heard anything unusual.

'Where were you an hour ago?' Dietrich asked when he'd finished.

'Me?' Rudy Krüger said. 'I was at a rally for Tacheles.'

'Anybody see you?'

'Hundreds,' he said. 'I was a speaker. I've been there since this morning.'

'Any idea who'd want to kill her?'

Rudy's expression turned to outrage. 'The same person who probably killed Chris Schneider: Hermann Krüger. Or someone working for him. I promise you. When will you arrest him?'

'I've got to find him first,' Dietrich said. 'Hear his side of things.'

'Jesus Christ,' Rudy Krüger moaned. 'Jesus, it's just...'

'What?'

He was racked with anguish when he answered more to Mattie and Katharina than to Dietrich: 'After you left, on the way to the rally, I talked with my mother on the phone. I asked her what she'd decided to do about Hermann. She said she was going to stay married to him.

'Isn't that just perfect?' he asked bitterly. 'So Agnes, she went for the money. She'd decided to go on with their separate lives because of it. But he killed her before she even had the chance to tell–'

Down the street, they had his mother's body in a black bag and were loading it into an ambulance.

Rudy Krüger let loose a sigh and seemed on the verge of crying again, but instead he said, 'I better check on the house.'

'I prefer you leave it the way it is,' Dietrich said. 'We'll want to search it.'

162

That surprised the billionaire's stepson for a moment, but then he said, 'Of course, I'm sorry. I ... I guess I'll go home now?'

Dietrich nodded. 'You'll want to notify her friends and family.'

Rudy Krüger hung his head and said, 'I have my first opening in two days. She was coming, you know? My mother said she was coming.'

Then the high commissar's cell phone rang. Dietrich answered it and walked off several paces.

Rudy Kruüer got up, appearing beaten. He looked at Mattie and Katharina. 'Thanks. I couldn't have done that alone.'

'You have someone to go home to?' Katharina asked.

'Tanya might be there after the rally,' he said. 'I don't know.'

'You call us if you need us,' Mattie said.

He nodded absently and walked off, a shattered man.

Mattie heard Dietrich complaining, 'I'm tied up here. Send someone else.'

He hung up, shaking his head.

'What is it, High Commissar?' Inspector Weigel asked.

Dietrich hesitated, and then said, 'Halle police found a floater in the river down there. They've identified him: a doctoral student at Berlin Technical University. Some kind of computer super-genius. They wanted our help. We've got too much to do already. I want Hermann Krüger found.'

Mattie had wanted to tell Dietrich about the files stolen from the archives, but now she was consumed by this information in light of the fact

163

that someone of tremendous skill had hacked into Private's computer.

So was Katharina, who said, 'You have a name for this dead student?'

'Weigel can get it for you,' Dietrich said, walking away.

'I think I'll go to the Technical University then,' Katharina said. 'Dig around.'

'Not me,' Mattie said. 'I'm heading to Halle.'

Chapter 52

Friends, fellow Berliners, it's only three in the afternoon, but I must admit that I'm already bone tired from the many long and difficult tasks I've been forced to attend to already today. But I like to have things cleared away, cleaned up and polished like glass before I move on to something new.

That's the way of an invisible man.

Some old habits never die.

I look at my hands a moment and entertain the notion that I've never really seen myself, not without a mirror anyway; and mirrors are part of life's illusion, aren't they?

I really don't know what I look like at all, I decide, and I never will.

And if I don't, who will?

Certainly not all those I've been forced to eliminate in the last two weeks. Not one of them recognized my new face.

164

But they knew my voice.

Before they died, when I was speaking to them, they looked at me like I was a scary puzzle with pieces missing.

I laugh, feeling buoyed as I smear instant tanning lotion on my face and hands, and then use colored contact lenses to turn my eye color from brown to green. Then I glue on thick, dark eyebrows and a moustache and stuff rolls of cotton in my cheeks.

I pull on a blue workman's coverall embroidered with the name of a local plumbing company. It's amazing what you can find in thrift stores if you really know what you're looking for. I even found the matching cap there too.

When I'm finished and satisfied that no one from my current life would recognize me, I fill a toolbox with wrenches, screwdrivers, and a mini blowtorch, making gentle clicking noises in my throat. It's so important to have the right tools for the job, isn't it, my friends? Hmmm?

Chapter 53

It was midafternoon by the time Mattie returned to Private Berlin, requisitioned a car, and drove the one hundred seventy kilometers south to the city of Halle.

A gray, bleak city dominated by GDR-era architecture, Halle looked even more grim and somber in the mist that was swirling in advance of another storm.

Mattie parked, wondering again if the body of the computer genius was indeed linked to the hacking at Private, Chris's death, and now the murder of Agnes Krüger in broad daylight. Was Hermann Krüger behind all of it? Could someone of his stature afford to be so brazen and cold-blooded?

In an effort to answer those questions, Mattie went to city hall and inquired at the clerk's office about Waisenhaus 44. The tattooed emo girl who waited on her said she'd never heard of the orphanage, much less its records.

But a middle-aged woman working at a desk behind the emo girl told Mattie that Waisenhaus 44 was out on the road from Klepzig to Reussen.

'It's still there?' Mattie asked.

'Not for long,' she said. 'Someone's tearing it down next month and building a green lightbulb production facility.'

'Records?' Mattie asked.

'I think they were transferred to the Federal Archives after reunification.'

'No other place they could be?'

'Not that I know of.'

Mattie considered throwing in the towel. But then she decided to make the drive out to see the orphanage. She told herself it might help her to understand whatever it was that Chris went through as a kid.

The thought of Chris as a boy made her think about Niklas. The two brought a lump to her throat, and tears to her eyes, and it took every bit of her strength to stay on the wet highway leading

166

east out of Halle.

The wind began to gust and the rain fell harder as Mattie drove north on the pot-holed secondary road from Klepzig to Reussen. The road wound through farmland, by stands of hardwood trees partially stripped of leaves, and past giant white wind turbines, their blades slicing the iron sky.

At last Mattie spotted the roofline of the orphanage through a tangle of brush and woods. It sat next to a field being tilled by a farmer on a tractor.

Between two stout wooden posts, a new steel cable stretched across the orphanage's overgrown driveway. There were notices of condemnation in plastic sheeting stapled to both posts. A sign dangled from the cable: No Trespassing.

Mattie parked her car on the shoulder, pulled up the hood of her rain jacket, and got out. She trotted across the road, jumped the cable, and moved down the driveway through sopping weeds and thorns that clawed at her slacks.

Vines strangled the off-kilter walls of Waisenhaus 44, a large three-story building with a sagging roof. The windows of the old orphanage were gone, except for teeth-like shards that clung to the frames.

Mattie stepped up on the front porch, which sagged off the building. The orphanage's front door lay broken on the floor in the mouth of a long, gloomy central hallway.

Something in her stomach told Mattie not to enter and to leave the secrets of Waisenhaus 44 alone.

167

But then thunder cracked in the distance and the rain fell even harder.

Feeling keenly on edge, wondering if she was crazy, she stepped inside.

Chapter 54

In the hallway, Mattie stopped to get out her flashlight. She shined it around, finding a room to her right that held the last relics of an office lying in leaves, fungus, and mold: a desk with two legs, a chair with the stuffing and rusted springs visible, and an overturned file cabinet with no drawers.

This was where the headmaster or mistress must have done their business, Mattie thought. She walked on, moving about the orphanage's lower floor, which had been stripped of nearly everything.

She found the kitchen and the eating hall. They were stripped too.

As she climbed the stairs, she tried to imagine Chris in this horrid place, eight years old, motherless, fatherless. She thought of Niklas having to be put in an orphanage and felt on the verge of weeping again.

On the second floor, Mattie discovered the ruins of old classrooms and became aware that something about the background din of the rain falling and the tractor plowing had changed.

She ascended to the third floor and found dormitories set to either side of a long central corridor. The first was empty. The one across the hall held rusted bunk-bed frames bolted to the wall.

Mattie walked over creaking floorboards to the second set of dorms. In the first one she inspected, the roof was caved in on top of one of the steel bunk beds, the only one she'd seen that still had a mattress on it.

The mattress was black with filth and mold. There were puddles on it, and on the floor. For reasons she could not explain, Mattie felt drawn into the dorm, toward that bunk bed mattress.

The floorboards felt soft and rotted underfoot. But she went anyway and stood in the rain teeming through the hole in the roof, transfixed by the mattress and the splintered joists that stabbed it in several places.

Was this bed once Chris's?

Mattie saw him lying on the bed as easily as another memory that came flooding in around her.

She and Chris were in bed at a ski condo they'd rented at Garmisch, a rare separation from Niklas.

Chris made her breakfast and brought it to her on a tray with a single rose, and a small box of chocolates wrapped in a bow. He watched her eat, amused. And then he was interested to see her opening the chocolate box.

Inside was a ring, two emeralds surrounding an emerald-cut diamond.

Suddenly, there in the wreckage of the orphanage, loss flowed everywhere around Mattie, an invisible, terrible hydraulic pressure built, making the room feel as menacing to her as the subbasement in the slaughterhouse.

Lightning flashed, almost blinding her.

Thunder cracked right overhead.

Mattie ducked, desperate now to leave this place, to get back to her car and go home to Niklas.

She ran from the room.

She raced to the staircase and then froze.

Standing in the shadows at the bottom of the staircase was a man in a long, black, hooded rain slicker.

His face was hidden beneath the hood.

He was aiming a double-barreled shotgun at her.

Chapter 55

'Who are you?' the man with the shotgun growled. 'And what in God's name are you doing in here?'

For an instant, Mattie couldn't answer.

He adjusted his aim. 'I asked you–'

She reached to her coat pocket.

'Easy,' the man said, still aiming the gun.

'I'm going for – my badge – and ID,' she stammered.

He picked his head up off the butt of the shotgun. 'You police?'

'I work for Private, Private Berlin.' She showed him the badge.

He made a motion for her to come down the stairs toward him.

'The gun, sir?' she asked. 'It's making me nervous.'

At last he lowered the gun, and then pulled back the hood, revealing a rawboned man in his late thirties. He said, 'I saw the car after I quit plowing. You're not supposed to be in here. They're demolishing this place next month.'

'I'm sorry,' Mattie said, her wits returning. She started down the stairs toward him. 'This was an orphanage. A ... a close friend of mine lived here.'

'Lot of people lived here. Can't say many liked it, from what I've heard.'

She stuck out her hand. 'Mattie Engel.'

'Darek Eberhardt,' he replied, not taking her hand. 'You should leave, Frau Engel. This place is dangerous. Floorboards are all rotted. You could go through anywhere. Break a leg. Or a neck.'

'My friend is ... dead, murdered,' Mattie said. 'He was more than my friend. He was my fiancé, and I'm just trying to understand his childhood.'

Eberhardt studied her without emotion. 'I'm sorry for your loss, but you won't learn anything here. This place was abandoned twenty years ago. Looters stripped most of it. Took the government forever, but they finally got the land sold to some green energy company.'

'I heard that. Lightbulbs.'

Eberhardt turned without comment and started down the hall.

Mattie hurried after him, saying, 'The records about Waisenhaus 44 that are in the Federal Archives, they're ... they're incomplete.'

171

Eberhardt said nothing as he headed toward the front door.

Mattie called after him, 'I was hoping I could find someone who knows about the orphanage, someone who might have known Chris.'

Eberhardt went out the front door. The rain had slowed. The thunder boomed and the lightning flashed to their east now.

'I've got to get back to my tilling,' Eberhardt said.

Mattie followed him, saying, 'I'm sorry. I'd hoped...' She started to choke up. 'It's just so hard not understanding ... why he died, who he was, this place.'

She wiped at her tears with the sleeve of her rain jacket. Eberhardt had turned to face her, the shotgun held low at his side, his face a mystery.

'I'm sorry,' she said again. 'I'll be going. I'm sorry to have bothered you and taken you away from your work.'

Mattie pivoted and took several steps down the overgrown driveway toward the road.

'Hariat Ledwig,' the farmer said. 'She lives in a nursing home in Halle.'

Mattie stopped and looked at him, puzzled. 'Who is she?'

'My father's second cousin. She ran this place for twenty-two years.'

Chapter 56

Thirty-five minutes later, Mattie knocked and entered a room that reeked of old age, disease, and an antiseptic that smelled like citrus.

Hariat Ledwig sat upright in a chair by a hospital bed, connected by a tube to an oxygen tent. A little bird of a woman in a nightgown, robe, and slippers, she was having a coughing fit. A blanket covered her legs. There were books stacked around her. One lay open in her lap cradling a magnifying glass.

When the coughing subsided, Hariat Ledwig spit into a tissue and dropped it in a trashcan set among the books.

'What do you want?' the old woman croaked suspiciously.

Mattie identified herself, showed her the Private badge, and then said, 'I met your second cousin's son, Darek, out at the old Waisenhaus 44 building. He suggested I come talk to you.'

Hariat Ledwig now turned highly guarded. 'Who do you work for? The state?'

'No, I...'

The old woman picked up the magnifying glass and shook it at Mattie. 'I was not a part of any forced adoptions. Never. Not once. I can prove it...'

Mattie understood what she was talking about. During the communist reign in East Germany, children were sometimes taken from parents thought disloyal. The children's names were changed, and then they were given over to families deemed true to the state.

'That's not why I'm here, Frau Ledwig,' Mattie assured her. 'And there is no client. I'm just trying to find out about a very dear friend of mine who lived at Waisenhaus 44 in the seventies and eighties.'

Hariat Ledwig watched Mattie the way a cobra might a mongoose. 'Your friend's name?'

'Chris, uh, Christoph Schneider.'

The old woman blinked. Confusion and then pain rippled through her.

She started coughing again, hard and spastic convulsions, and she would not meet Mattie's gaze.

When the fit eased, Mattie said, 'Did you know Chris?'

Hariat Ledwig seemed in some kind of internal battle, but then she glanced sidelong at Mattie and said, 'I had nothing to do with whatever happened to that boy. Absolutely nothing.'

Chapter 57

Mattie felt a pit opening in her stomach. She stared at the woman who'd run Waisenhaus 44 and said, 'What *happened* to Chris?'

'I don't know,' Hariat Ledwig whispered.

'You do.'

The old woman shifted painfully. 'I *don't*. Why are you here? Why now?'

'Because Chris was murdered last week.'

Hariat Ledwig's eyes unscrewed a moment as if she'd fallen into some time warp. Then she said, wheezing, 'I'd always hoped he'd be safe and live a long life. I'd hoped they all would... I ... I did nothing but try to help him as best I could, but it was beyond me. I was a good person caught in an impossible situation!'

The old woman blubbered these last words: 'I'm innocent.'

'Innocent of what?' Mattie demanded. 'Was Chris abused in your orphanage?'

Hariat Ledwig forced herself to sit straighter. 'Absolutely not. Whatever it was, it happened before he came, before they all came to Waisenhaus 44.'

'All?'

The old woman hesitated, but then, between hacking fits, she described the snowy winter night of February 12, 1980.

A car and a police van came. A man got out of the rear of the car. He told Hariat Ledwig that he was with the state. Three girls and three boys between the ages of six and nine had been found wandering the streets of East Berlin. Waisenhaus 44 was the only orphanage around with vacancies.

The children appeared to be in shock when they arrived. They clung to each other obsessively. Most had violent nightmares, and would wake up screaming for their mothers. Two of the girls were sisters and rarely let the other out of their sight. They all feared men.

Over the course of years, Hariat Ledwig tried to coax out of them what had happened, but every time she did, they'd become terrified and refuse. The only thing Chris ever said about it was that some things were best forgotten.

'So I did,' the old woman croaked. 'From then on, I saw to their care as best I could. Made sure they were fed and clothed and educated. Some of the six did better than others, Chris and Artur probably the best.

'And then they were teenagers, and word of the uprising in Berlin had reached even Waisenhaus 44. They all went up there one night. They came back, but not for long. They were of age. They could do what they wanted. I lost track of them, though I heard that Chris chose the army.'

Mattie nodded. 'But other than that and the fact that Chris lived at the orphanage, there's nothing about his childhood that's real. At least as far as documents go.'

Hariat Ledwig fought for breath. 'Because of me. I did that.'

The old woman explained that after seeing the traumatized state the six children were in, and their pathological fear of being asked to talk about it, she came to believe that someone had threatened them if they ever talked.

'I didn't want whoever had tortured those children to be able to find them,' she said. 'They came to me with no documents, so I invented documents for them. Even when the children were able to tell me their parents' names, I changed them, and made the children memorize the new names I had written.'

'And you told no one?'

'It was a different time. As Chris said, one best forgotten.'

'What was Chris's real name?'

'Rolf Christoph Wolfe.'

'And his mother and father?'

'I never knew. I guess I didn't want to know.'

'Earlier today, a man posing as a professor stole six of the Waisenhaus 44 files from the Federal Archives. I believe Chris's file was among them.'

Hariat Ledwig blinked, and then she seemed to shrink right in front of Mattie. 'How could that possibly...?' She choked hard as if someone or something was strangling her. Then she said, coughing, 'My God, they all came in on the same date. I sent the Federal Archives the chronological copy of the files.'

The old woman broke down sobbing. 'No, this is not right. I wanted them to be safe!'

Mattie went to her side, squatted down, and put her hand on the blanket, through which she could feel the woman's legs. They were like twigs. 'Hariat, do you remember the names of the other five children?'

Hariat Ledwig's crying slowed. 'I knew what would happen when the wall fell. I knew there would be a witch hunt. I kept copies of the files of every child who lived in my orphanage.'

Mattie's heart skipped a beat. 'Can I see them? Make copies?'

The old woman nodded. 'They prove I was a decent person, not part of the sickness that seemed to afflict everyone around me in those days.'

Book Three

THE MOTHERLESS CHILDREN

Chapter 58

'Find these people, Gabriel,' Mattie said, slapping down six blue files on the hippie scientist's workbench at Private Berlin. 'They're the key.'

'Wait a second,' Katharina complained. 'I've got first dibs on him.'

Dr. Gabriel was hunched over a computer, removing its hard drive.

'Kat–' Mattie insisted.

Her friend cut her off. 'That computer belongs to Ernst Neumann, dead computer genius, doctoral student at Berlin Tech, and, according to his roommate, a freelance hacker who'd come into a lot of cash recently.'

'Really?' Mattie said, impressed. 'I'll do my own research then.'

Gabriel did not look up, just gestured with his screwdriver toward an iMac. 'Use that machine.'

Mattie started toward the machine with Katharina in tow. 'What's in those files?' she asked.

'Fiction,' Mattie said, sitting down in front of the computer.

The door to Gabriel's lab opened and Jack Morgan entered with Daniel Brecht. They were on their way out to catch Cassiano's game at the stadium, but they wanted to bring everyone up to speed on Pavel, his background in the KGB, and his disappearance last evening, sometime after he'd vacated the room he'd shared with Perfecta.

'And I spoke with some old friends in Vegas,' Morgan said. 'There was heavier than normal betting on the games where Cassiano played poorly. And get this: in every case, Hertha went into the games as five to three favorites.'

'I'm not following,' Katharina said.

'The odds were such that few flags would be raised on someone betting on Cassiano's opponents,' Morgan said.

'Pavel?' Mattie asked.

'That's where my money is,' Dietrich said. 'Here's a picture of him.'

Mattie studied the photograph of the nightclub owner, but she could not tell if it was the man she'd seen at the Federal Archives that morning.

Then she told them all what she'd discovered in Halle.

When she finished, Gabriel abandoned the hard drive of the computer genius, went to Mattie, and pushed her out of her chair, flipping open the first file. 'Why didn't you say so in the first place?'

'Gabriel!' Katharina protested.

'The computer will take me hours,' he said. 'This, minutes.'

The first file belonged to Ilse Frei, who had been one of the younger of the six children who'd arrived at Waisenhaus 44 on February 12, 1980.

Morgan and Brecht left for the game just before Gabriel found an Ilse Frei, correct age, living near Frankfurt.

'She's a paralegal and lives in the suburb of Bad Homburg,' the old hippie said, now giving his computer a command to cross-reference her name against the various law-enforcement databases to which Private had access.

He immediately got a hit and looked pained.

'What is it?' Mattie asked, coming around the back of his chair.

'Ilse Frei was reported missing fifteen days ago.'

Chapter 59

My friends, fellow Berliners, twenty years ago it would have taken me weeks to track down the address of Greta Amsel. I know this because nearly two decades ago, shortly after recuperating from my surgeries, I decided to find and kill the bitch that bore me.

It took me a solid month of painstaking document research to locate my dear sweet mother and end her life. But that is a story for another time.

It had taken me all of an hour on Google to pin down the fact that Greta Amsel was a nurse who lived alone in a small apartment building in the outskirts of West Berlin not far from Falkensee.

At the moment, I'm sitting in my blue workman's van diagonally across the street from the apartment building, reviewing the actions I took after finding her. I'd had the good sense to call her phone number once I'd arrived. The voice on the machine was a stranger's. Funny, I never would have recognized it.

I called the apartment manager next, a man

named Gustav Banter, and posed as an electrical supply salesman from Mannheim who wanted to drop by later, around five thirty. Impossible, Banter told me. His shift ended at four thirty.

How sad, I said, and settled in to wait for Greta.

Again, I did not recognize her voice on her answering machine, but I know her the moment she rides by me on her bicycle at a quarter to five. She's still got the naturally blond hair, the high cheekbones, and that lost look about her.

Greta Amsel locks her bike in a rack in front of the apartment building. I wait until she's been inside ten minutes before taking the tool bag from the floor and setting it on the passenger seat beside me.

I wait until a man carrying a book bag comes down the street and heads for the front door of Greta's building. As he puts his key into the lock, I'm angling in behind him.

In a heavy Slavic accent, I say, 'Do you knows where I finds Herr Banter? The superintendent?'

The young man turns to look at me. 'Banter? He's long gone by now.'

I shake my head angrily. 'I get call to come fix toilet leak on third floor.' I pat my pockets. 'I got number and name here somewhere, but I supposed to meet Banter.'

The young man shrugs. 'Banter's a worthless piece of shit. It's just like him not to hang around when someone's toilet's leaking. I'm in two twelve. It's not above me, is it? My ceiling could be falling in.'

'No,' I say. 'Three forty-seven, or something. Can I go in?'

The young man nods absently, stopping at the mailboxes.

By the time he's got one open, the elevator door is shutting on me.

I get off at the third floor, find the stairwell, and climb to the fourth floor.

I find apartment four twenty-nine and knock. I look right at the peephole, and a shiver of excitement passes through me.

'Yes?' I hear her call in that unfamiliar voice. 'Who is it?'

'It is plumber, Frau Amsel,' I say. 'Herr Banter called. He says tenant in three twenty-nine is complaining of water from the ceiling. He wants me to check toilet.'

There's a long pause.

And then I hear a chain slide and a dead bolt thrown.

Chapter 60

'Who reported her missing?' Mattie asked, studying the PDF of a document carrying the letterhead of the police department of Frankfurt am Main.

'Her sister, Ilona,' Dr. Gabriel said, tapping the section that identified the concerned relative.

Mattie felt a chill. 'Ilona was also one of the children who entered Waisenhaus 44 with Chris. She give an address?'

'Just a cell number,' said Katharina, who was

also looking at the document.

Mattie whipped out her cell and dialed just as Tom Burkhart entered. He went straight to her. 'I think I've got something.'

She held up her finger, hearing Ilona Frei's phone ring. A synthesized voice answered, telling her to leave a message and a callback number.

'Hi, Ilona. My name is Mattie Engel. I am a friend of Chris Schneider's. He and I work together at Private here in Berlin. If you could call me, I'd appreciate it. Any time. Day or night. Please, it's important that I speak with you.'

'Here's a Greta Amsel, Mattie,' Dr. Gabriel said when she hung up. 'She lives out by Falkensee. That's twenty minutes, tops.'

Mattie jotted down the address and moved toward the door. Again Burkhart said, 'Engel, I said I think I've got something.'

Mattie hesitated and then replied, 'Come with me. Tell me on the way.'

Chapter 61

When my dear old friend Greta Amsel opens her door, she's wearing an apron and I smell bacon frying. She studies my plumber's disguise and then stands aside. 'Down the hall on the right. You don't suppose it's a burst pipe?'

I shrug, smile, and respond cheerily, 'Who knows? I look, okay?'

The smell of bacon surrounds me as I walk

down a hall with bare walls. When I go into the toilet I notice she does not have the array of cosmetics, lotions, and soaps you'd expect.

Greta Amsel lives a simple, austere life.

I set the toolbox down and pull on rubber gloves. I look over my shoulder. She's watching me. I smile again. 'You cooking, yes? I knows in a minute if this is problem. If no, two minutes I be gone.'

She hesitates, and then moves out of the doorway.

I wait until I hear dishes rattle, and then a radio sputtering with news. I fish in the toolbox and come up with my flathead screwdriver and a clipboard with blank paper on it. I flush the toilet, and then, holding the screwdriver beneath the clipboard, I walk toward the smell of the bacon.

'Hallo there?' I call pleasantly.

Greta stands at the stove in a galley kitchen about six feet from me. She's rolling bacon onto a paper towel on a plate. She looks up. 'All done?'

'Yes, no problem with toilet. Must be neighbors.' I hold out the clipboard. 'You sign that I am here, make trip, for Banter, okay?'

Greta steps toward me. And then I can't help it. Being this close to her pleases me more than I'd anticipated, and I make that clicking noise in my throat.

Puzzlement and then disbelief twist through Greta's face.

'You know me, Greta, hmmm?' I say. 'A long time and still you know me.'

She's paralyzed with terror, but I'm thrilled and fluid when I drop the clipboard and launch my-

187

self at her.

Greta grabs the skillet and throws the bacon grease at me. It scalds my face. But that only serves to infuriate me.

She starts to scream, but I knock the pan from her hand and jam my fist into her mouth before she can get out much more than a squeal.

She looks at me wide-eyed and makes soft whimpering noises.

'You remember, don't you, Greta?' I ask in a hoarse whisper. 'All the fun we used to have? You and your mother, hmmm?'

Chapter 62

Burkhart parked the Private car down the street from Greta Amsel's apartment building just as an older man in a blue jumpsuit and matching cap left by the front door, carrying a toolbox.

Mattie was trying Greta Amsel's number for the third time. No answer. The workman climbed into a dark-blue panel van.

Mattie was barely conscious of him. She was running through the information Burkhart had given her on the way over.

The counterterrorism expert had discovered no other documents regarding the auxiliary slaughterhouse in Ahrensfelde. He'd looked in the Berlin city archives and in records repositories in Ahrensfelde, and there was nothing more than what they'd found already.

People in the area immediately surrounding the blasted abattoir told Burkhart that they'd already spoken to Risi Baumgarten's agents and knew nothing about the place other than they'd thought it represented a hazard to their children.

Then Burkhart had stopped for lunch at a café not far from the slaughterhouse and met a retired shopkeeper and his lady friend.

The shopkeeper grew up on a farm that used the slaughterhouse. He said a man he knew only as 'Falk' ran the place, and he described Falk as an alcoholic with a bitter and gloomy attitude.

Falk had a son who worked at the abattoir too. He couldn't remember the younger Falk's name, but he remembered that he was in his late teens the last time he saw him, and very smart despite limited schooling.

The shopkeeper's lady friend told Burkhart that she walked by the abattoir in the late seventies, late at night, and thought she heard a woman screaming, but it could have been a pig squealing. Pigs are smart, she told Burkhart. They know when there's killing going on. She told her late husband about the incident, and he'd told her to plug her ears from now on.

The blue workman's van began to pull out.

'You want to knock on the door?' Burkhart asked.

'We're here, right?' Mattie said, climbing out.

The van drove past them. They barely gave it a glance.

They tried the buzzer to Greta Amsel's apartment twice. No answer.

'Let's come back tomorrow,' Burkhart said.

An older gentleman walked up behind them. 'Who are you looking for?'

'Greta Amsel,' Mattie said.

The man looked around. 'That's her bike. She's here.'

'She's not answering her buzzer.'

'Lots of the buzzers don't work. But if her bike's here, she's here.'

Burkhart flashed his Private badge. 'Mind if we go upstairs and try her door?'

'Hell, I don't care,' he said, and let them in.

They went to Greta Amsel's apartment on the fourth floor, knocked, and got no answer. Then they noticed a strange smell coming from inside, a mix of bacon smoke and the acrid taint that lingers after hair catches fire.

'Something's wrong,' Mattie said.

'I agree,' Burkhart said. He crouched and proceeded to pick the lock.

Guns drawn, they entered the hallway. The smell was worse here, crossed with human feces.

The light was on in the bathroom. The toilet seat was up. The fan was running.

So was the one in the kitchen where Greta Amsel's corpse lay, sprawled on her belly.

Her hands were singed and her fingers charred black.

Chapter 63

Thirty yards out from the goal, Cassiano came to a full stop, juggled, and then popped the ball over the head of the final Düsseldorf defender. With explosive speed, the Brazilian wove around the stunned sweeper and half-volleyed the bouncing ball left-footed into the upper right-hand corner of the net.

The crowd inside the Hertha Berlin stadium went nuts. Jack Morgan and Daniel Brecht were up on their feet applauding.

'That's three,' Brecht crowed. 'Absolutely super.'

'No wonder Manchester United is interested,' Morgan said. 'He's incredibly good.'

'Why would he risk his career to get involved with someone like Pavel?'

'That's exactly what he said, remember?' Morgan said.

'But there's no denying the way he looked in those six games,' Brecht countered. 'He was simply not the same player.'

Out on the field, the referee blew the whistle, ending the game. Cassiano jogged off, sweating, smiling, and waving to his adoring fans.

Jack was silent for several moments watching him.

'I think he's telling the truth,' he said finally. 'I don't think he'd risk his career for someone like

Pavel, but maybe Perfecta would.'

'She did get naked for him.'

'She did,' Morgan agreed. 'I want to talk to Cassiano again. And his coach. And the club's general manager. All together. Think you can set that up?'

'When?'

'Now sounds good.'

Chapter 64

'Hauptkommissar Dietrich?' Mattie said into her cell phone. She was standing in the hallway of Greta Amsel's apartment.

'Who is this?' Dietrich replied in a thick, slow voice.

'It's Mattie Engel,' she said. 'There's been another murder.'

There was a long silence before Dietrich said, 'Who? Where?'

'A childhood friend of Chris's,' she said. 'Greta Amsel. They lived in an orphanage together near Halle.'

Another long silence. 'And she's dead?'

'We just found her in her apartment. We haven't touched a thing. I think we saw the killer. He was posing as a plumber. He was leaving as we arrived.'

'Did you get a look at him?'

'No,' she admitted.

Dietrich's third silence was the longest. She

thought she heard him drinking something. 'Call Inspector Weigel,' he said at last. 'Have her bring in a forensics team and three Kripo detectives to canvass the building. I'll see to this all tomorrow around noon.'

Mattie hesitated, incredulous. 'Tomorrow? With all due respect, Hauptkommissar, I think you should come here right now and listen to what we've found. Another of Chris's childhood friends is missing.'

The high commissar breathed heavily in response, almost laboring.

Then he said, 'Frau Engel, I must confess to you that it would be unprofessional of me to be at a crime scene in my current state. I am to bury my father in the morning, and I am drunk and well on the way to being drunker. You'll have to call Weigel. I've left her in charge for the night. She'll be helped by the rest of the Kripo homicide team.'

The phone clicked dead.

Chapter 65

My friends, I can't help it. Two hours after the fact and I'm still shaking like a calf about to become veal. The smell of flesh burning and bacon still poisons my nose. The grease burn on my right cheek throbs.

And thoughts crowd my head.

I was in Greta's apartment barely twelve minutes.

I left the fans running.

It should have been days until her body was discovered.

But then I saw Mattie Engel and the big bald guy. And ever since then my mind's been throttled with questions: How could they have found Greta? I took all the files from the archives. What do they know? What did Christoph tell them before he came after me?

For the first time in nearly twenty-five years, I feel almost overwhelmed by the thought that my mask, my invisibility, might be weakening.

Then I shake it off. They'll find nothing that will link to the Invisible Man.

But I am, above all, a realist. I can clearly see now that I have limited time in which to fully erase my past. Three other children are still unaccounted for.

Just three and I'll be free.

Like it or not, my friends, tomorrow is shaping up to be a busy, busy day.

Chapter 66

It was nearly eleven by the time Burkhart turned onto Mattie's street.

They'd been at the Amsel crime scene for hours, watching Inspector Weigel and the team of Kripo investigators and crime scene specialists document the body and the apartment.

Weigel had seemed overwhelmed to be in

charge of an investigation, even if it was only for one night, but she'd listened attentively and took copious notes when they gave their statement.

Mattie had held nothing back. She told Weigel about the files stolen from the archives, Hariat Ledwig's assertion that something terrible had happened to Chris and his friends, and the missing-persons report on Ilse Frei.

Weigel had duly noted all of it before saying, 'So you're saying that there's no connection between the deceased and Hermann Krüger?'

'I don't know.'

Weigel looked uncomfortable as she said, 'This afternoon, the higher-ups put a lot of pressure on the Hauptkommissar about Agnes Krüger's murder. They think that is the key to all of this. Dietrich thinks so too.'

Burkhart said, 'You mean it's more high-profile than, say, a nurse's death?'

Weigel appeared even more torn, but then she nodded and told them that she had talked with Hermann Krüger's secretary in person. Weigel had gotten the secretary to admit that five days before, the billionaire told her he was going to be off on personal business for the next week, and then quite simply he'd vanished. Berlin Kripo had intelligence specialists trying to track his finances, but so far they were as shadowy as the man.

No matter what had happened to Greta Amsel, Weigel believed the focus of the official investigation would be on Krüger until he was found and cleared.

'It's the six children,' Mattie insisted to Burkhart as he pulled up in front of her apartment building. 'They're the key, not Hermann Krüger.'

'I agree,' Burkhart said. 'But I can see how someone like Agnes Krüger being slain in broad daylight would have a way of distracting attention.'

'We have to find the other children from Waisenhaus 44. We have to warn them.'

'Gabriel said he was staying at the office until he found them,' Burkhart said.

Mattie nodded, but she felt insanely frustrated that they'd been so close to saving Greta Amsel. The killer had walked right by them, and then driven right by them!

She put her hand on the door handle and was about to pull it, when she stopped and looked at Burkhart. 'Have you eaten anything?'

'Not since lunch,' he admitted.

'Feel like a home-cooked meal?'

'You're gonna cook after the day you had?' Burkhart asked.

'My aunt does the cooking. When I get home this late, I warm it up.'

Chapter 67

Cassiano roared in Portuguese when his wife dropped her coat in the video Brecht had shot of the entrance to Pavel's hotel room.

Hertha Berlin's star striker leaped from his chair in the team's conference room and lunged toward the door, shouting like a wild man.

Brecht grabbed the Brazilian and said something forcefully in his language. For a second Morgan thought Cassiano was going to pulverize Brecht, but then the striker softened and sat back down in his chair.

'What was he yelling?' demanded the team's general manager, Klaus Bremen, who sat next to the coach, Sig Mueller.

Brecht said, 'He wanted to get a machete, cut off Pavel's balls, and shove them down Perfecta's throat until she suffocated. I told him it was a bad idea for someone bound for the World Cup.'

'So he's saying he had no idea about this?' the coach asked. 'Or about the betting?'

Brecht posed the question in Portuguese. Cassiano shook his head.

'Ask him about those games where he played horribly,' Morgan said.

Brecht did so and the Brazilian began to shout at Morgan.

Brecht said, 'He says he told you yesterday, he was sick. He did not take a dive and would like to slap you for saying so right after he found out his wife was having sexy-time with some old Russian bastard.'

Morgan said nothing.

Cassiano looked at his coach and babbled in Portuguese.

'You believe me, yes, Sig?' Brecht translated.

Bremen, the general manager, replied, 'It's not a matter of belief, Cassiano. We need proof you're not involved.'

After Brecht told Cassiano so in Portuguese,

the Brazilian began to shout again indignantly.

'How can I do this?' Brecht translated. 'My wife is a whore and I am the victim of rumors. How can I prove that I am clean?'

'Tell him to give us a hair sample,' Morgan said. 'Private will take care of the rest.'

Chapter 68

'Mommy!' Niklas cried when Mattie opened the door to the apartment.

Her son was in his pajamas and ran to her.

She took him up in her arms, scolding, 'What are you doing up so late?'

Aunt Cäcilia came behind her wearing her robe and curlers. 'He wouldn't listen. He's been a crazy man, bouncing off the walls since that game ended, wanting to wait up and tell you all about it.'

'Cassiano was unbelievable!' Niklas exulted. 'He scored three. Three!'

Burkhart appeared in the doorway looking somewhat awkward.

Mattie smiled. 'Niklas, Aunt C, this is Herr Burkhart. He works at Private too.'

Aunt Cäcilia blushed, pulled her robe tighter, and complained, 'Ohhh, Mattie, I didn't know you were bringing company home.'

'He drove me home and we both realized we were starving.'

That broke whatever spell Burkhart's arrival had held over her aunt, who turned and bustled toward the kitchen. 'I have cold sausages, potato pancakes, and homemade applesauce. And cold beer. Give me just a minute!'

'Say hello, Niklas,' Mattie said, setting down her son, who appeared shy.

Burkhart crouched and held out his hand. 'Nice to meet you, Niklas.'

Niklas hesitated and then shook it, saying, 'You're big.'

'I know. You will be too someday.'

'Am I gonna lose my hair too?'

'Niklas!' Mattie scolded.

But Burkhart just laughed. 'Being bald has nothing to do with being big, Niklas. Being bald is a state of mind.'

Mattie grinned. The tension of the day faded toward exhaustion. 'I've got to get him to bed.'

'Sure,' Burkhart said. 'Maybe I better go?'

'No, no, my aunt would not hear of it. Someone going hungry is a major injustice with her.'

'I heard that!' Aunt Cäcilia shouted from the kitchen.

Mattie put her hand on Niklas's shoulder and said, 'Say good night.'

'Good night, Herr Burkhart,' Niklas said.

'You can call me Tom.'

Niklas grinned and took his mother's hand and they went to his room. She tucked him into bed. Niklas said, 'Are you and Tom going to catch whoever killed Chris?'

'Most definitely.'

Mattie kissed him on the forehead. 'Get some sleep, my little man.'

'Tom said I'm going to be big.'

199

'He did, didn't he?'

She went to the door.

'Mommy?'

'Yes?'

'You're not going to get killed trying to find out who did it, are you?'

Mattie turned and went straight back to him and wrapped her arms around him. 'No. I'm going to be safe and here with you until you're as big as Burkhart is.'

Niklas hugged her fiercely. 'I love you, Mommy.'

Mattie started to tear up. 'I love you too, Nicky. More than you can know.'

Chapter 69

Friends, fellow Berliners, it's not quite six in the morning, and I'm already on the road in the ML500. I have a long drive in front of me, four and a half hours to Frankfurt am Main if traffic on the autobahn cooperates.

Can there be a better time to hear a story than over a long stretch of road? I confess I love those audiobooks, don't you?

Sit back, now, and listen closely:

As I indicated once before, two years after the wall fell, well after the surgeries in Africa, it took me a month to locate the bitch that bore me.

She was living in the sleepy hamlet of Biedenkopf near the Rothaargebirge Nature Park in west central Germany.

Do you know the place?

It doesn't matter. Suffice it to say that my mother lived alone in a cottage on the outskirts of a rural village threatened by forest.

On a chill, dark, November night, I knocked at her door.

'Who's there?' came a tremulous response.

'It is me, mother,' I said, and I repeated the name she'd given me at birth.

After a moment's hesitation, the wooden door opened slowly, revealing an old, frail woman I almost did not recognize.

She was carrying an old Luger, which she pointed at me suspiciously.

'Who are you?' she demanded.

'A lover of masks, Mother,' I said, and made that clicking noise in my throat. 'Don Giovanni's most of all.'

Her eyes peeled wide, and her mouth sagged open in sheer disbelief as her pistol slowly lowered. 'Is it really you?'

'Of course,' I said. 'Do you still have that old *Papierkrattler* mask?'

'They told me you died in Hohenschönhausen Prison!' she cried and threw herself at me, weeping.

I caught her as any loving son would. 'They told me you died there too.'

She pushed back in horror. 'No!'

'Yes.'

'But they said you'd be told I went into the West.'

'They said many things,' I replied. 'I didn't believe any of it.'

'And I should not have. Come in! Come in out of the cold!'

I smiled dutifully at her mothering, followed her inside, and shut the door behind me.

My mother's living area was a simple place with an overstuffed reading chair and a lamp and a fire burning in a wood stove. There were no photographs, which made my mission seem all the easier.

She was looking at me in wonder and joy again. 'I did not recognize you.'

'It's been too long,' I said.

Timidly, she said, 'Your father is dead, yes?'

'Five years now.'

'I'd heard that,' she said with a pained expression. 'But I guess all things must pass,' she went on, and then swallowed and looked at me pleadingly. 'Do you forgive me?'

I could not control my reaction.

My right hand shot out of its own accord and grabbed my dear mother by the throat. I lifted her dangling, bug-eyed, and choking into the air.

'As a matter of fact, Mother,' I said, 'I can honestly say I will never, ever forgive you for leaving me.'

Chapter 70

Private's corporate jet was a sleek Gulfstream G650, the gold standard in business aviation. At nine forty-five that morning, the jet's landing gear descended in anticipation of landing at Frankfurt am Main airport.

Mattie finished her coffee and handed it to the steward, and then looked at the front page of the *Berliner Morgenpost*. The newspaper was plastered with stories about Agnes Krüger's murder and Hermann Krüger's disappearing act.

Berlin Kripo was executing a search warrant on his offices and all his known residences in the city. The price of Krüger Industries stocks had fallen in overseas trading. At the same time, Olle Larsson, the Swedish financier, had filed documents that indicated he'd increased his position in Krüger Industries from 5 to 10 percent.

Mattie shook her head, puzzled, trying to stitch it all together. Was Krüger involved? Had he somehow known Chris when he was a child? Krüger was born in East Germany, wasn't he?

She turned to look at Burkhart. The counter-terrorism expert was in the tan leather captain's chair opposite her. His eyes were closed – his great shaved head lolled to the right – and his breath came slow and rhythmic.

Mattie decided that she might have under-estimated Burkhart. After shutting off Niklas's light, she'd gone back to the kitchen and found Aunt Cäcilia laughing and Burkhart grinning, a plate of sausages and potato pancakes before him.

'He's funny,' Aunt Cäcilia said.

'She's a great cook,' Burkhart said, sipping his beer.

'I know that,' Mattie said, taking her own plate and beer.

They'd talked and eaten for almost an hour. Burkhart was funny and entertaining in a mordant way, a quality she attributed to the line of work he'd been in prior to joining Private Berlin.

He thanked Aunt Cäcilia twice after he'd finished, and then Mattie saw him to the door.

'That was the best meal I've had in a long time,' Burkhart said. 'Thanks.'

'You're welcome.'

He smiled and said, 'I'll see you at the meeting, Engel?'

'Call me Mattie. And I'll be there,' she promised and shut the door.

Burkhart *was* a good guy. But she didn't think of him as she went to bed. All she could see as she plunged toward sleep were images of Chris and Greta Amsel walking into Waisenhaus 44.

Her cell phone rang at 6:20 a.m., less than six hours after she'd gone to sleep. Dr. Gabriel had found another orphan. His real name was Artur Becker. He'd changed it to Artur Jaeger. He was a design engineer for BMW in Munich.

Mattie called BMW security, looking for a phone number for Jaeger, but was told that he had gone to the IAA Motor Show in Frankfurt am Main, and the company had a policy against disclosing personal cell phone numbers. But Mattie insisted that Jaeger could be in danger, and the security person on duty relented.

Mattie called the number immediately. Jaeger answered groggily. She identified herself and asked if his real name was Artur Becker.

A pause. 'I don't know who you're talking about. My name is Jaeger.'

'Please, sir, I'm trying to warn you about–'

Jaeger almost screamed at her, 'I don't know anyone named Artur Becker!'

'I think you do, and other orphans,' she said. 'You're all in–'

'This is a sick, sick joke,' he said, and hung up.

She tried him back several times but got his voice mail. She left a detailed message, describing what had happened to Greta Amsel and to please call her back. Then in frustration she called Morgan, who told her to take the jet to Frankfurt.

Finally she had called Burkhart, and he'd met her at the corporate terminal.

She reached over and tapped him on the forearm. He startled and jerked awake.

'We're landing,' she said.

Burkhart yawned. 'Thanks. How far to the auto show?'

'Fifteen-minute drive, tops,' Mattie said as the jet touched down.

He sat up straighter, all business, and checked his watch, and his face turned grim. 'Let's hope we get there in time.'

Chapter 71

Following six old men who carried the colonel's ashes, Hauptkommissar Hans Dietrich trudged through wet grass toward an open grave in Zentralfriedhof Friedrichsfelde, the central cemetery in the Lichtenberg district of East Berlin. The high commissar's head pounded from the vodka he'd consumed so copiously the night before, trying to deaden his mind so he would not drown in the dark, twisted quagmire that was his father.

It had not worked.

Dietrich's drunken thoughts had not been where they should have been – on the slaughterhouse, say, or on Christoph Schneider, Agnes Krüger, and now this Amsel woman. Instead, he'd wallowed in memories of the colonel and the ruthless manner in which his father raised him.

Indeed, brutally hungover, moving unsteadily toward the grave, the high commissar's mind was still recalling the cold and often inexplicably cruel acts to which his father had treated him growing up.

Dietrich was fifty-two. He'd been trying to understand the colonel since he was a child. But as he watched the old men observing his father's urn being lowered into the grave, he realized once again that he could neither explain his father nor come to terms with him.

The colonel was dead and about to be buried,

yet the high commissar had the shuddering realization that the threat of the man might never die.

Dietrich gazed blearily at the men gathered around his father's final resting place. They were in their seventies and eighties, and they wore somber gray suits, dark raincoats, and fedoras.

There was no minister present. The colonel might have risen from the grave in fury had there been.

But one of the men, stout with rheumy eyes and gin blossoms on his nose, stepped forward at last, and said: 'Conrad was one of the last of his kind, and to me it is fitting that he be given a final resting place close to the greats.'

Dietrich looked off toward a circular brick wall strangled in vine. He knew there were many burial urns sealed in the wall. A tall upright stone slab cut like an ancient tombstone stood dead center of the yard inside the brick wall. Surrounding the tombstone were the graves of Karl Liebknecht, Rosa Luxemburg, Wilhelm Pieck, and seven other titans of the German communist movement.

My father's heroes, Dietrich thought bitterly. So close and yet so far.

He looked back at his father's mourners. They were looking at him expectantly and he realized the stout one had stopped speaking.

The high commissar said nothing. He took two steps forward, picked up a clod of wet black earth, thought to hurl it, but then dropped it on the urn. He stepped back, aware of the mud on his hand and not caring.

One by one, the pallbearers tossed dirt into the grave and then shook Dietrich's hand, blackening it further.

The last mourner, the stout man, said, 'You have the condolences of the inner committee, Hauptkommissar. Your father was a valued member.'

With a dull, flat expression, Dietrich nodded. 'Thank you, Willy.'

Willy hesitated, and then hardened. 'I suppose *you* must feel relieved then, now that he's gone.'

Dietrich had to fight to quell the nausea roiling in his stomach as he said, 'Actually, I feel cursed by him, by all of you. I won't be free of that until I know that every last one of you is dead, and all your secrets are buried with you.'

Chapter 72

It is just past 10 a.m. when I turn the Mercedes into a parking structure on the northwest corner of the grounds of the IAA Motor Show, the largest car exhibition in the world. Gleaming exotic rides litter the parking lot, and I'm instantly a happy man. I love cars. They're one of the best disguises there is.

In the right car, my friends, you can be anyone, don't you think?

I park and study a photo of Artur Jaeger downloaded from the Internet, thinking about the helpful secretary who told me where I might find the engineer.

208

I look in the mirror, checking the makeup job that makes me appear bald and much older. I zip up a blue windbreaker, and then put on a red one with an Aston Martin logo over it.

I tug on a matching ball cap.

I pause, forcing myself to breathe deep and slow.

I know what a terrible risk I'm taking.

It's unlike me. I prefer to have the odds in my favor. But I have no choice.

So I get the pistol and the suppressor from under my seat and slide the weapon into a holster I wear beneath the windbreaker.

I open the door and make a show of pain as I get out. I've got a bad hip, or arthritis, or at least I do today.

I gimp toward the galleria entrance, telling myself that if I am as cold and deadly as my father taught me to be, I just might leave Frankfurt an even more invisible man.

Chapter 73

The taxi from the airport dropped Mattie and Burkhart in front of the unequal twin towers called Kastor and Pollux that front the city entrance to the Frankfurt Messe trade fair. They paid for admission at the Festhalle entrance and entered a sprawling campus of gigantic halls linked by moving walkways and escalators.

It was the second to last day of the show, but

the place was still packed. Using a map, they navigated toward the BMW stand in hall number one and began looking for Artur Jaeger using a photo Dr. Gabriel had sent to their cell phones.

Mattie spotted him up on a stage beside a beautiful woman in an evening gown. He held a microphone and was describing the intricacies of the sleek concept sports car that was turning on a revolving platform behind him.

Mattie worked through the crowd toward the front. It was loud inside the massive hall, a general din that competed with Jaeger's spiel, so she did not hear what caused the engineer to suddenly jerk, drop the mic, and collapse backward.

But when Jaeger hit the stage floor, she saw the fine plume of blood that burst from his lips.

'Shooter!' Burkhart roared. 'Everyone down!'

Chaos bloomed into pandemonium as people around the BMW exhibit began screaming, diving for the floor, or tripping toward the exits.

Mattie drew her gun, her mind computing the rough angle from which Jaeger had to have been shot. She looked along that line of sight and spotted among those trying to flee an older man in a red windbreaker limping quickly away.

'The guy in the red jacket!' Mattie shouted at Burkhart.

He heard them. The old man began bulling his way through the melee, showing tremendous strength and agility.

But Burkhart was like a rhino on steroids. He brushed people aside as if they were scarecrows, with Mattie trailing in his wake.

The killer disappeared out into a crowded passage. Ten seconds later, Burkhart and Mattie exited the same doors and scanned the crowd, which was beginning to pick up on the frenzy inside the hall as more and more people ran from it talking about the shooting.

The old man was gone.

Or was he?

Mattie spotted a red jacket on the floor.

'He's changed jackets,' she shouted at Burkhart.

Suddenly, toward the west entrance to the convention hall, they heard a gunshot and screaming.

Chapter 74

A security guard had confronted the assassin at point-blank range and been shot in the chest, his gun discharging as he fell.

Beyond the guard, outside the entrance, and running toward Brüsseler Strasse, a man in a blue windbreaker and black cap dodged through the crowd. Burkhart took off in a full sprint with Mattie gasping to keep up behind him.

By the time Mattie and Burkhart reached the entrance, the killer had dragged a man from a Maserati, pistol-whipped him, and climbed in. The sports car squealed away as they ran out onto the sidewalk. Rain was starting to fall again.

As he ran, Burkhart flashed his badge at a man standing shocked beside a red BMW coupe. 'Call Frankfurt Kripo,' he shouted at the man, snatching the keys from his hand.

'Hey!' the man shouted. 'That's not mine! You can't–'

'Report this vehicle taken by Private Berlin and the Maserati stolen by an assassin,' Burkhart commanded as he jumped in the driver's seat. 'He killed two.'

Mattie was in the BMW's passenger seat, strapping herself in. 'He's got a head start.'

'And he's got more horsepower,' Burkhart said, slamming the sports car in gear and popping the clutch. 'But he can't drive like I can.'

They went screeching after the Maserati, which had downshifted and drifted through a hard U-turn, heading due east toward Osloer Strasse. The killer went right past them. He looked out the window directly at them.

Bald. Dark glasses. A moustache. Hard to tell his age.

The killer had already taken a right on Osloer Strasse by the time they'd made the U-turn. They sped after him through a series of right-hand turns that led them around the perimeter of the fairgrounds and through a red light out onto Route 44, heading west. The Maserati was four hundred yards ahead of them when it took the ramp onto Autobahn 648.

Due to Burkhart's remarkable driving skills, the killer could not widen the gap between them all the way to the interchange with the Autobahn 5. The Maserati headed north.

'Call Kripo,' Burkhart told Mattie. 'Tell them to put a chopper in the air and give them his position.'

But right then the skies opened up – a deluge came in sheets and a gale overwhelmed the windshield wipers. Burkhart did not slow. Instead, he seemed to drive by braille on the three-lane high-speed route, weaving in and out of cars as if the skies were clear.

It scared the hell out of Mattie, who could not bring herself to take her eyes off the blurry road.

'Call them!' Burkhart snapped.

Mattie shouted, 'Slow down and I will!'

'I slow down, we lose him!' Burkhart yelled back.

'We can't even see where he is!'

'I can see the brake lights where he's cutting people off!'

Mattie held on for dear life as Burkhart got them closer and closer. She heard herself tell Niklas that she would not die trying to find Chris's killer.

For a second, north of Rosa-Luxemburg-Strasse, Mattie thought Burkhart would eventually reel in the Maserati.

But then the killer did something absolutely crazy. The rain let up enough for her to see the Maserati speeding up as it passed the exit for the village of Bad Homburg. The car flew over an underpass with Burkhart still gaining ground. Then the killer must have hit his emergency brake just shy of the on-ramp for vehicles leaving Autobahn 661 for the northbound A5. On the slick pavement, the Maserati drifted and turned 160 degrees, and then it roared down the entryway to the autobahn.

Mattie's eyes widened and she gasped as they shot past the lane. 'He's going the wrong way!'

Chapter 75

Friends, fellow Berliners, accelerating straight into traffic feeding off the 661 is the best move I think I've ever made.

It's remarkable how easy it is to get vehicles to turn out of your way when you're hurtling right at them, fully prepared to die.

A Lancia swerves right off my front fender, catches the guardrail, and does a cartwheel. The driver's face was so terrified I start laughing. This has to be the most fun I've had in years.

Better yet, I glance in the rearview mirror and see the red BMW that's been after me has failed to make the radical move that I did. Do the unexpected, my friends. It always pays off.

At the far end of the on-ramp, I downshift, throw the car through a one-hundred-eighty-degree turn, and hit the gas.

The road to Bad Homburg is miraculously clear ahead. I keep looking in my rearview mirror as I pass through the town, but I still don't see the red BMW. They missed the turn. The next exit was five miles away. They're not coming any-time soon.

Still, I know that the Maserati is a car that's easy to recognize, one that I will have to lose as

214

soon as possible.

Ten minutes later, I pull the car deep into a wooded lane inside the Hochtaunus Nature Park northwest of Bad Homburg. Do you know it?

It doesn't matter.

Just know that I have no time to lose. There will be police swarming the area soon and I have some distance to cover.

I park the car in the darkest spot I can find, wipe down the steering wheel and the door, and get out, heading due northeast into the sopping-wet forest.

As I walk, I tear off the skullcap, the nose prosthesis, and the moustache. I find a stream and use mud and cold water to strip the makeup from my face. I ditch the blue windbreaker and continue on in the rain, my mind a whirl.

I keep seeing the look on the driver's face before he flipped.

I can't help it, my friends.

I stop out there alone in the woods, throw up my fists, punch them at the weeping sky, and start to laugh.

Soon, I'm hysterical and I've fallen to my knees.

I've done it. Two more to go and I've done it. No one will ever know who I am or what I've done.

Some may suspect.

Others may offer conjecture.

But as I get to my feet, and continue to make my way northeast toward the train station in the hamlet of Friedrichsdorf, I'm more certain than ever before that the person I was will never be linked to the person I have become.

Chapter 76

'Where did you last see him!' Burkhart shouted as they roared north toward the next exit.

Mattie was craned around in her seat, still shocked by the move.

'Engel?' Burkhart demanded.

Mattie blinked and pointed. 'He went off the road back there.'

'Bad Homburg,' Burkhart said.

But by the time they covered the fifteen miles and reached the sleepy little village of smooth-walled gray houses, they knew they had little chance of catching the Maserati. It could have gone in any one of several directions.

Burkhart smashed his fist on the wheel.

Mattie felt the same way. They'd been so close, but they hadn't saved Artur Jaeger or the security guard, nor had they prevented the injuries resulting from the crashes. The killer had beaten them once again, and she was beginning to fear he might be unstoppable.

'We should go back,' Burkhart said, 'and find the police and give our statement.'

Mattie almost agreed, but then something clicked in the back of her mind.

'No, wait,' she said, digging for her cell phone. 'Pull over.'

She dialed Dr. Gabriel's number and got the aging hippie right away. Without pretext she asked,

216

'Where is Ilse Frei from? The missing woman?'

'Bad Homburg,' he replied.

'You have the address?'

He told her to wait a moment and then came back with it. 'What's happening? Where are you?'

'Bad Homburg,' she said and hung up. She looked at Burkhart. 'Ilse Frei lives less than a mile from here. The killer knew this place. That's why he ran here.'

Burkhart put the car in gear.

Six minutes later they drove past a modest duplex on the outskirts of town at the edge of farm country. The rain had slowed to a drizzle and in the distance they could hear sirens wailing.

Burkhart parked the red BMW in the alley so as not to attract police attention. They went to the back door and knocked.

A few moments passed and they were about to knock again when a pleasant-looking blond woman in her early thirties appeared in the window and eyed them suspiciously before opening the door on a security chain.

'Yes?'

Mattie held up her badge. 'We're with Private Berlin. We–'

The woman's hand went to her throat and she cried, 'Did Chris send you? Has he found Ilse?'

Chapter 77

'Dead?' Tina Hannover said twenty minutes later in a soft, sad voice. 'And Ilse, too?'

They were sitting at a small table in a spartanly equipped kitchen, drinking coffee she'd made for them.

Mattie's mind flashed on the woman's corpse beside Chris's. 'I can't say for sure. Her remains have not been tested, but there was a woman's body with his.'

Ilse Frei's roommate's shoulders slumped. Tears trickled down her cheeks as she shook her head slowly. 'Poor Ilse. She was right to be afraid. I told Chris she was afraid and to be careful. I guess I...'

She bit at her knuckles and turned away from them.

'Why was Ilse afraid?' Burkhart asked. 'And why did Chris come to you?'

Tina Hanover made a puffing noise and wiped her tears with her sleeve. 'He came because Ilse's crazy sister, Ilona, asked him to. He said they were all friends from childhood.'

Mattie put it together in an instant. Ilona Frei had to be the mystery woman who'd visited Chris a week before his disappearance.

'Start at the beginning,' Burkhart insisted.

Over the course of a half hour, Tina Hanover explained that Ilse Frei came home from work about two weeks ago as upset as she'd ever seen

218

her. But Ilse had refused to tell her roommate what had gotten her so worked up.

Stranger still, Ilse had gone straight to her room and called her sister in Berlin, which was very unusual. According to Tina Hanover, Ilona Frei was the bane of Ilse's existence. Ilona was a methadone addict who'd been diagnosed with schizophrenia. She'd been in and out of institutions and was forever hounding her sister for money.

'How did you know Ilse called Ilona?' Burkhart asked.

Tina Hanover blushed and squirmed in her chair. 'I ... uh...' She turned defensive. 'I listened at her door. She was so upset, I couldn't help it.'

'What did she tell her sister?' Mattie asked.

Ilse Frei's roommate fidgeted again before replying, 'I didn't catch all of it because the doors are pretty thick. But I caught the gist of it. She'd recognized someone from their past. She called him Falk and seemed terrified. I mean absolutely terrified of him.'

'Falk?' Burkhart said. 'Are you sure?'

Tina Hanover nodded and Mattie looked at Burkhart, puzzled.

He said, 'The man who ran the slaughterhouse was named Falk.'

'But he couldn't...' Mattie said, and then she remembered. 'He had a son.'

'He had a son,' Burkhart said, nodding.

For the first time since she'd gotten word of Chris's disappearance, Mattie believed they were homing in on the killer. 'Did you tell Chris all this?'

Tina Hanover nodded. 'He seemed to know

219

who Falk was.'

'What did he say?' Mattie pressed.

'Say? Nothing. But you could see it in his body language. He knew him.'

There was a moment of silence in the room before Burkhart said, 'So where did Chris go from here? Ilse's law firm?'

'The law firm?' Tina Hanover said, surprised.

'But you said she recognized Falk at work,' Mattie said, confused. 'Was Falk a client at the firm? Someone she saw at the courthouse?'

'No, no,' she protested, her face flushing. 'Ilse ... she...'

She got defensive again. 'Ilse stopped working at the law firm eighteen months ago when she found out she could make more money in half the time working at the Paradise FKK club north of town. She was a licensed, professional sex worker.'

Chapter 78

The Paradise FKK club was situated amid agricultural fields on ten manicured acres north of Bad Homburg. Trees and a white wall surrounded the compound. Despite the dismal weather there were fifteen or twenty high-end cars parked in the lot and taxis were traveling to and fro.

Mattie and Burkhart walked on a cement path past gardens appointed with pale Grecian statues of naked men and women in erotic poses. They came to a white building with columns that supported a portico over a grand entryway.

'A little over the top, don't you think?' Mattie cracked uncomfortably as two men leaving the building walked by, staring at her.

'I told you to stay in the car,' Burkhart replied.

Mattie's cell phone rang and she answered it.

'You stole a car?' Katharina Doruk shouted in her ear.

Mattie cringed and held the cell at arm's length a second before replying, 'We were chasing Chris's killer. He was getting away.'

'You're not the police!' Katharina shouted. 'You don't have the right to commandeer vehicles! Frankfurt Kripo is going ape-shit. You're wanted for questioning and—'

Mattie turned off her phone. 'I'll deal with her later.'

'When she's calmer,' Burkhart agreed.

They went through wooden doors carved with explicit scenes from the *Kama Sutra* into a surprisingly utilitarian and small lobby. Loud disco music played somewhere beyond the room.

Two older women sat behind a counter at one end of the lobby. Stacks of Turkish towels and robes were piled on shelves behind them. They eyed Burkhart and then Mattie and then each other.

One smiled knowingly.

The other shrugged and said, 'Sixty-five-euro admission fee. You get use of the facilities, dinner, and coffee and soft drinks. The girls are extra. Fifty euros for half an hour of straight loving. Fifty euros to climax orally. One hundred euros for thirty minutes of anal eroticism.'

She said this all while smirking at Mattie, who refused to react even when the woman said to her, 'You want them to go down on you, honey? Negotiate.'

Chapter 79

Mattie pulled out her badge.

The lady behind the counter stiffened. 'This is a legal establishment.'

'We're not police,' Burkhart growled. 'We're investigators with Private Berlin.'

Mattie added: 'We're looking into the disappearance of one of your workers, Ilse Frei, and the murder of a man we believe came here looking for her last Tuesday.'

'I don't know–' she began.

'I remember him,' the other old woman said. 'He paid his way in, talked with several of the girls, and left in a hurry.'

'You know who he spoke with?'

'No. But go inside and find Michelle. Michelle knows all.'

Burkhart and Mattie moved toward the door into the brothel.

'No. Rules are rules,' the lady behind the counter said, holding out a robe to Mattie and a towel to Burkhart. 'If you want to take a walk through Paradise, you pay and you change out of your street clothes.'

Mattie thought to protest, but Burkhart said,

'You take Visa?'

'Of course,' the woman said and cackled.

A few moments later they walked through a door into a T-shaped hallway with signs for men's and women's locker rooms.

Mattie soon found herself in an empty and surprisingly clean locker facility that easily rivaled the one where she worked out. She hesitated but then took off her jeans and blouse and hung them with her holster and gun in the locker.

She put on the robe, which was entirely too large for her, and she had to cinch it tight about her waist. She found a pair of sanitized rubber sandals and headed toward a staircase at the other end of the locker room that featured an arrow and the word *Spa*.

At the top of the stairs, Mattie emerged into a large room with pools and Jacuzzis and exotic flowers growing everywhere. There were beautiful naked women walking around and floating in the pools.

A dozen men dressed only in towels around their waists mingled about, appraising the women. Burkhart was one of them. He stood near a bank of orchids, behind it actually. The towel they'd given him was barely enough to cover his massive physique, and he was holding on to both ends of it for dear life.

Mattie couldn't help it. She started laughing. 'Don't slip,' she said.

'You coulda stayed in the car, made this much easier,' Burkhart shot back.

'And miss the expression on your face?'

A tall blond woman with large natural breasts

223

strolled up to them. She put her ruby fingernails on Burkhart's chest, looked at Mattie, and said in a Hungarian accent, 'Is the rest of him as big?'

Mattie fought off a smile. 'I wouldn't know.'

The blonde's eyes sparkled. 'First date and you agree to come to Paradise? You must be sexy, girl. So, you want to party with Michelle?'

Chapter 80

My friends, fellow Berliners, cruising at one hundred and thirty kilometers an hour, I should make it home to my city of scars just in time for a late-afternoon appointment I cannot afford to miss.

I yawn. It took me more than an hour and a half to reach the train station and ride back to the auto show. But the Mercedes was right where I left it, far from the police sure to be jamming hall number one.

I've been driving ever since, and I confess I'm tired.

I should pull over and sleep, my friends.

But there is so much left to do before I can even think of resting.

So I reach in the glove compartment and get out a bottle of amphetamines. I take two, think about it, and then down another.

I turn on the radio and listen to descriptions of Artur Jaeger's murder and the chase on the autobahn. They've found the Maserati and are taking

DNA samples from it.

It doesn't bother me. There's nothing that can match me to the car.

As the uppers kick in, I glance over at the folder on the seat beside me. I open it and turn over the picture of Artur and his mother from his archived file. Beneath it is a picture of two girls, one nine, one six. They're hugging each other.

Ilona and Ilse.

I tried every trick I knew to get Ilse to tell me where Ilona lived. But she refused right up until the end. The only thing she'd tell me was that Ilona was mentally ill and a methadone addict because of me.

And then it hits me.

Methadone addict.

It means she has a license. It means Ilona goes to a clinic.

She can be found.

She can die tonight, if I'm lucky, and with her almost all my secrets.

Ilona Frei? I muse. Ilona?

I glance at the photo.

Such a name someone gave you. Ilona. What did your name used to be?

No matter. I'd remember you no matter what they called you. You looked so very much like your younger sister, not like your mother at all.

Chapter 81

Burkhart and Mattie followed Michelle as she sashayed down a hallway at the Paradise FKK. There were doors on both sides.

'Where are we going?' Mattie asked, feeling uneasy.

'To talk to Genevieve,' Michelle said as she rounded a corner.

Mattie followed reluctantly, with Burkhart walking beside her, still clutching his towel. Set against the walls of the hall and between the doors were gilded sofas with deep purple velvet upholstery. On one couch, a naked woman's head bobbed in the lap of a man whose eyes were closed.

'They're doing it in public?' Mattie whispered sharply at Burkhart.

He sputtered, 'It's not my idea of fun.'

Michelle meanwhile went to the last door on the right, rapped loudly, and said, 'It's Michelle, Genevieve. Please stop what you're doing, and tell your client he will incur no charges for time spent.'

A moment later, an irate Italian man appeared in the doorway and started to upbraid Michelle for the interruption. Burkhart stepped forward, towering over the guy, and told him to hit the showers. The man hesitated but then stormed away, railing in Italian.

Genevieve, a beautiful young woman from

226

Guadeloupe with smooth cocoa skin and long wavy hair, came to the door.

'I'm out a hundred and fifty euros,' Genevieve complained.

'We'll compensate you for your time,' Mattie assured her.

Genevieve squinted and studied her. 'Who are you?'

Michelle said, 'Perhaps we'd better go inside.'

Genevieve shrugged and turned into the room, which was small and filled almost entirely with a bed. The walls were mirrors. So was the ceiling. There were reflections of the two naked women, Mattie, and Burkhart at every angle.

Michelle introduced the Private investigators and told Genevieve that they were here to find out what happened to Ilse Frei, and to Chris Schneider. Reluctantly Genevieve agreed to talk.

She corroborated much of what Tina Hanover had told them, but with more detail. She said that she was in the women's locker room two weeks before when Ilse ran in shaking and crying. Ilse told Genevieve that she had just overheard a customer talking to one of the other girls in the lounge.

'Ilse said she did not know him by sight,' Genevieve said. 'He looked completely different than she remembered him. But she thought she knew his voice.'

'Why?' Mattie asked. 'Whose voice was it?'

Genevieve bit her lip before replying, 'Ilse said she thought he may have been the man who killed her mother.'

Mattie absorbed that, her mind wanting to leap

in a dozen directions, but she reined it in when Burkhart said, 'But she wasn't sure?'

'She was pretty sure,' Genevieve allowed. 'But when we went back upstairs together to try to hear him again, he was gone.'

Mattie groaned. 'So you can't identify him?'

Perplexed, Genevieve looked at Michelle, who said, 'If he's the punter we think he is, he's been here six or seven times in the past few years.'

'So you know what he looks like?' Mattie said, excited.

'Not exactly,' Michelle cautioned.

'What does that mean?' Burkhart said.

'We think it's the same guy,' Michelle explained. 'But he looks different every time he comes in. Sometimes he's blond and blue-eyed. Other times brown with dark hair. His eyebrows. His cheeks. One time his hair was slicked black like a helmet. Another time he wore a devil's beard and–'

Genevieve interrupted. 'He was green-eyed and redheaded last week when I saw him, about eight days after Ilse disappeared.' Genevieve was openly agitated by the memory. 'He's a freak, you know? He likes to make you feel threatened. Gets off on it.'

'He give you a name?'

Genevieve's eyes flashed darkly. 'That night he called himself the Invisible Man.'

Michelle nodded grimly. 'But we all call him the Mask.'

Chapter 82

Aboard Private's corporate jet, returning to Berlin two hours later, Mattie finally got up the nerve to call Katharina Doruk.

She answered in an infuriated rave: 'You hung up on me?'

'Calm down,' Mattie said. 'We've made a break. A big one.'

'I don't care!' Katharina shouted. 'Where are you?'

'On the jet. We'll land in half an hour.'

Katharina fumed, 'You didn't talk to Frankfurt Kripo?'

'We'll do it by phone,' Mattie said. 'We – uh, Burkhart and I – felt like we needed to get back to Berlin ASAP.'

'That makes you a fugitive!'

Mattie had had enough. 'Only if we don't catch the bastard who killed Chris and Ilse Frei and Artur Jaeger and who knows how many others!'

That silenced Private Berlin's managing investigator for several moments before she said in a hoarse, barely controlled voice, 'What did you find?'

Mattie gave Katharina a wrap-up of their trips to Ilse Frei's home and the Paradise FKK, including the vague description she'd gotten of the Mask man.

'Did you show them pictures of Hermann

Krüger or Maxim Pavel?' she demanded.

'Both,' Mattie said. 'They said they couldn't be sure in either case because the only reason they know it's one guy coming back is the fact that he always shows up with a new mask.'

'So, what, he's an art collector like Krüger?' Katharina asked.

'They didn't know, but one of the women said he knew everything about the mask he wore while they had sex. It's called a Chokwe tribal mask. She says it was leather and ebony and ivory and depicts a monster.'

'My money's on Krüger,' Katharina said. 'High Commissar Dietrich thinks it's him as well. He called here looking for you about an hour ago. Berlin Kripo found a gun in the trunk of one of Kruger's cars this morning. Ballistics tests show it's the same .40 caliber that killed Agnes. They're preparing an arrest warrant, but I'll call Rudy Krüger, see if his stepfather collected masks.'

'Good idea,' Mattie replied, then asked Katharina to tell Dr. Gabriel that Ilona Frei had been in and out of mental facilities and was a methadone addict. She also told Katharina about their suspicions regarding the son of the man named Falk who'd run the slaughterhouse.

After Katharina promised to start running those leads down, Mattie called her aunt Cäcilia to warn her that it was going to be another late night. Mattie felt a few moments of guilt at not spending time with Niklas. But she told herself that it was justified. Niklas wanted to know who killed Chris as much as she did.

Mattie hung up just as the pilot came on over

230

the intercom to tell them they were in their initial approach to Berlin and to turn off all electronic devices.

She looked over at Burkhart, who turned off his iPad.

'Any luck?' she asked.

Burkhart nodded as he slid it into a neoprene sleeve. 'There's a professor at Potsdam I found, an expert on masks and primitive art. He's roughly the right age. And there are several galleries in the city that specialize in primitive art. I'm thinking that if our boy is a serious collector, they just might know him.'

Chapter 83

They landed during a sunset that made the skies over Berlin look bruised.

At least to Mattie, who immediately began making calls on her cell phone while Burkhart went to retrieve the car.

The line of Franz Hellermann, the art professor at Potsdam University, went directly to a voice mail prompt. She hesitated and then decided not to leave him a message. It would be better to talk with him face-to-face in the morning.

She called two of the art galleries Burkhart had found and got recordings that listed their addresses and hours of operation. She looked at the third number and address and realized that the I. M. Ehrlichmann Gallery was just south of

Savignyplatz on Schlüterstrasse, not far from where Agnes Krüger had died.

'Let's swing by this place on the way to the office,' she told Burkhart.

They were outside the I. M. Ehrlichmann Gallery in less than ten minutes, only to find a man lowering metal-grate security gates on the establishment.

'Hello,' Mattie called.

'I'm closed,' he said and turned, revealing a trim, academic-looking man with black-framed glasses, close-cropped salt and pepper hair, and a tweed jacket and tie.

He blinked at Mattie, and then glanced up at Burkhart. 'You're a big fellow.'

Burkhart nodded. He showed the man his badge, identified himself, and said, 'This is Mattie Engel. We work for Private Berlin.'

'Isaac Ehrlichmann,' the man said agreeably. 'But my gallery is closed.'

'We were hoping you could help us,' Mattie said.

'Tomorrow, I would be glad to,' the gallery owner said. 'But I have a dinner engagement to attend, a birthday dinner actually. My lady friend's.'

'Just one question,' Mattie insisted.

Ehrlichmann sighed. 'One question.'

'Is Hermann Krüger a collector of masks? Have you sold any to him?'

'That falls under client privilege, I'm afraid. And that's two questions.'

'You know he's under suspicion in his wife's murder?' Burkhart asked.

'That's your third question, and I did read

232

about that in the paper. Yes.'

'This could be part of it, Herr Ehrlichmann,' Mattie said. 'Please, off the record, does Krüger collect masks? If he doesn't, we're on our way.'

The gallery owner checked his watch, going through some inner struggle before replying: 'Herr Krüger has bought many masks from me over the years.'

'Any recently?' Burkhart asked.

Ehrlichmann paused and then nodded. 'As a matter of fact, early last week he bought a valuable Chokwe tribal mask.'

Chapter 84

Forty minutes later, the Chokwe mask showed on the big screen in the amphitheater at Private Berlin.

Before hurrying off to his dinner engagement, Isaac Ehrlichmann had told them where to find a digital photo of the mask in his online catalogue and promised to make himself available to them in the morning.

Jack Morgan had ordered take-out food and the entire Private Berlin staff and Daniel Brecht were in the amphitheater eating. Morgan sat next to Mattie and studied the mask skeptically.

'So let me get this straight,' he said. 'Hermann Kruger goes to brothels in disguise and then wears these masks while having sex?'

'That's evidently the long, strange journey he's

233

on,' Mattie replied.

'And I thought LA was the world capital of twisted.'

Mattie laughed. 'Berlin will definitely give LA a run for its money. What about Pavel? Does he have any interest in masks?'

'No idea,' Brecht answered. 'He hasn't surfaced in more than two days now. But I'm predicting he makes an appearance about an hour or two after Berlin's game tomorrow night.'

'Why?'

'We're setting up a little surprise for him,' said Morgan cryptically.

Staring once again at the Chokwe mask, Mattie felt lingering doubt. Did Hermann Kruger kill Chris, his wife, and the others? Or could Pavel be somehow involved? Were they in on it together? And where were they?

Mattie said, 'I can't believe Interpol can't find Krüger.'

'They'll find him,' Katharina Doruk said. 'You can't hide a billionaire for long, especially when his stock's taking such a beating. In the meantime, call Frankfurt Kripo and give them a statement.'

Dr. Gabriel's phone rang. He answered it.

'So, Burkhart,' Brecht said. 'Explain again how he got away from you.'

Mattie laughed and said, 'The story of the skimpy towel he had to wear at the FKK club is better.'

Burkhart frowned at her. 'I thought we had an understanding about that.'

Mattie tried to swallow her grin. 'I couldn't resist. It was just so classic.'

234

'Mattie,' Katharina said. 'Frankfurt Kripo?'

Mattie sighed and nodded.

But then Dr. Gabriel hung up his phone and said, 'I've got the sister. Ilona Frei. She *is* a registered methadone addict, and she lives in Wedding.'

Chapter 85

The air had warmed during the break in the storm, and a mix of recent immigrants and low-income workers was out strolling the streets of Wedding – northeast of the Berlin Technical University – when Burkhart turned onto Amsterdamer Strasse, where Ilona Frei lived in a government-subsidized apartment on the second floor of a shambles of a building.

They parked, climbed a front stoop blackened with grime, and found the front door unlocked. Rap dueled with Middle Eastern music as they ascended a bare wooden staircase to a second floor that smelled of jasmine and curry.

Mattie heard an infant squalling with the distinctive rattle of colic and her mind flashed back to Niklas as a five-month-old racked with the affliction. She felt instant pity for the poor woman who must care for the child. Mattie had had no husband while raising Niklas as a baby, but she'd had Aunt C and her mother, and that had saved her.

'Mattie?' Burkhart said, startling her from her thoughts.

Mattie blinked, surprised to find herself stopped in the hallway, looking at the door to the apartment where the infant was crying and coughing.

'Sorry,' Mattie said, feeling slightly bewildered and suddenly more tired than she thought possible. 'What number is she?' she asked, yawning.

Burkhart gestured toward the far end of the hail. 'Twenty-seven.'

They'd no sooner passed apartment twenty-five – a mere ten feet from Ilona Frei's door – than they heard a woman shrieking in abject terror.

Chapter 86

At the first scream, I spin and leap down the fire escape and reach the ladder just as the screeching turns hysterical. I hear pounding and yelling mixed with the screaming as I swing off the ladder and then land in the alley behind the apartment building where Ilona Frei lives.

I sprint away. People are yelling from windows above me. But I'm wearing a simple black ski mask. No one has seen me, the real me, I'm sure.

Approaching the mouth of the alley where it gives way to Turiner Strasse, I tear the mask off, stick it in my back pocket, and force myself to step out slowly and deliberately, and I continue down the sidewalk.

From there, with all the traffic, I can't hear the screaming at all. I tear off the dark anorak as I

236

move, revealing a bright yellow jogging coat with reflectors.

My heart is racing and I'm berating myself for being so bold, so cocky after so many years of careful movement. I never should have attempted to use the fire escape to reach her apartment.

I should have slowed down, watched her, and patterned her movements.

But I no longer have the luxury of time.

On what was supposed to be a scouting mission, I spotted the fire escape leading up past an open window of what had to be her apartment. I'd glanced around, seen no one in the alley, and opted for a quick, improvised plan.

I pulled the mask on.

I started climbing.

When I reached the landing, I squatted there a moment and then slipped to the window. My old and dear friend Ilona had been right there, right in the hallway of her apartment with her back to me.

I couldn't help it. My throat clicked in that way it does when I'm pleased.

She must have heard it because she twisted, saw me, and screamed.

Now I start to jog toward Schiller Park. When I reach it, I dump the anorak in the first trashcan. Then I keep jogging, figuring that I'll go thirty minutes or so before looping back to the Mercedes.

Stay calm, I tell myself. You know where she lives. And she's an addict. My friends, we know exactly where she'll be come morning, don't we? Hmmm?

Chapter 87

As the shrieking intensified, Mattie pounded on Ilona Frei's door and shouted, 'Frau Frei? Ilona Frei?'

'That one,' said a woman's voice. 'She crazy.'

She stood in the doorway of apartment twenty-five, a disgusted old Vietnamese woman wearing a maroon scarf on her head. 'She always screaming and crying 'bout ghosts and something. Crazy.'

The screaming inside had turned into hysterical sobs.

'Stand back, Mattie,' Burkhart ordered.

Mattie got out of his way. Pistol drawn, Burkhart hurled his weight against the door. The jamb splintered and the door blew open.

They followed the sound of the woman sobbing, 'No! No! God, no! Please, Falk! Please!'

At the mention of Falk, Mattie ran past Burkhart into a bedroom that featured a mattress, a few blankets, and a lamp burning a naked bulb.

The same disheveled woman Mattie had seen on video embracing Chris in Private Berlin's lobby the week before he died was now rammed into the deepest corner of the room. Ilona Frei's hands were wrapped tightly around her head as if to protect it from a beating.

'No,' she moaned. 'No, Falk. No.'

'We're not here to hurt you, Ilona,' Mattie said

softly, walking to her slowly. 'We're here to help you.'

Ilona Frei blinked through her tears and began to whimper, 'No. Please. I want to stay here. I'm taking my meds. I promise you. There *was* someone at the hallway window. He wore a mask. I promise you. Don't take me away again.'

'We won't take you anywhere you don't want to go,' Mattie soothed.

Ilona Frei panted and sweated like a wild woman, but Mattie's tone of assurance caused her to lower her arms. She spotted Burkhart and pressed backward in fear.

In her mind, Mattie heard Frau Ledwig telling her that all of the children who arrived at Waisenhaus 44 on the night of February 12, 1980, feared men.

She looked at Burkhart. 'Do me a favor? Check the hallway window and that fire escape. And then hang outside.'

Burkhart squinted, but then he nodded.

When he'd gone, Mattie turned back and said: 'We're friends of Chris Schneider's, Ilona. We worked with him at Private Berlin.'

Something unknotted in Ilona Frei at that point and she peered at Mattie as if she were a distant light in a fog. 'Christoph?'

Mattie sat on the bare floor next to her. 'The man you went to see at Private Berlin a couple weeks ago. The boy you lived with at Waisenhaus 44.'

Ilona Frei wiped her tear-streaked face and choked: 'Where is he? He was supposed to come see me and tell me he'd found my sister.'

239

Mattie sighed and said, 'Chris is dead, Ilona.'

At that Ilona Frei began to hyperventilate. She began scratching at her wrists, whining, 'No. No. Please tell me that's not true.'

'I'm sorry. But it is true. He died last week.'

Ilona Frei lowered her head and began to weep. 'How?'

'Chris was murdered, Ilona. I found his body in a slaughterhouse in–'

'No!' Ilona gasped before her entire body went seizure-stiff and trembling. Her lips rippled with terror as she said: 'Not there. Not the slaughter-house. Oh, God, not there.'

She tried to get up but then doubled over on her knees, and retched.

Mattie was completely upended by Ilona Frei's reaction. But while the poor woman dry heaved and choked, Mattie got to her feet, and in the bathroom she found a threadbare towel that she wetted in the sink.

She returned to the bedroom to find Ilona Frei slumped against the wall looking like she'd been punched and kicked into dumbness.

Mattie wiped at the sweat on Ilona's brow and daubed away the mucus lingering at the corners of her mouth, saying: 'What do you know about the slaughterhouse, Ilona?'

But Ilona Frei said nothing as she stared off into space, her mouth first loose and agape and then tightening as she began to weep. 'He said he'd kill us if we talked, and here he's killed Chris and he was here to kill me.'

She hunched over and sobbed.

Mattie reached out and brought Ilona into her

arms, feeling her agony pulse through her. When her crying slowed, Mattie asked again, 'What do you know about the slaughterhouse, Ilona?'

At last, shuddering at the burden, Ilona Frei whispered, 'I know everything about the slaughterhouse in Ahrensfelde. Everything.'

Book Four

THE MASK

Chapter 88

An hour later, Mattie sat in a state of shock on a rickety chair across a small table from Ilona Frei as she wound down her terrible story.

Wrung out from the telling, Ilona Frei's voice had gone hoarse when she said: 'That was the afternoon before the men came and took us to Waisenhaus 44. It was also the last time I saw the slaughterhouse or Falk. I wanted to forget it, and forget everything that had happened there. I could not get myself to go back later and look at it. Never. And for Chris to have gone in there ... and...'

She threw up her hands and fought back tears.

Mattie had been involved in police work for most of her adult life and had cynically believed she'd heard every sort of brutal tale there was to tell. But none was even remotely like the horrific story she'd just heard, and for several moments she could not utter a word. A heavy silence seized the room.

Ilona Frei studied Mattie, tears seeping past the corners of her mouth as she gripped her arms tightly. 'I've never told anyone about the slaughter-house. You two are the first.'

Mattie glanced at Burkhart, who stood in the doorway looking skeptical. She knew instantly what he was thinking: Ilona Frei was a schizo-phrenic. A narcotics addict. How much of what

245

they'd just heard was real, and how much of it was an invention of her disturbed mind?

Burkhart had checked the fire escape and the alley, but he'd seen nothing that could corroborate Ilona Frei's claim that a man had been outside her window, which had increased his skepticism.

But then Mattie thought of Chris's nightmares and that haunted space he used to shield inside him. If Ilona Frei's story was true, it was certainly a big enough trauma to create a festering wound in even the strongest of men.

'Why was this never reported to the authorities?' asked Burkhart. 'Why didn't you tell your doctors?'

'Falk said he'd kill us,' Ilona Frei said. 'We believed him. I believed him. And tonight he was true to his word, wasn't he?'

'Did Greta Amsel believe him?' Burkhart asked.

Ilona Frei pushed her hair back from her face. 'Greta? Why Greta?'

'She's dead, too, Ilona,' Mattie said sadly. 'And Artur.'

Ilona Frei's lips stretched wide and her body began to sway and contort as if something were racking her muscles. 'Then Ilse's dead too. Isn't she?'

Mattie's mind flashed on the image of the woman's corpse in the subbasement of the slaughterhouse, but she did not have the heart to tell her. 'We don't know...'

'He has killed her and he's going to kill me,' Ilona Frei whined. 'That *was* him at the window. Of course it was. I'm one of the last! He's got to

246

kill me!'

'We are not going to let that happen,' Mattie said, reaching across for her hand. 'Just calm down. We talked to one of the girls who worked with your sister. She said Ilse heard him speak where she worked, is that right?'

Ilona Frei hugged herself, shivering as she nodded. 'Falk has a distinctive voice. He makes these clicking noises in his throat when he's pleased. And he likes to finish sentences with this hum that rises to a question. *Hmmm?*'

'But that was thirty years ago,' Burkhart said. 'How could she be sure?'

Ilona Frei glared at him. 'You don't forget someone like Falk. He's burned into your brain.'

'Was that why you came to our office? To tell Chris that Falk was alive and Ilse was missing?' Mattie asked.

'I was petrified,' Ilona explained. 'Chris was the only person I could turn to, the only one I knew who would believe me and could do something about it.'

Burkhart said, 'So Chris investigates, finds out it's true, that Falk's alive. He tracks Falk down, and follows him to the slaughterhouse.'

'And Falk kills him,' Mattie said dully, feeling the haunted space in her own heart growing with every tortured beat.

Chapter 89

My friends, my fellow Berliners, at this moment I'm sitting behind the wheel and tinted windows of my old Trabant 601 sedan.

Do you know the Trabant? The worker's car?

No matter. My well-maintained Trabi is parked on Amsterdamer Strasse south of Ilona Frei's apartment building. I've been here almost half an hour and I'm starting to shiver in my sweaty clothes.

No police, I think. That's good. A neighbor was probably in the hallway when I was on the fire escape, heard her scream, and...

I suddenly want to break something. No, I want to shatter it. No, pulverize it into dust.

My friends, Mattie Engel and Tom Burkhart just came out the front door of the apartment building, and they're flanking Ilona Frei.

They walk away from me heading north and instantly my confidence feels like it's suffered a thousand razor cuts.

Has she talked? Will they believe her?

No, no, I tell myself. Ilona Frei is certifiably insane. The state says so. She hears voices. She has other personalities. She's a registered opiate freak, for God's sake.

Even so, there's an impulse shooting through me right now that wants to start the Trabi, haul ass down the street, and shoot them all dead, right

248

there on the sidewalk or in that BMW they're climbing into.

A moment later, they pull out, still heading north.

I wait a few moments, cool down, and ultimately decide not to follow them.

I think I know where they might end up eventually tonight.

I'll go there. I'll be invisible.

I'll wait for my chance to strike.

Chapter 90

Twenty minutes later, Mattie walked up to her own apartment door. Ilona Frei shuffled along uncertainly behind her with Burkhart bringing up the rear.

As she fumbled for her keys, the odor of sautéed onions and meat came to her. So did Niklas's voice as he chattered to Aunt C about the possibility of Hertha Berlin and Cassiano becoming champions of the second division.

'You don't want someone like me staying with your family,' Ilona Frei said somberly. 'Especially if you've got kids. I might…'

'You might be surprised,' Mattie said. 'In any case, you're not staying anywhere else until this is over.'

'I need my meds in the morning,' Ilona said, scratching at her arms.

'We can arrange that,' Mattie said, and she un-

249

locked and opened her door.

Ilona Frei followed Mattie into the apartment in a slow trudge. Burkhart closed the door behind him and turned the dead bolts.

As Mattie knew she would, her aunt Cäcilia welcomed Ilona Frei like an old friend caught in a storm. 'Have you eaten?' she asked.

'Smells real good,' Burkhart said, sniffing the air as Ilona shook her head.

'It was good, Tom,' Niklas announced after hugging his mother hello.

'*Maultaschen* with venison and onion stuffing,' Aunt C said, moving toward the kitchen. 'But the noodles are already cold. I'll fry them and you can have them with sour cream and a beer, ya?'

'Uh ... ya,' Burkhart said, rubbing at his stomach.

Ilona Frei still looked lost, and Mattie was trying to figure out what she could say to set the woman at some ease when Socrates pranced into the room. Chris's cat went straight to Ilona and rubbed against her legs.

'That's Socrates,' Niklas said, reappraising the woman his mother had brought home to a late dinner. 'He doesn't usually like new people.'

Mattie shook her head, saying, 'It's true. He was Chris's.'

Socrates purred loudly and contentedly until a weak but growing smile crossed Ilona Frei's face. She bent down and picked up the cat. She sat in one of the chairs and rubbed Socrates's belly as Niklas surged again into a high-spirited explanation of why Cassiano was such a great striker.

Niklas's argument was directed at Burkhart,

250

who listened attentively and in total agreement while Mattie helped her aunt fry the stuffed pasta crispy and golden.

Burkhart praised the fried *Maultaschen* as the best he'd ever had after eating the last one in the bowl. Ilona Frei ate only one, but she agreed with Burkhart's assessment of the meal, which pleased Aunt Cäcilia to no end.

After clearing the plates, Burkhart said to Mattie, 'If you'll give me a blanket and a pillow, I'll sleep on the couch tonight.'

Mattie frowned. 'That's not–'

'It is necessary,' Burkhart said firmly. 'She's one of the last two.'

'Last two of what?' Niklas asked.

Ilona Frei looked upset and Socrates jumped off her lap.

'She's one of the last two really nice ladies we know,' Mattie said quickly, irritated with Burkhart. 'Now off to bed, you. I'll be in to say good night in a minute.'

Chapter 91

Mattie kept her irritation in check until Aunt C had taken Ilona Frei to show her where she could sleep and she'd heard Niklas's bedroom door shut.

She crossed her arms and faced the counter-terrorism expert. 'I try to shield Niklas as much as I can from what I do. I don't want to explain all the murders to him. It will frighten him. He's only nine.'

Burkhart's face fell. 'You mean my line about Ilona being one of the two left?'

Mattie nodded. 'He's smart, but he's also very sensitive.'

'I apologize,' Burkhart said sincerely. 'It won't happen again.' He paused. 'He's a good kid, you know. You're doing something very right with him.'

Mattie softened. 'Thank you, Burkhart. It's nice of you to say so.'

He hesitated. 'His dad in the picture?'

She didn't know whether she wanted to respond, but said, 'No. Niklas's father was someone inconsequential in my life, an ill-considered fling that became the miracle that is my son. He wanted no part of Niklas, and I, frankly, wanted no part of him.'

'So you raised him alone?' Burkhart said. 'That's impressive, considering.'

'Aunt C and my mother helped until she passed,' Mattie said, feeling defensive. 'And *considering* what?'

'Well, the job of course. I know how demanding it can be.'

Mattie's shoulders fell. 'You don't know the half of it.'

'Tell me,' Burkhart said.

She studied him, wondering whether to explain or let it lie. Something about his compassionate expression made her decision.

'I lost my position at Kripo because I refused to compromise when it came to Niklas,' Mattie said. 'I won't bore you with the details, but one night

252

when I should have been at a murder scene, I was, instead, home with him. He was very ill: a horrible cough and fever. For that I was transferred to the press office and away from investigations. I sued the force. I lost.'

Burkhart's eyebrows rose. 'Is that what Dietrich meant when he first came on the case and said something about your reputation preceding you?'

Mattie's cheeks reddened. 'Yes, I expect so. And speaking of the Hauptkommissar, I think it's time to tell him everything that happened today.'

Aunt C came into the living room with a blanket and pillows. 'You sure you'll be comfortable on that couch? Your legs will hang off.'

Burkhart grinned and took the bedding from her. 'I'll be fine.'

'Good night, Burkhart,' Mattie said. 'And thank you for staying.'

'I wouldn't have it any other way.'

Chapter 92

The moon was near full and glowed through a vent in the storm, casting Treptower Park in a pale light that threw dark shadows past the statues of the kneeling Russian soldiers.

High Commissar Dietrich sat bow-backed amid those shadows on the stone steps of the memorial. He was drinking from a bottle of vodka and staring blearily out over the graves of Stalin's men toward the silhouette of the great Soviet warrior carrying the German child.

Dietrich was recalling how he'd come here as a boy shortly after his mother's death from pneumonia. He'd been no more than six or seven. The colonel had brought him to these very steps.

His father had pointed across the graves toward the huge statue, saying: 'Your mother is now like the heroes buried here, Hans. And you, you are like that child cradled in that soldier's arms. Do you understand?'

Dietrich had not understood. At that moment, he had felt only confusion and loss. And yet he had nodded at the colonel for fear of disappointing him.

Sitting there in Treptower Park some forty-odd years later, the high commissar felt the same emotions whirl through him, and anger, and desperation, and...

His cell phone rang. He thought about ignoring it but then dug it from the pocket of his coat. 'Dietrich.'

'High Commissar,' Mattie said. 'It's–'

'I know who this is,' Dietrich grumbled. 'Weigel called me two hours ago. She informed me of the murder of Herr Jaeger and the fact that you and Herr Burkhart are wanted in Frankfurt on charges of grand theft auto and for questioning in regards to that murder.'

'It's irrelevant. We *know* who the killer is, High Commissar,' Mattie said.

Dietrich's head snapped back.

'Hermann Krüger?' he asked, feeling much drunker than he had a minute ago.

'No,' Mattie said firmly. 'His name is Falk. No

254

first name yet. He's the son of the man who ran the slaughterhouse in Ahrensfelde. Have you been drinking again, sir?'

'I have,' Dietrich acknowledged. 'I buried my father today. My last family.'

There was a silence on the phone before Mattie said, 'I am sorry, sir. Should I take this information to Inspector Weigel?'

A war erupted inside the high commissar, part of him wanting to push it all Weigel's way, but his insatiable curiosity got the better of him. 'No. Tell me.'

Clouds closed in on the moon, leaving Dietrich and the war memorial in darkness save a saber of dim light that cut across the statue of the Soviet as Mattie gave him a thumbnail report on their actions in Frankfurt am Main and a rough outline of Ilona Frei's story.

As she spoke on, bile crept up and burned the high commissar's throat. When she finished, Dietrich felt weak, almost disjointed, almost like a marionette clipped of strings, and he hunched over his bottle.

He was silent for many moments, his drunken mind reeling, trying to think through the implications of the tale. He saw several lines of possible inquiry that he did not like. Not one bit. Despite his pride, his ethics, and his devotion to duty at Berlin Kripo, the high commissar began to think openly in a different manner, one that was more extremely self-interested.

'High Commissar?' Mattie said. 'Are you there?'

Finally, Dietrich cleared his throat and said, 'Your sources are prostitutes and a schizophrenic

255

methadone addict. Is that correct?'

'Yes,' Mattie said, again defensive. 'But I believe them.'

The high commissar laughed scornfully. 'That's why you work for Private and I still work for Berlin Kripo. As a public servant, I have to take sources into account when I'm judging where to put my manpower.'

'Greta Amsel is dead,' Mattie insisted. 'I was an eyewitness to Artur Jaeger's murder. And I think that body with Chris's was Ilse Frei's.'

'Agnes Krüger is dead too,' Dietrich shot back. 'And I'm beginning to believe Hermann killed Chris and the others.'

'No, that's something different. I think.'

'Is it? Seems more likely than some crazy story about the slaughterhouse and a bogeyman named Falk.'

'Maybe Krüger is Falk,' Mattie said. 'Or Pavel is Falk.'

Dietrich gritted his teeth. 'Perhaps. I'll ask them.'

Mattie's voice came back bitter. 'You're saying you won't talk to Ilona? Hear her entire story firsthand?'

Dietrich felt stronger now, charting his own way. 'I will in due course, Frau Engel. Meanwhile, my time will be best spent hunting for Hermann Krüger.'

The high commissar stabbed the End button on his phone, and the moon fell full victim to the clouds, leaving the war memorial grounds so pitch-black that Dietrich thought for a moment he'd been blinded.

Chapter 93

I confess, friends and fellow Berliners, that I've been drinking absinthe, the green fairy, since midnight.

Ordinarily I don't indulge in any sort of intoxicant. But for the first time, I truly understand what it must be like to have escaped prison with dogs baying behind me. The green fairy is the only thing stopping me from panicked flight.

The instinct is, of course, to run and run hard. My drunken heart races at the idea I might have to abandon my life and disappear into yet another mask.

But I've done so much to craft this one, as carefully as the masks that line the walls of the room where I'm drinking absinthe and brooding.

My mind feels sullen and foggy, and I keep seeing myself sitting down the street from Mattie Engel's apartment building, waiting for Tom Burkhart to leave. But he did not leave. The lights in her place went off with him inside, and me filled with the sudden and intense longing for the green distillation I'm using to deaden my growing agitation.

What did Ilona tell Engel and Burkhart?

It doesn't matter. An insane woman's ravings. That's what they'll think.

Unless they find Kiefer Braun.

But I've been using every search engine at my

disposal. I've even hired several tracking services, and there's no trace of him. Maybe my dear old friend Kiefer just decided to disappear into another life as I did.

Or maybe he left Germany.

Or died?

Well, then. If that's the case, I've got nothing to worry about, do I? Kiefer's long gone, and Ilona Frei's a most unreliable witness, and I'm good. It's as likely a scenario as another, I tell myself as I pour another drink.

Now the green fairy begins to seriously toy with my brain, and I look up at my collection of masks, running my eyes fondly over the creatures I have become behind them.

I'm smiling, my friends. I'm feeling among allies as true as you.

They say absinthe has hallucinatory properties. I can't say for sure. But then, among the masks hanging on the wall, the faces of Mattie Engel and Tom Burkhart materialize and sharpen. They seem to laugh at me.

At first I'm shocked at this intrusion into my inner sanctum.

Then I turn violent.

I reel to the wall and pick off the masks where the faces of Private Berlin had mocked me, one carved of wood, the other molded and ceramic.

I beat them to shards and splinters on the tile floor.

When I'm done, when I've totally destroyed them, I get up and stand there weaving, panting, using the absinthe to summon every bit of my cunning while forcing myself to face the fact that if Ilona Frei talked someone will eventually believe her, which means the dogs are most certainly behind me.

No panic, my friends. It's not in me. I'm a Berliner. I know how to defend my ground. The trick here is to be smarter than the dogs, to go to water if need be, to double back, or better yet to make a move they're totally not expecting.

Double back, I think again. Make a move that will floor them.

Suddenly, the green fairy tosses up an idea from deep in my subconscious.

I grab it, and consider it like a gift.

Private Berlin

A treasured gift.

I smile. How perfect.

Yes, I think at last, this particular option is the best way to handle the situation once and for all. How goddamn perfect!

I set the glass of absinthe down and cross to a laptop on my desk. I reattach Chris Schneider's hard drive and call up the pictures.

I scroll down, looking for the one I want. Ahhh, there it is.

I double click the icon and up pops a photograph of Mattie Engel's son. Niklas is on one knee, soccer ball in hand, shooting the camera an impish grin.

What a lovely little boy, my friends, my fellow Berliners. Quite captivating.

I'll bet he's the apple of his mother's eye.

Chapter 94

Mattie woke up to the smell of bacon frying and coffee brewing. She actually felt rested for the first time since getting word of Chris's disappearance.

But then she thought of High Commissar Dietrich. Why was he being so obstinate in his pursuit of Hermann Krüger? Was he getting pressure from above because of her status? Or was he just a man in grief, trying to put one easy step in front of another for fear of falling?

Rather than stew any further, she took a quick shower, got dressed, and went out to find Niklas at the breakfast counter. He was already dressed for school. An empty plate and juice glass sat on the counter in front of him.

Aunt C was nowhere to be seen. But Burkhart was at the stove, working a wooden spoon in a cast-iron skillet.

'He's making his specialty,' Niklas informed her. 'Eggs Burkhart.'

'The one and only,' Burkhart said. 'Want more?'

'I have to go to school,' Niklas said.

'Mattie?'

'When I get back,' she said. 'I like to walk him.'

It was a chill, blustery day, and Niklas's hands got too red and cold for her to hold as they walked.

'I like Tom,' Niklas said. 'He doesn't treat you

260

like you're a kid.'

'Is that right?'

'He said I knew more about soccer than most adults.'

'Well, that's true,' Mattie said and mussed his hair.

'Mom,' Niklas groaned, 'I just combed it.'

'For who? For me? Or is there another lady in your life?'

Niklas looked slightly taken aback, but he said nothing.

'Friends?' Mattie asked.

Niklas shrugged and nodded before asking, 'What's wrong with Frau Frei?'

They were nearing John Lennon Gymnasium. Mattie paused, wondering what to tell him. Then she said: 'She's had a hard and difficult life, one I could not imagine, Niklas. People like that can be delicate. Easy to break.'

'Is that why she's staying with us?' he pressed.

'Yes,' Mattie said. 'And the fact that she was one of Chris's childhood friends, and so was her sister.'

They reached the corner down the street from the school. Niklas said, 'I can walk from here. Okay?'

Mattie could see the school entrance and children streaming into it clearly from where she stood. But she still had a moment's hesitation before thinking that she had to give him his independence slowly and in small increments.

'Okay,' she said. 'And–'

'Aunt C will be here when practice is over,' he said in a mild grumble. 'You sure I can't walk home alone?'

She shook her head. 'Maybe next year.'

'Ahhh,' Niklas groaned. 'That's not until I'm ten.'

'Exactly. Love you, Niklas.'

He pursed his lips and said grudgingly, 'I love you too, Mommy.'

Mattie watched her son until he'd disappeared inside his school, and then she felt odd, as if someone were watching her.

But she looked around and saw no one at all.

Chapter 95

The feeling of being anonymously scrutinized had fallen away from Mattie by the time she bought the newspapers and returned to the apartment where Aunt Cäcilia and Ilona Frei were finishing up plates of Eggs Burkhart.

'This is very good,' Aunt Cäcilia said. 'I'm going to get the recipe.'

Ilona Frei smiled at her, fidgeted, and started scratching at her wrists.

'Here's yours,' Burkhart said, sliding a plate with an egg dish and toast to her.

'Thanks,' Mattie said. She tossed the papers on the table behind her and took a bite of Burkhart's egg concoction. It was good. Really good.

'What's in this?' she asked. 'Bacon and...'

'It changes every time,' Burkhart said. 'Like stone soup.'

'I need to go to the clinic soon,' Ilona Frei

announced in a worried voice.

'As soon as I'm done,' Mattie promised, before looking at Burkhart. 'I'll take her by her apartment to get the things she needs.'

'And me?'

'You're going to look for proof of Falk's existence.'

'Where am I supposed to do that?'

'Start in Ahrensfelde, then go to the special archives,' she said. 'They're right here in Berlin.'

'I know where they are,' Burkhart retorted. 'But don't you think if Falk was in there that his story would have come out by now?'

'We're just looking for his name and some connection to the slaughterhouse,' Mattie said. 'Some tangible proof that Falk was real.'

'He was real,' Ilona Frei insisted.

'We know that,' Mattie soothed. 'But–'

Her cell phone rang. Katharina Doruk began the conversation by saying, 'An Inspector Weigel just called here for you. Hermann Krüger has surfaced. He's going to appear voluntarily for questioning at central Kripo this afternoon.'

'Really?' Mattie said, surprised. 'Where's he been?'

'Kripo's not exactly sure *where* he's been,' Katharina admitted. 'His lawyer's been brokering the surrender deal with the higher-ups. But I figured you'd want to be there. You should probably call Dietrich to arrange it.'

'The high commissar is probably too hungover to care,' Mattie said before describing her frustrating conversation with him the evening before.

'You're saying he's sticking his head in a hole?'

Katharina responded.

'Yes, but why would he?' Mattie said. 'It doesn't make sense. It's not like he's somehow linked to...'

She stopped, puzzled at a possibility that she hadn't considered before.

'You all right?' Katharina asked.

'I'll get back to you,' Mattie said and hung up.

She sat there thinking a second, then jumped up, spun around, and went for the morning newspapers on the table behind her. She checked the indexes and then tore through them before stabbing a finger on a page deep inside the *Morgenpost*.

'No obituary,' she said out loud. 'Just a death notice.'

'Whose?' Burkhart asked, confused.

'High Commissar Dietrich's father. Conrad Dietrich Frommer.'

Chapter 96

Cassiano stirred at the sharp knock on his bedroom door and asked in Portuguese, 'Who is it?'

'It's me, silly,' a woman's lilting voice called back. 'Open up. Why is your door locked?'

Cassiano got out of bed wearing a warm-up suit. He glanced at the bathroom before going to the suite door, and then he twisted the dead bolt and opened it.

Dressed in skimpy black lingerie, Perfecta stood there holding a tray heaped with fruits and breads and a pot of tea.

Cassiano feigned surprise. 'I didn't know you were in Germany.'

Perfecta smiled at him as if he were addled, then brushed by him saying, 'Of course I am. Right when I said I would be. With enough time to prepare your favorite pregame meal.'

Cassiano grinned. 'Put it down over there.'

Perfecta did and then turned, skipped into her husband's arms, and kissed him hungrily. 'Miss me?'

'Every day you've been gone,' the soccer star said coolly.

'I'm home for a whole month now,' Perfecta promised. 'No trips until November.'

'That's excellent,' Cassiano said. 'We should celebrate. Go out after the game somewhere. Eat. See a show.'

Perfecta hesitated. 'Yes. Of course. Why don't you eat, and then we'll burn some calories in bed, get you relaxed before your game.'

She made to head toward the bed, but the striker stopped her, saying, 'Sit first. We'll eat a little snack together. It will make us stronger for love.'

Perfecta looked uncomfortable, but then she smiled brightly. 'I just ate.'

Cassiano poured from the teapot. 'Tea then? You love green tea.'

He held the teacup out to her. 'So good for the skin.'

Perfecta looked worried, and then she shook her head. 'No. I've already had three glasses this morning.'

'I insist,' her husband said.

She appeared insulted and her nostrils flared. 'No.'

'I insist,' Cassiano retorted with a hard edge to his voice.

Perfecta stepped toward him but did not take the teacup. She ran her hand across the front of his training pants. 'Let's see if we can—'

The door to the bathroom burst open. Out jumped Jack Morgan, Daniel Brecht, and Georg Johansson, an agent with the Bundeskriminalamt, or BKA, the German Federal Criminal Police.

Agent Johansson flashed his badge and said, 'Perfecta Delores, you are under arrest for wire fraud, conspiracy to commit wire fraud, and the attempted murder of your husband.'

'You bitch,' Cassiano snarled, throwing the tea at her.

Chapter 97

Morgen, Brecht, and Johansson grilled Perfecta for almost an hour on her whereabouts and activities during the last ten days. She spoke decent English. At first she indignantly claimed that she had been in Africa on a photo shoot and threatened to sue them all for defamation of character.

Then they showed her Dr. Gabriel's analysis of Cassiano's hair, which indicated that he'd been exposed to low doses of cyanide. Not enough to kill him, but enough to make him nauseated and 'off' for a couple of days.

'I have no idea how that could have happened,' Perfecta insisted.

'No idea?' Morgan said, picking up the teapot. 'I'm betting there's some form of raw Brazilian manioc in this tea. The raw stuff contains cyanide, as I'm sure you know. Everyone in Brazil has to know that.'

Perfecta denied her involvement again before Cassiano shouted at her: 'Who did you poison me for? Maxim Pavel?'

For the first time, Morgan saw a crack in the fashion model's façade even as she started to say, 'I don't–'

Cassiano hit the remote and the screen was filled with the image of Perfecta stripping for Pavel in the hotel hallway.

'How could you do this to me with him?' her husband shouted in outrage. 'He's twice my age!'

'And he knows how to use his hands, not his feet!' Perfecta shot back.

They got it all out of her eventually.

She'd done it out of greed. It was true that her husband might make good money at Manchester United, possibly as much as 1.5 million euros a year. But Pavel had offered her twenty times that in the betting scam.

'Did Pavel kill Chris Schneider?' Brecht demanded.

'Who?' Perfecta asked, her puzzlement undisguised.

'Who?' Brecht echoed.

'He worked at Private,' Morgan said. 'We think he was on to the swindle.'

'I've never heard of him.'

'Where's Pavel now?' Brecht asked.

She shrugged. 'I don't know. He disappears for days at a time. He's very secretive, but frankly I didn't want to know where he goes.'

'Uh-huh,' Morgan said. 'Well, I can tell you that after the beating he's going to take this afternoon on the Hertha Berlin game he's going to come looking for you, Perfecta, and he's not going to be happy. As a matter of fact, I expect him to be homicidal.'

Chapter 98

Mattie walked out of the methadone clinic with Ilona Frei, who was glassy-eyed and moving slowly with a contented expression.

But Mattie craned her head all around, looking everywhere, knowing that the clinic was a choke point in Ilona's life, a place where she could be counted on to show up, a place where someone like Falk might try to attack her.

But they made it to the car safely.

'Do you think Burkhart will find the records?' Ilona asked.

Mattie wanted to say that she doubted it, but she replied, 'I've learned that he's a very determined man.'

Ilona blinked several times. 'I heard they were shredding everything they could at the end. It's what started it all. The end I mean. Do you remember?'

'Other than Niklas's birth, they were the greatest days of my life.'

'People were dancing and singing,' Ilona recalled as Mattie pulled away from the curb. 'Ilse and I left the orphanage with Chris and Artur and Kiefer and Greta and came to Berlin. We wanted to see what was happening for ourselves.'

Mattie remembered everything about those days, how extraordinary it felt to be sixteen with everything suddenly new and everything possible.

She started to sing the Jesus Jones song, 'Right Here, Right Now.'

"A woman on the radio talks about revolution..."

Ilona joined in with her.

"When it's already passed her by..."

They stopped singing. Their smiles sagged.

In a faraway voice Ilona said, 'When we got to Berlin, I saw the crowds and got scared. I kept looking for him in the crowds. For Falk. Chris tried to convince me that we would never see him again.

'But I think he was there somewhere that night, Mattie. I could feel him. Everyone else was so happy. But I felt like he was right there as the wall was coming down. Even though we'd been freed from the state, I knew I would never be safe from Falk. Until yesterday, I hadn't seen him in almost thirty years, but he was in my thoughts constantly. Falk, he ate at my mind. He...'

Mattie glanced over to see tears streaming down Ilona's face again as she said, 'I didn't know who I was half the time; I invented things, lives. I...'

She started to rub her hands as if washing them and began a slow rocking motion. Mattie wanted to pull over and calm her, but then her cell phone rang.

'Engel,' she said.

'I've been at it all night, Mattie,' Dr. Gabriel said. 'I tried every database I could think of. There's no Kiefer Braun in Germany that comes close to matching our guy.'

Mattie's heart sank. 'What? Is he dead? Left the country?'

'No, he's here in Berlin,' the scientist replied. 'He changed his name. Three times.'

Chapter 99

I look in the mirror as I apply the last bit of makeup.

Sadly, I think, this may be the last mask in my superb collection of original, onetime creations.

When I'm finished with my disguise, I return to my masks, letting my eyes linger on old favorites – the Dogons and the Indonesians – and new friends like the Chokwe and Jaguar masks.

But as I know I must, I leave them all in favor of Chris Schneider's Private ID and badge, doctored now with my disguised face in place of his.

I gather up the other things I need: rope and parachute cord. Cigarettes, and a little something to light them with. A screwdriver. Leather gloves. Two pistols equipped with suppressors, and six magazines of ammunition. And four passports and supporting documentation for four different

270

identities. I also have a heavy-duty trunk with wheels. It's filled with enough cash and gold coins to allow me to live well for a very long time, a nest egg amassed and set aside years ago in the event that I ever had to leave my beloved Berlin for good.

And now here I am, my friends, my fellow Berliners, about to shed my skin and flee my beautiful city of scars forever.

I smile bittersweetly as I return to my private place one last time.

I look around at what I've built for myself, the collage of my life, thinking of all the events and experiences that have changed me, made me a different person than the one I once was – certainly better spoken, more calculating, and slyer than that bloodthirsty young bumpkin.

I check my watch. It's almost two. I shut off the light and close the door.

After one more errand, I'm off to school.

After the trouble I've gone to, I can't take the chance of missing little Niklas, now can I? Hmmm?

Chapter 100

When Mattie and Katharina Doruk followed Inspector Weigel into a darkened observation room at Kripo headquarters around quarter to three that afternoon, Hermann Krüger was sitting at an interrogation table on the other side of a two-

271

way mirror.

The billionaire was an extremely fit man in his early fifties who wore a 5,000 black suit and had skin so smooth that Mattie swore he was wearing a little makeup.

At the same time, Krüger's posture was ramrod straight, and the bearing of his head was both imperious and enraged, as if he were disgusted to even be in such a predicament and eager to rip off the head of whomever had had the gall to summon him to Berlin Kripo.

Krüger's lawyer, a slight, intense man named Richter, must have picked up on his client's aura, because he nudged him and then whispered something in the billionaire's ear just as the door to the interrogation room opened.

High Commissar Dietrich shambled in wearing a rumpled suit and holding a bulging manila file under one arm and a coffee in the opposite hand. His eyes were bloodshot and his hair in disarray, and Mattie thought his skin looked as sallow as candle wax.

'See?' Mattie muttered. 'I'll bet his head is just pounding.'

Inspector Weigel frowned, but then she sighed and nodded before replying, 'I'm going to give him the benefit of the doubt and let him prove you wrong.'

'We're not wrong, Inspector,' Mattie said. 'You heard–'

'Just the same,' Inspector Weigel replied curtly before turning her attention to Dietrich, whose hand trembled as he set the coffee on the table.

He spilled a little, apologized, and got a napkin,

making a show of cleaning it, moving so slowly that Hermann Krüger's patience was tested and Richter, his lawyer, once again had to whisper in his ear.

At last Dietrich sat and with mock cheer said: 'We're hoping you can clear up a few things for us, Hermann.'

Krüger's cheeks flushed. He wasn't used to having someone of his station in life addressed with such familiarity by someone like Dietrich.

'Herr Krüger wants to cooperate, High Commissar,' Richter said.

'Good. That's fine. But I think we'll let your client talk from now on.'

The billionaire cleared his throat. 'What do you want to know?'

'For starters, where have you been?'

Krüger hesitated, and then replied: 'I can't discuss that for another hour or so. There would be severe financial consequences if it were to come out too soon.'

Chapter 101

A beat of silence passed before Dietrich growled, 'I don't care about financial implications. There are legal implications if you don't start talking to me. Think murder charges, Hermann. Did you kill your wife?'

Kruger looked outraged and sputtered, 'I most certainly did not.'

'You most certainly had reason to,' the high commissar said in such an agreeable and inviting conversational tone that Mattie found herself thinking differently of Dietrich. Despite his faults, the man was a master interrogator.

In short, quick succession, he hit the billionaire with the mistresses, the prostitutes, and the Private Berlin investigation into his life.

'You found out that Private Berlin was looking at your extramarital activities on Agnes's behalf,' Dietrich said. 'You decided word of your perversion would harm your reputation, so you killed Christoph Schneider and then your wife in revenge, and you fed their bodies to rats in a secret basement in an old, abandoned slaughterhouse in Ahrensfelde.'

Krüger got beet-red and choked out, 'That's – that's–'

His attorney snarled, 'Slanderous, High Commissar. My client did no such thing. He had absolutely no involvement in his wife's murder or Schneider's.'

The billionaire found his voice. 'And I have no idea what goddamn slaughterhouse you're talking about!'

'Your stepson thinks you killed your wife,' Dietrich said calmly. 'Or had her killed.'

'He would, the little leeching bastard,' Krüger said evenly. 'I repeat, I had nothing to do with Agnes's death.'

'And yet, you did not rush home when you heard about it,' the high commissar remarked.

'As I understood it, she was dead,' Krüger replied. 'Not sick. Not dying. Dead. I was upset,

274

and grief-stricken, but I knew I could not change that sorry state of affairs, and I had vital business to conclude.'

'With who, Hermann?' Dietrich demanded. 'Tell me where you've been, and now, or that will be the story presented in your indictment, the one the press and the bloggers will devour and spit out at the corporate world.'

Krüger acted like he had bugs on his skin. He squirmed and said to his lawyer, 'I pay you enough. Make him understand what's at stake here.'

Richter checked his watch. 'As a matter of fact, I think it's safe to talk now, Herr Krüger. The markets close in one hour. As long as the high commissar agrees not to talk about this conversation until four, you're free to speak.'

Hearing that, Mattie checked her watch. Three o'clock. School was getting out. She flashed on an image of Niklas leaving with Aunt C, and then returned her attention to the billionaire, who finally looked ready to tell all.

Chapter 102

Friends, fellow Berliners, it's five past three when my soon-to-be young friend Niklas Engel walks out the front of the John Lennon Gymnasium. He's looking for his mother's aunt. But the poor dear won't be making an appearance today. I've made sure of that.

The boy looks upset. How perfect. I make my move and pull the Mercedes forward and roll down the window. 'Niklas?' I call in an affected Dutch accent. 'Niklas Engel?'

I'm holding out my Private Berlin badge and identification and smiling at him. 'I'm Daniel Brecht. Your mother's probably mentioned me. She asked me to come get you and take you home.'

Niklas looks at me suspiciously. 'Where's my aunt Cäcilia?'

I give him a sad smile. 'That's why your mother asked me to come. Your aunt is sick, very sick. She was taken to the hospital.'

That does it. The dear boy's defenses drop and, clearly worried, he moves straight to the car door and climbs in, asking, 'What's wrong with her?'

'They don't know,' I say. 'She collapsed at home and they're running tests. Now buckle your seat belt.'

Niklas does. Right away. No argument.

What a remarkable boy. So earnest. So obedient.

'Where's my mom?' Niklas asks as I put the Mercedes in gear and pull away from the school.

'Don't worry,' I say. 'She'll be joining us shortly.'

Niklas frowns, looks around, and says, 'This isn't the way to my house. Where are we going?'

'A special place,' I say. 'A very special place for a very special boy.'

Chapter 103

'For the past ten days I've been in Sweden,' Hermann Krüger announced. 'I've been staying at a hunting lodge near Östersund that belongs to the Swedish financier Olle Larsson. Olle and I have been negotiating the sale of my empire. I wished to enjoy the rest of my life and do some good with my money. I'd hoped Agnes would like to stay with me and help me do good. But the last time I spoke to her, she told me she wanted a divorce–'

'Not how we heard it,' Dietrich said. 'She was staying.'

Krüger shook his head. 'She was leaving me.'

'Your stepson says otherwise,' Dietrich replied.

'My stepson is a jackass, High Commissar,' Krüger snapped. 'In the meantime, I've got pressing things to attend to and unless you plan to arrest me, I must leave now. Herr Richter will provide you with Herr Larsson's private number. He and several of his aides and the staff at the lodge will attest to my whereabouts. Remember, you are sworn to secrecy until four.'

Krüger got to his feet as if the meeting were over. Dietrich did as well, and Mattie could see he looked bewildered at the sudden turn of events.

But then he regained his footing. 'Do you own a Chokwe mask?'

That startled him. 'Yes. Why?'

'Have you ever been to the Paradise FKK in Bad Homburg?'

He shrugged. 'Once, perhaps. I don't know.'

'We found the murder weapon in one of your vehicles,' the high commissar said. 'I can place you under arrest based solely on that.'

'The weapon is an obvious attempt to frame Herr Krüger,' the attorney said. 'And I don't see any connection between a Chokwe mask and an FKK in Bad Homburg. If you're sure of yourself, arrest Herr Krüger, but rest assured we will sue for damages. Otherwise, we're leaving.'

Dietrich hesitated but then said, 'I'll need to know where you're going, whether you intend to leave the country again.'

'I need to attend to Agnes's funeral arrangements,' Krüger replied, imperious once more. 'Right after I place orders to buy more shares in my company. With all this talk of murder and takeover, Krüger Industries is undervalued now but will most certainly jump in price once word of the deal gets out. You should buy, too, High Commissar. I promise you'll make a killing.'

Mattie watched as the billionaire left the room. His lawyer placed a piece of paper in front of Dietrich and followed.

Inspector Weigel looked at Mattie and sighed. 'You were right. Do we do this now or do we wait a little bit?'

'Sooner the better,' Mattie said. 'You want him on the defensive.'

Katharina had been silent during the entire interrogation, but now she said, 'I just thought of something else.' She headed toward the door.

'What?' Mattie said. 'Where are you going?'

'I have a follow-up question. I've got to catch Krüger before he leaves the building.'

Chapter 104

'Hauptkommissar?' Inspector Weigel said. She stood uneasily at the door to the interrogation room where Dietrich was sitting at the table, looking like he'd lost a crucial game.

'Go away, Weigel,' he said. 'I have to think.'

'Sir, if you please–' she began.

'I'm not pleased,' the high commissar snapped.

Inspector Weigel stood straighter and with a firm voice said, 'Sir, I believe that with the help of Private Berlin I've made a major break in the case.'

Dietrich's brow knitted and he looked up at her. 'With Private Berlin?'

'Yes, sir.'

'You mean, you've been cooperating with them without my knowledge?'

'Sir, you have not been yourself lately, and you placed me in charge while you dealt with your father's–'

The high commissar slammed his hand on the table. 'Don't tell me who I've been, Weigel! I could destroy your career for this. You'll have to leave Kripo. You'll be lucky to find a spot with city police, a meter maid, a traffic cop.'

Inspector Weigel's face had turned a rose color

and her voice shook as she said, 'Be that as it may, sir, I've had a witness brought in for questioning.'

'A witness?' Dietrich said, taken aback. 'A witness to what?'

'Sir, if you'll come with me, he's in interrogation room B. I thought you'd want to observe.'

'Observe?'

'My interrogation, sir.'

Mattie watched the entire scene from behind the two-way mirror before finding her way to a similar room and similar two-way mirror across the hall. A man in a beard and workman's clothes sat alone at the table, staring at his hands and picking at his calluses in frustration.

The door to the observation booth opened and High Commissar Dietrich entered. When he saw Mattie, his entire body tightened. 'You. What are you doing here? Who gave you permission to be here?'

'Inspector Weigel,' Mattie replied calmly.

'Weigel?' Dietrich cried as the door opened behind him. 'She has no authority. She—'

'She has my authority, Hans,' said the tall bald man behind him. His name was Carl Gottschalk. He was the high commissar's supervisor.

'Yours, Carl? You can't be serious,' Dietrich said.

'I'm always serious about murder, Hans,' Gottschalk said. 'Let's see where your young protégé takes us.'

On the other side of the two-way mirror, Inspector Weigel had entered the interrogation room and was moving toward the table and the man waiting.

The high commissar seemed to notice him for

280

the first time. He craned his head toward Mattie. 'What nonsense have you been feeding Weigel? Who is that man in there?'

Mattie gazed evenly at Dietrich and said, 'He goes by several names, none of them correct.'

Chapter 105

'Can you tell me your name for the record?' Inspector Weigel asked.

'Am I under arrest?' the man across the table from her demanded.

'We don't think you've done anything wrong. You were brought in for questioning. Your name?'

'Gerhardt Krainer,' he replied.

'Occupation?'

'I own a construction business. We rehab apartment buildings.'

'How long have you been at this business, Herr Krainer?'

'Fifteen years. Look, I don't understand what I'm being–'

'In due time, Herr Krainer,' Inspector Weigel said, cutting him off. 'You've changed your name four times in your life.'

Krainer's chin retreated toward his throat. 'So? It was done legally. Every time, I wanted a new start. A completely new start.'

'You were once known as Kiefer Braun?'

He hesitated, but then nodded. 'A long time ago.'

'You grew up in an orphanage, did you not? Waisenhaus 44?'

Krainer frowned and didn't answer for a moment. 'I did, but–'

Inspector Weigel cut him off again. 'Tell me about the slaughterhouse.'

Krainer blinked several times, and Mattie thought he looked like a man waking up from hypnosis. He replied in a thin voice, 'I don't know what you're talking about.'

'The slaughterhouse,' Inspector Weigel insisted. 'The abattoir south of Ahrensfelde.'

Krainer blinked again before saying, 'I'm sorry. I grew up in Leipzig. My parents died in a car accident. I don't know anything about any slaughterhouse.'

Inside the observation room, High Commissar Dietrich made a harrumphing noise as if in satisfaction.

'What about a man named Falk?' Inspector Weigel asked.

'No. I don't know him either. Never heard of him.'

Dietrich made that noise again and then said, 'This is a waste of time. I'm leaving right–'

Carl Gottschalk caught him by the elbow. 'Wait.'

Weigel had gotten up from the interrogation table. She went to the door and opened it. Ilona Frei shuffled in, her head bowed.

Krainer stared at her, trying to figure out who she was, until she said, 'Hello, Kiefer. It's me, Ilona. Ilona Frei.'

The man looked like he'd seen a ghost or a zombie, but he said, 'I'm sorry. I don't know you.'

282

Ilona took that like a slap to the face. 'I'm Ilse's sister, Kiefer. Please. You know me, and you know what happened to us in the slaughterhouse.'

'No, I don't,' he said, but he would no longer look at her.

'Chris is dead!' Ilona screamed at him. 'So is Greta! And Ilse! And Artur!'

Krainer's head rocked back in disbelief. 'What? I–'

'Falk's alive,' she blubbered. 'He tried to kill me last night. And he'll try to kill you if he finds out who you are.'

Krainer was suddenly wrapped up in a faraway expression, as if he were watching some horror from a great distance.

'If you don't tell, he's won,' Ilona pleaded. 'Please, tell them. They think I'm insane. Tell them or they won't believe me. Tell them, or we both die!'

Chapter 106

Krainer's jaw was trembling, and tears came to his eyes when he at last allowed himself to look at Ilona Frei. In a voice that sounded to Mattie like a lost boy's, he said, 'I've never spoken about it, Ilona ... not one word.'

Ilona walked to him and put her hand on his shoulder, weeping. 'I know. None of us did. None of us.'

'He said he'd kill us if we ever talked.'

283

'Falk's already trying to kill you,' Inspector Weigel said. 'We're offering you protection, but only if you tell us what we want to know.'

Over the course of the next hour, Krainer's story came out in fits and starts, but it corroborated much of what Ilona Frei had told Mattie and Burkhart the evening before.

Krainer was born in Leipzig, where he was christened Edmund Tillerman. When he was six, his father, an attorney who had been speaking out against the communist government, simply disappeared.

Ilona Frei's real name was Karin Klauser. Ilse's was Annette. They were born and raised in Thuringen. Their father, a scientist, vanished when Ilona was eight and Ilse was five.

Several weeks after their fathers' disappearances, both Krainer and Ilona Frei remembered men pounding on their doors in the middle of the night, and then their mothers crying and begging for mercy.

The men grabbed them from their beds.

They took their mothers too.

They were taken to the slaughterhouse in Ahrensfelde.

They were put in those rooms to either side of the anteroom hallway. There were bunks bolted into the walls, a metal pot, and little else. At one point, fifteen women were held there along with their sixteen children.

In the dead of night, a young man, no more than twenty, would come. They knew him only as 'Falk,' and most nights he would select a mother and her child or children and bring them into the

284

slaughterhouse itself.

Falk put the mothers through unimaginable pain, hanging them on meat hooks by their handcuffs so their arms dislocated. He burned their feet with cigarettes. He whipped them, cut them, and raped them, trying to get them to turn evidence against their husbands, their husbands' friends, and their families.

Falk made Krainer, Chris, Ilona, and the other children watch what he did to their mothers. Falk said he thought it made the mothers' torture even more unbearable, and therefore made them more likely to talk about their crimes against the state.

If and when that didn't work, Falk tortured the children in front of their mothers.

'And when he thought he'd gotten everything out of our mothers,' Krainer said, 'Falk killed them with a screwdriver and dumped their bodies in a well filled with rats.'

Chapter 107

Krainer broke down completely, and Ilona Frei threw her arms around him, saying, 'Thank you, Kiefer. Now they'll believe. They'll believe.'

'I'll give you two a moment,' Inspector Weigel said. She got up, ashen-faced, and looked right at the two-way mirror before heading to the door.

High Commissar Dietrich looked much sicker than a man with a brutal hangover, Mattie thought. He stared at the two people in the inter-rogation room with an expression that was drifting toward hopelessness.

But when Inspector Weigel came into the ob-servation room, carrying a manila folder that she handed to Carl Gottschalk, Dietrich said, 'This can't be true. It would have come out after the wall fell. A place like the slaughterhouse would have come out.'

Mattie crossed her arms. 'Not if all the files about it were destroyed before the uprising started, long before the wall came down.'

'They burned files in every state agency,' Inspector Weigel said. 'Everyone knows that. So which one was Falk working for? The Stasi? The secret police?'

Dietrich said nothing. Mattie noticed Dietrich's boss studying him intently.

'He had to have been Stasi,' Mattie said, watching Dietrich now as well. 'They used torture and execution at Hohenschönhausen Prison to make family members testify against one another. Starvation, sleep deprivation, mock drowning.'

'But this is beyond the pale,' Dietrich said in a hushed voice. 'Depraved.'

'Yes,' Mattie said. 'It was.'

The high commissar looked at his supervisor and said in a voice more sure of its convictions: 'Carl, without some kind of documentation–'

'Documentation?' Mattie cried, cutting him off. 'You've got eyewitnesses! Look at them, High Commissar. Do they look like they're lying?'

Inside the interrogation room, tiny Ilona Frei was still holding on to Krainer, who was sobbing,

286

'Falk stuck a screwdriver in the back of my mother's head, Ilona. And I just stood there and watched him do it.'

Dietrich's shoulders suddenly rolled so far forward that he looked like a wading bird cowering in the shadows. In a shaky voice, he said, 'I'm sorry, Carl, I ... I can't believe that–'

'High Commissar,' Inspector Weigel said sharply. 'Why have you been trying to steer this investigation as far from the slaughterhouse and Falk as possible?'

Dietrich looked shocked and then indignant in his response to Carl Gottschalk. 'I have not. And I certainly won't have a rookie investigator questioning my–'

'You *have* tried to slow or thwart this investigation from the beginning,' Mattie said firmly. 'Inspector Weigel says that you considered Burkhart and me enemies from the outset.'

'She was mistaken in my meaning,' he snapped. 'Why would I have any interest in doing such a terrible, unproductive thing?'

'Because, Hauptkommissar,' Mattie said, 'your father, Colonel Conrad Dietrich Frommer, was Stasi and, before *you* changed your name, you were Stasi too.'

Chapter 108

'That's an out-and-out lie!' Dietrich shot back. 'You have no proof of that.'

Carl Gottschalk looked pained and pitying when he said, 'Unfortunately, she does, High Commissar.' He placed a photocopied document in front of Dietrich. 'This is your application to become a trainee cadet at the GDR's Ministry for State Security as Hans Dietrich Frommer, son of Conrad Dietrich Frommer.'

Dietrich gazed in disbelief at the document. 'This isn't real. They–'

'That document is very real,' his supervisor stated flatly. 'After Frau Engel and Inspector Weigel came to me with Ilona Frei, I petitioned the Federal Commissioner for the Stasi Archives to do a rapid search for us. She balked at first, but when I told her it concerned an ongoing murder investigation, she agreed to help us.'

Carl Gottschalk's face turned stony as he placed another paper in front of Dietrich. 'This is a copy of your application to Berlin Kripo, six months after you changed your name and thirteen months after the wall fell. You did not mention the name change on your application. You did not disclose anything about the year you spent as a member of the East German secret police, Hans. Nor did you disclose your father's long involvement. You wrote in your application that your father was a carpenter, a conveniently dead carpenter.'

Dietrich sighed and said nothing at first. Then he looked up at them all, a broken man. 'I hid who I was because I wanted to be a policeman, as my father had been, and my grandfather had been. I did not care for politics. I still do not. I have only wanted to be one thing my entire life – a policeman.'

The high commissar explained that he had spent just eleven months as a recruit to the Stasi.

'I laid down my weapon after I was ordered to go to Gethsemane Church. I heard what they wanted me to do there, and I walked away. I'd heard about people shredding paper as well. So I walked away three weeks before the wall fell and joined the protests.'

'Why lie, then?' Carl Gottschalk demanded.

'It was a strange time after the wall fell, Carl, remember?' Dietrich said. 'I had no job. Little food. No place to live. And there were many people from the East who wanted revenge on anyone associated with the Stasi, and they were right to want it. I had done nothing wrong, but even so I could read the writing on the wall. Being a member and son of the Stasi would only hurt me in the new Germany. So I lied.'

'What about the slaughterhouse?' Mattie asked. 'Did you suspect it had been used as a torture chamber? Or did you know?'

Dietrich took a deep breath and said, 'Suspected.'

The high commissar described a night when he was in his early teens. His father came home drunk. He got on the phone and Dietrich overheard the colonel's side of the conversation.

'He was ranting and raving about all sorts of things,' Dietrich recalled. 'But then I heard him saying that he feared being caught up in what he called, quote, "barbaric secrets" associated with the auxiliary slaughterhouse in Ahrensfelde. He also said that he would not go down for, quote, "that man."'

'Who was he referring to?' Mattie asked.

'I don't know.'

'Did you ever ask him?' Inspector Weigel asked.

Dietrich cleared his throat. 'I did, Weigel. Twice. Both times within the last five days. The first time he told me to stay away from the slaughterhouse. The second time he had a stroke and died.'

'Who else knew about the slaughterhouse other than your father?' Mattie asked. 'Do you know who he was talking to that night?'

'I don't know for sure,' the high commissar replied. 'But I suspect it was one of the men who helped bury my father yesterday.'

Chapter 109

Inside a fourth-floor room at the Hotel de Rome, Jack Morgan paced, checked his watch, and glanced back and forth at the television and Daniel Brecht's iPad.

The television sportscaster was giving a spirited report on the manner in which Cassiano, in a rare afternoon match, had completely dissected the Düsseldorf defense, scoring four goals, two of them singlehandedly.

Brecht's screen, meanwhile, showed the exterior hallway, and the interior of the adjacent hotel room where Perfecta stood in a sheer white nightgown, looking in the mirror and tending to her makeup.

'I still can't understand why she went for Pavel's scam,' Georg Johansson said. 'I mean look at her. She could have anything she wanted.'

Morgan shrugged. 'I assume there's more to this than she's telling us. There always is. But twenty million euros is a solid motive for crime, no matter how beautiful you are.'

'Here we go,' Brecht said, gesturing at the hallway feed, which showed an irate Maxim Pavel storming past the camera.

They heard him pounding on the door offscreen and through the other feed inside Perfecta's hotel room.

The Brazilian model did not move, but then Brecht said, 'Answer the door. Get him to talk.'

Perfecta had a radio bud in her ear. 'I can't,' she whispered.

'You can and will if you want any chance at a judge giving you leniency.'

Perfecta nodded but went hesitantly to the door and opened it, saying, 'Maxim! You're early! I only just–'

The Russian nightclub owner smacked her in the face so hard she stumbled backward and crashed to the hotel room floor. 'You whore!' he seethed, kicking the door shut behind him. 'You stupid Brazilian whore!'

'What, Maxim?' Perfecta cried, cowering from him. 'What did I do?'

'Do?' he shouted. 'Your husband played brilliantly this afternoon, and I lost millions on the spread! Millions!'

With that Pavel threw himself on her, got his hands around her neck, and began to choke her.

'Now!' Morgan said.

Agent Johansson burst through the door into the next room, gun drawn, yelling, 'BKA! German Federal Police!'

He grabbed the nightclub owner by the collar and swung him up and around and slammed him against the wall. 'You're under arrest.'

'For what?' Pavel managed to demand.

'Assault, to start,' Johansson said, snapping the handcuffs on. 'Fraud. Conspiracy. Attempted murder. There will be other charges, I'm sure.'

'Like four counts of premeditated murder,' Morgan said as Johansson spun Pavel around and Brecht helped Perfecta up from the floor.

Pavel looked at her and Morgan with contempt. 'I've never killed anyone.'

'That right?' Brecht said. 'Where have you been the last few days? Take a trip to Frankfurt? Spend some time with Greta Amsel, Herr Falk?'

'Falk?' the nightclub owner said. 'Frankfurt? I don't know any Greta.'

'Then where have you been since we saw you last?' Morgan demanded.

Pavel hesitated and then shrugged, saying, 'I have an ironclad alibi. I was with my lover, my real lover. His name is Alex. He lives in Vienna.'

'Alex?' Perfecta asked, incredulous. 'You said you were straight.'

The nightclub owner laughed at her. 'And you're dumber than I thought. I own a drag-queen club for God's sake.'

Chapter 110

Forty minutes later, as the sun began to set, Katharina Doruk wandered off Oranienburger Strasse into Tacheles. She walked through the art collective's archway, which led to the large outdoor art area behind the building. The dusk throbbed with a blend of hip-hop and techno and glowed like a movie set.

Spotlights were trained on the opening of Rudy Krüger's *Rude, Rot, Riot* exhibition, which had attracted a crowd of anarchists, punks, street people, artists, musicians, poets, and other assorted Berliners who were drinking heavily from an open bar.

Katharina Doruk spotted the man of the hour, dressed entirely in black, standing with his arm around his 'student' Tanya. He was holding a beer bottle and shaking hands with an admirer who had a fluorescent green mohawk and tiny skulls on chains hanging from his pierced nose.

Rudy Krüger spotted Doruk and grimaced when she came up to him after the mohawk man moved on. 'Why are you here?' he asked caustically. 'I'm not talking to you or anyone. You and

Kripo let Hermann go, and now he's shutting me out of planning for her funeral!'

'I work for Private – letting your stepfather go wasn't my call, and I can't control his actions either,' Doruk said. 'I came to support your opening. I figured you could use it. But I see you've got more than enough, and I'm not wanted here, so I'll go.'

Tanya frowned and squeezed him around the waist. 'Rude, be nice. She's just trying to help.' Doruk noticed then that Tanya was wearing a black leather jacket that had to have cost at least 1,500. It made Doruk more confident.

'Okay, all right, I'm an asshole sometimes,' Rudy Krüger said. 'I'm sorry.'

'Apology accepted,' Doruk said. 'Quite the bash.'

He shrugged. 'One thing I learned from Hermann, you want to be known, you better yell a lot. Want a beer?'

'Maybe later,' Doruk said. 'Did you know your stepfather maintains that your mother *was* divorcing him?'

'He's lying,' Rudy Krüger said immediately, and then hesitated. 'I don't know why, but he's lying. That was the irony. She was staying with him, selling out for the money.'

Katharina Doruk shook her head. 'According to him, your mother had laid down the line. Despite the fact that he'd pledged to turn his pursuits to philanthropy, she'd decided to leave with her dignity intact. That's the irony. If she'd done it, you were the one who would have been screwed, Rudy.'

Chapter 111

Rudy Krüger's lips thinned. 'What the fuck you talking about?'

'Your mother's prenuptial agreement,' Doruk said. 'Before he left Kripo headquarters I asked Hermann if you were mentioned in the agreement. Know what he told me?'

The billionaire's stepson shrugged.

'He said the deal worked like this,' Doruk said. 'If your mother stayed married to Hermann until his death, she would inherit his entire fortune, which meant *you* would eventually inherit a fortune.'

'I don't care about money,' he said flatly. 'And so what?'

'It also stated that if your mother divorced Hermann, she would get only ten million.'

'*I* told you that,' Rudy Krüger replied.

'You did,' Doruk said. 'But what's interesting is that the third provision in the agreement states that if Agnes died first in marriage, her husband would provide you, Rudy, with a full tenth share of his fortune, which as of the close of trading today was worth close to four hundred million euros.'

He stared at her. 'If you say so. I told you I don't care about money. I'll probably give it to this place. Make sure it survives.'

'Maybe some of it,' Doruk replied. 'But the

295

rest, I think, you'll use for your own gain and leisure.'

He laughed bitterly at her. 'Fuck you. Who are you? You don't know me. What are you trying to say, that I killed my mother? I wasn't anywhere near my mother when she was shot. I was here at a rally for Tacheles.'

'I know,' Katharina Doruk said. 'We checked.'

'There you go, then,' he shot back. 'So why don't you take your vicious innuendo and get the hell out of here.'

Katharina ignored him, looking instead at his girlfriend and saying, 'But you know, Tanya, very few people seem to remember you being at the rally.'

'Me? I was there,' she said indignantly. 'Lots of people saw me.'

'Name one,' Doruk said.

'Rude,' she said.

'Convenient.'

'There were others,' she protested.

Doruk shook her head. 'No. You left the rally shortly after it began and went to Wilmersdorf. You knew Agnes was going out to lunch because Rudy told you she was going to lunch with her friend Ingrid Dahl at Restaurant Quarré. You knew the route she'd likely take leaving. You waited and you shot her.'

'You have no proof of that,' Tanya said, her voice breaking toward a whine.

'We will,' Doruk said. 'Or rather Kripo will. They're searching Rudy's studio right now.'

'What?' Rudy Krüger yelled, pulling away from his girlfriend.

For a moment, Tanya looked too stunned to move. But then she tried to take off. Doruk was too quick. She grabbed Tanya and shoved her arm up behind her back.

'I had no idea!' Rudy Krüger was shouting at Doruk. 'If she did this, she did it on her own. Stupid, crazy bitch!'

At that Tanya went berserk and started spitting words at him. 'What? This was your idea! You said no one would ever suspect me! This was your idea! You said we could do good with that money. We could save Tacheles, and other places, and live a righteous life.'

'That's not true,' he said, and turned as if to get away from her.

But Inspector Weigel stood in his way.

Chapter 112

Mattie and High Commissar Dietrich exited the S-Bahn at Alexanderplatz. They crossed the plaza where the protests had peaked before the fall of the wall.

Dietrich was on his cell phone. Mattie snapped hers shut in frustration; since leaving central Kripo headquarters, she'd been trying unsuccessfully to reach her aunt Cäcilia, Niklas, and Tom Burkhart. She'd not heard from any of them the entire day.

Mattie glanced at the high commissar, who was listening closely. She had thought his career was finished when he admitted to lying his way into Berlin Kripo, but his boss, Carl Gottschalk, had surprised her, telling Dietrich he would face a severe disciplinary hearing and probably suspension, but in the meantime he was to use his father's contacts to find Falk.

Dietrich hung up and smiled at her in chagrin. 'Your associate, Frau Doruk, was right. Weigel just placed Rudy Krüger and his girlfriend under arrest for Agnes's murder.'

Mattie shook her head. 'The anarchist did it for the money.'

They turned onto Karl-Marx-Allee just as night fully seized Berlin. The temperature had been climbing all afternoon, but a wind was picking up. As they passed the Café Moskau, Mattie smelled ozone.

A storm was coming. Fast.

'There he is,' Dietrich said, slowing and gesturing toward a glass-walled and steel-framed box of a building that exuded a soft, silvery glow. 'Other side of the bar, his back to the wall.'

Mattie peered into the Bar Babette, one of the hippest watering holes in Berlin, with a retro 1960s décor and an artsy clientele. The place was sparsely populated at this early hour of the evening. Even so, the stout old man in the gray suit and dark topcoat looked jarringly out of place.

'Let me do the talking,' Dietrich said and went to the front door.

Mattie followed him into the bar and looked over his shoulder at the man sitting in the suit and topcoat before a tumbler of vodka.

His face was rectangular, sloughing, and pale.

298

Pouches of wrinkled skin hung below his watery eyes, which were huge, dull blue, and watchful. He studied Dietrich and Mattie in turn.

'Who is this woman, Hans?' the old man asked.

'Her name is Mattie Engel, Willy,' Dietrich said. 'She used to be a valued member of Kripo, but we lost her talents to Private Berlin a few years ago. She's been working on the same case.'

The man nodded and held out his hand. 'You can think of me as Willy Fassbinder. It's not my real name, but no matter. Hans tells me you wish to talk about life in the East before the wall fell. Are you new to Berlin?'

'I grew up in West Berlin,' she said. 'But to be more exact, we–'

But Fassbinder spoke right over her. 'Did you know that this was the cultural center, the nucleus of the arts and society in the GDR?' He pointed out the window. 'The Kino International across the street was where all the great films premiered. The Café Moskau was the most famous club in the East. Just next door here was the Mokka-Milch-Eisbar, the best place for children to eat ice cream in all of East Germany. They had these little slivers of chocolate they'd put on sundaes that they called *Pittiplatsch*. My daughter loved them. Do remember the Eisbar, Hans? They wrote a song about it. A big hit.'

Dietrich replied, 'I remember the song, but I never came here, Willy.'

'No?' Fassbinder said, seeming surprised. He smiled at Mattie. 'And this place was a beauty salon: Babette's Cosmetique. My late wife would come here every other Tuesday to have her hair

299

and nails done in the latest styles from Moscow and Leningrad.' His face was melancholy with nostalgia. 'It's why I suggested this place to meet when Hans said you wanted to speak of the past. I often come here to think of those days.'

Chapter 113

A waitress came to take their orders, espressos for Mattie and Dietrich and two more fingers of vodka on the rocks for Fassbinder.

As soon as she walked away, Dietrich said, 'Actually, Willy, we wanted to talk to you about things and events that may have occurred within the Ministry for State Security, things and events that my father may have described to you in a drunken late-night telephone conversation many, many years ago.'

Fassbinder's nostrils flared instantly, and Mattie sensed a wall go up around him. She doubted they would get cooperation from the old man.

'Most Berliners have moved on, Hans,' Fassbinder said crisply after several moments of silence. 'They no longer wish to talk of the ministry.'

'Please, Willy. I tried to talk of these things with my father right before he collapsed and died. His secrets killed him. I saw it with my own eyes.'

Fassbinder's attitude changed several degrees, as though he were wondering about his own impending fate. Finally, he asked, 'What things?'

Mattie said, 'The slaughterhouse in Ahrensfelde and a man named Falk. We believe he worked there for the Stasi.'

The waitress returned with their drinks. While she set them out, Mattie watched as the old man maintained a blank expression, zero reaction.

'*Did* Falk work for the Stasi?' Dietrich asked when the waitress left.

Fassbinder took a long sip of his vodka, coughed, and said carefully, 'No. Not in any official capacity, and by that I mean that I believe you will never find a trace of him in the special Stasi archives, nor in the logs of Hohenschönhausen Prison, or anywhere else, I imagine. And, as I understand it, that slaughterhouse was destroyed just a few days ago. So there isn't anything I can say that would not be conjecture and hearsay on my part.'

Mattie felt herself growing angry. 'Well, Willy, or whoever you really are, there's no hearsay or conjecture in the fact that I was in the subbasement of that slaughterhouse before it blew. I saw where the corpses of the tortured mothers were fed to rats while their children watched. I saw the bones myself.'

That turned Fassbinder aghast and his skin ashen. 'I ... I had no idea that these things were occurring there, absolutely no idea. I will go to my grave telling you that.'

'But my father knew, didn't he?' Dietrich demanded. 'He found out about the slaughterhouse – he got very drunk one night, and he told you he could not stand being a part of these heinous crimes, and that he would not go down with whoever ordered the tortures and killings. Didn't he?'

Fassbinder's head tilted back as if pulled by some heavy weight before he sighed and nodded ever so slightly.

Chapter 114

Fassbinder cleared his throat and said, 'He, your father, had heard rumors, just as I had heard rumors of the secret crematoriums we were running where the bodies of the disappeared were being taken. Your father made a personal investigation. He found some truth, and more rumors. But it was enough to shake him, and Conrad Frommer was largely an unshakeable man.'

'He offered you no concrete proof?' Mattie asked.

Fassbinder looked at her as if she were naive and laughed. 'Concrete? Frau Engel, there was nothing concrete inside the Ministry for State Security. Everything was illusion, smoke and mirrors, gossip and accusations, outright lies and intricately manufactured half-truths. No one knew that better than Conrad.'

'Why?' Dietrich asked. 'What exactly did my father do in the Stasi?'

Fassbinder's eyebrows rose. 'He never told you?'

'No,' the high commissar replied.

That surprised the old man even more. 'You honestly have no idea?'

'None.'

Fassbinder laughed again, this time in some

bewilderment at the mystery that had been Dietrich's father. Then he leaned forward conspiratorially and in a voice that Mattie had to strain to hear, he said, 'Your father was a good policeman, Hans, an excellent detective like you. He was so good, however, that he was chosen to work behind the scenes on secret investigations for Mielke. He was one of Mielke's get-things-done men.'

'Mielke?' Dietrich cried. 'You mean Erich Mielke, head of the Stasi?'

'I said your father was talented,' Fassbinder replied as if the high commissar were an imbecile. 'Conrad worked for him directly on projects vital to Mielke's personal agenda.'

Although Mattie was shocked and fascinated by this revelation, she asked, 'But what about the slaughterhouse? What about Falk? Tell us what the high commissar's father told you.'

The old man turned grim. 'He said that he'd somehow discovered that the slaughterhouse in Ahrensfelde was being used as Mielke's personal torture chamber, the place people were taken when he absolutely wanted to know their secrets.'

'And Falk was the torturer?'

'And executioner, as I understand it now,' Fassbinder said.

Over the course of the next half hour, the old Stasi told them what he knew, the fact, the rumor, and the conjecture.

Dietrich's father never mentioned Falk's first name, or if he did Fassbinder did not remember it. Falk's father ran the abattoir for the state in the sixties and seventies. The boy grew up working in the slaughterhouse, and was said to be very close to his mother.

When Falk was ten, however, his mother was arrested, charged with crimes against the state, and taken to Hohenschönhausen Prison. She was a makeup artist with the German State Opera who had become involved in the underground railroad helping East Germans escape into the West, a crime considered high treason at the time.

The younger Falk was said to be extremely smart; he read all the time and excelled in school. But soon after his mother's imprisonment, for whatever reason, he discovered that he enjoyed killing the animals coming in to slaughter.

Mattie squinted one eye, saying, 'And what, Mielke recognized that part of him and encouraged it?'

'You're asking me to explain a paranoid mad genius, Frau Engel. I can't claim to know Erich Mielke's mind or how he came to know of Falk. But however it happened, the high commissar's father told me that the boy was enlisted into Mielke's private army shortly after the slaughterhouse was closed as an abattoir in the late 1970s.'

Chapter 115

Dietrich watched the old Stasi take a deep draw off his vodka and asked, 'How long was it used as a torture chamber?'

'I don't know that either,' Fassbinder replied.

304

'But certainly until your father got wind of it, sometime in January or February of 1980. He was frightened to confront Mielke. That was what that drunken call you overheard was about.'

In his mind, the high commissar could see himself outside his father's bedroom, listening to him rant. It was like yesterday. 'Why was he so upset?'

'Your father, though a great patriot and party loyalist, refused on principle to engage in character assassination, torture, or murder. He dealt with facts. He confronted Mielke with facts, and demanded the operation be shut down. It was a very brave thing to do, Hans. It could have gotten your father sent to Hohenschönhausen, or to the slaughterhouse himself.'

Dietrich was stunned. For so many years, he'd thought of his father in a single, ruthless way – cruel and unprincipled, except for his devotion to the state. And now it turned out that he may have been the one who rescued the motherless children of Waisenhaus 44? Was the colonel there that night when they were all brought to the orphanage?

Before the high commissar put voice to these thoughts, Mattie asked Fassbinder, 'Why would Mielke back down like that?'

Fassbinder shrugged. 'I don't know, though I suspect that Conrad must have had something on Mielke aside from the slaughterhouse, something that could not be simply found or erased. In any case, he closed the torture chamber and had all paper evidence of it destroyed, sometime in the spring of 1980, I'd presume.'

'And Falk?' Dietrich asked.

Fassbinder's laugh was curt and cruel. 'They threw him in Hohenschönhausen Prison for a few months. And then they retrained him.'

'Retrained him?' Mattie said. 'As what? He was a sadistic psychopath.'

The old Stasi's lips puckered before he asked, 'Other than being an executioner, what's the best profession for a man who genuinely enjoys killing?'

'Assassin?' Dietrich said.

Fassbinder reappraised him. 'You are as quick as your father, Hans. The rumor was that Mielke had Falk trained to be a more perfect killer, one run by the state, or rather the head of the ministry.'

That took Dietrich aback. 'He murdered people for Mielke? I didn't think assassination was part of the Stasi playbook.'

'I can't say that he actually carried out killings for Mielke, only that he was trained to do so,' Fassbinder replied.

'And then?' Mattie pressed.

Fassbinder shrugged again. 'We were an institution fueled by suspicions invented by despots. Who could keep track of everything that happened and everyone who was involved in the last few years? Suffice it to say that one day, long before the wall fell, your father discovered that all records concerning Falk had disappeared. Until you walked into this bar tonight, I had not heard one word of Falk since then. He vanished as many people did when the wall fell. A myth. End of story.'

Fassbinder's information gelled with much of what Ilona Frei and Kiefer Braun had testified to.

But it also raised as many questions as it answered. Dietrich was about to launch into a litany of them when he noticed a reflection in the window behind the old Stasi.

Both Dietrich and Mattie twisted in their chairs to find Tom Burkhart looking at them with a somber expression. 'There are no records of Falk in the special Stasi archives,' he said. 'I spent most of the day there.'

'We just found that out ourselves,' Mattie replied.

Burkhart broke into a victorious grin. 'But there *were* records in a church not far from the slaughterhouse. I found Falk's baptismal certificate there. I know his first and middle names, and I believe I know exactly where we can find him.'

'Where?' Dietrich and Mattie demanded almost in unison.

'At his art gallery in Charlottenburg.'

Chapter 116

Less than an hour later, the intense flame of an acetylene torch cut through the iron security gate at the I. M. Ehrlichmann Gallery of Fine Art. Police barricades had gone up around the entire block.

Special weapons and tactical Kripo officers surrounded all exits, including the roof, which was being monitored by a helicopter flying in high winds.

Mattie was there with Burkhart and Dietrich, all suited up in bulletproof armor. To one side, Ilona Frei watched, wrapped in a blanket and trembling in the arms of the former Kiefer Braun.

'Three-story building; he owns the whole thing,' Dr. Gabriel told them. 'He claims his residency on the second and third floors above the gallery.'

The torch died. Burkhart said, 'We are go.'

The SWAT team assaulted the building from front and rear, blowing open the doors with rams and following with stun grenades.

They should have saved the explosives and the doors.

Matthias Isaac Falk, aka 'I. M. Ehrlichmann,' aka 'Isaac Matthias Ehrlichmann,' was gone.

The name switch seemed obvious when you saw it on paper, but Mattie decided she had to admire Burkhart's clever instinct in making the connection so quickly once he'd seen the baptismal certificate.

When they were cleared to go inside, Mattie held a kerchief to her mouth because the air was still acrid from the stun grenades. Falk's gallery was a warren of a shop, crammed wall to wall and floor to ceiling with primitive art, including a huge collection on the walls surrounding his office area that featured masks from every corner of the world.

On the second floor, High Commissar Dietrich discovered a makeup kit. In the basement garage, he found eight vehicles, including a blue panel van and an impeccably maintained Trabant 601.

Mattie made the biggest discovery. When she tried to open a locked upright filing cabinet behind the gallery desk, she noticed that it rocked oddly.

She pushed and twisted the cabinet to the left and nothing happened. It felt bolted into the ground and to the wall. But when she twisted it to the right, it disengaged and swiveled out along with a piece of the wall.

She pulled out a light, drew her pistol, and eased inside, finding herself in a narrow, high-ceilinged passage that ran the length of the outer room. When she'd determined the space was clear of threat, she groped the wall by the door, felt a switch, and turned it on, illuminating a secret gallery behind the gallery.

Mattie stood there, looking all around, confused at first as to what she was seeing, and what it all meant. The walls of the secret gallery were decorated with a loose collage of trinkets, jewelry, and odd pieces of clothes; and toys, newspaper clippings, and purses and wallets; and older and more recent snapshots of people, men and women and children.

Mostly children.

And suddenly, the collage made sense and the shock that followed was a blow to her stomach that rocked her mind.

'Mattie?' Burkhart called from outside. 'You in there?'

'Yes,' she managed.

Burkhart ducked inside and looked around. 'What is this?'

'I think it's a trophy room.'

Chapter 117

High Commissar Dietrich wanted the secret gallery sealed the moment he saw it, which Mattie understood completely. It was a forensics investigator's mother lode of information and evidence.

'Let them see it before you do,' Mattie suggested.

'Who?' Dietrich asked.

'Frei and Krainer,' Mattie said. 'See if they recognize anything. I think that gallery is a trophy room, but unless someone can identify something in there, it's just somebody's weird obsession.'

She thought he was going to argue, but then he nodded and said, 'I suppose it can't hurt.'

Mattie went outside. There were television trucks at either end of the block and klieg lights flaring. She found Ilona Frei still standing with Krainer. She told them what they'd found and asked if they'd be willing to go inside. Krainer said he did not think he could. The tidal wave of emotions in the past several hours was too much to deal with as it was, though he did say he'd be willing to look at a later time.

But Ilona Frei said, 'I'll go.'

'You sure?' Krainer asked.

She nodded, tucked her chin, and walked with Mattie into the main gallery. Her eyes perked up and she looked all around her at the jumble of art as they walked toward the doorway into the secret gallery.

But then Ilona Frei stopped suddenly and stared up at the mask collection, her eyes roving all over them and fear building in her carriage.

'What is it?' Mattie asked.

'They're almost all of monsters, aren't they?'

Mattie had not noticed before. But it was true. Falk's monsters leered down as Mattie led Ilona inside the secret gallery.

Burkhart, Weigel, and Dietrich watched Ilona as her attention rolled slowly and carefully over the collage on the wall, her mouth open as if in a trance, her fingers passing above the items.

'Don't touch,' Mattie said, following her closely.

'No,' Ilona said. 'These are haunted things, aren't they?'

'I suppose they are.'

Ten feet into the gallery, looking at the right wall, Ilona made a little gasp and halted. 'No.' Tears boiled from her eyes as she moaned, 'No.'

Chapter 118

The old, curling snapshot was thumbtacked to the wall. In it two girls in bathing suits were leaning up against the legs of a woman in a bathing suit. Beside it, hanging on a chain from a nail, was an open tarnished silver locket with a tiny photograph inside of a beautiful young woman.

'Is that you and Ilse at the beach?' Mattie asked her.

Ilona nodded through her tears. 'And that's my locket and my mother. She gave the locket and the picture of her to me when I turned eight. It was her mother's locket. Falk took it from me the night we were brought to the slaughterhouse.'

She wiped away her tears and reached for the locket with joy and disbelief, saying, 'I haven't seen a picture of her in thirty years.'

Mattie caught her hand. 'You can't touch, Ilona. Not yet. But you'll have the locket, I promise you.'

Ilona looked at it longingly and then suddenly appeared exhausted. 'I need to go home, Mattie,' she said in a dull, flat voice. 'I need to sleep. And we need to be at the clinic early in the morning.'

Mattie wanted to look further, to see if there was any memento of Chris in the collage, but she checked her watch. It was nearly 10 p.m. Niklas was already in bed. Aunt C probably was getting ready.

'Take her home,' Dietrich said. 'There's nothing more you can do here.'

'I'll come with you,' Burkhart said.

Mattie said, 'I don't–'

'You do,' he said. 'Falk is still out there.'

Mattie gave in because now she was suddenly too tired to argue. She'd done her job. They'd all done their job. They knew who Falk was. They'd exposed his role in the death of Chris and dozens if not scores of others. Beyond this, the case was a manhunt and nothing more.

They went out the back of Falk's building with Dietrich, who was making sure that Kripo provided Krainer with protection overnight. Krainer told Ilona Frei he would contact her soon.

Leaving by the rear allowed Mattie, Burkhart, and Ilona Frei to avoid the media circus at either end of the closed block and to arrive quickly at Mattie's car.

Mattie heard thunder rumbling in the distance as she climbed in the passenger seat. She thought to call home but then was overwhelmed by fatigue. She drowsed in the front seat as Burkhart navigated them north toward Ernst-Reuter-Platz and Strasse des 17 Juni, the street that celebrates Berlin's reunification.

They were heading east when Mattie's cell phone rang in her pocket.

She tugged it out and was surprised to see that Niklas was calling.

'What are you doing up?' she asked by way of greeting. 'And why have you and Aunt C not been answering your phones?'

She heard a clicking on the line and then a smooth voice purred, 'Dear Frau Engel, I'm afraid Aunt C's rather tied up at the moment. And Niklas has been with me since school let out, such a pleasant young man. We've taken a drive in the country. Why don't you and Ilona Frei come out and join us?'

Book Five

THE VISIBLE MAN

Chapter 119

Stunned and cored through with fear for Niklas, Mattie whispered, 'Falk?'

Burkhart snatched the phone from her and turned on the speaker just in time to hear Falk say, 'An old name.'

Panic-stricken now, Mattie pleaded, 'Let him go. Please, he's just a boy.'

'Yes, he is,' Falk said icily. 'So listen carefully if you ever want to see him alive again. I want you to get Ilona Frei, and I want you to bring her to me. You and Ilona. No one else. If you do bring someone else, anyone else, I will cut your son's throat, ear to ear, just the way I used to bleed out hogs for my father.

'Do you understand?'

Mattie glanced at Burkhart, who had gone cold and hard at the wheel, slowing, looking for a place to stop. Ilona Frei softly whimpered in the backseat. Burkhart looked at Ilona, pressed his finger to his lips, and nodded to Mattie.

'All right,' Mattie said shakily. 'Where do you want me to bring her?'

'Where any mother might have looked for a lost child in the last days of the East German Republic,' Falk snarled. 'You have ninety minutes to get here or your boy dies.'

'That's not enough—'

'It's what you've got,' Falk said and hung up.

Chapter 120

Racing south as the storm threatened, Mattie stared into the darkness, doing everything in her power not to collapse.

In the backseat, Ilona Frei was turning hysterical. 'You're not going to let him have me, are you? You wouldn't trade me for your son, would you?'

For a second Mattie was so stunned at the question that she did not know what to say, but then she shook her head. 'No. No, of course not.'

'Call the police,' Ilona pleaded.

'That could get Niklas killed,' Burkhart said.

'Then call your friends at Private!'

With Falk's warning about bringing anyone else along still ringing in her ears, she looked to Burkhart and said: 'You're the hostage rescuer. What do we do?'

'Is there specialized gear in the trunk?'

'Yes, it's Private's car.'

'Give me the particulars.'

Mattie struggled to think. 'Two bulletproof vests. One 9 mm Heckler and Koch automatic assault rifle. Two twenty-shot magazines in 9 mm.'

'Night vision?' he asked.

'A scope.'

'No goggles.'

'Just the scope.'

'Radios? Cameras?'

'Two earbuds with Bluetooth mics, and two

fiber-optic units.'

'Can they feed wireless to a website?'

'Private Berlin's.'

'So I could access a feed from my phone?'

'If coverage is good.'

'Describe the layout of the orphanage.'

Between Mattie and Ilona they gave it to him. The front entry. The offices on the immediate right. The kitchen. The dining hall. The staircase. The rooms upstairs. The rotting floors. The caved-in roof.

'Is there a rear entrance?' Burkhart asked.

Ilona said there were three: one at the kitchen, and two others at either end of the building that led to back staircases to the upper floors.

They passed Halle and headed east. With every mile, Mattie felt more and more on the verge of a nervous breakdown. First her mother. Then Chris. And now Niklas? Though she considered herself spiritual, Mattie was not by nature religious.

Still, as they got closer and closer to the ruins of Waisenhaus 44, she found herself praying to God to save her son. He was only a boy. Nine years old. Her little boy. Her most precious gift.

Chapter 121

Burkhart's first plan called for Ilona Frei to remain behind in the car and call Private and Berlin Kripo while he and Mattie made a rescue attempt.

'But he'll kill Niklas if I'm not there,' Ilona said.

'I'll tell him I couldn't find you,' Mattie replied. 'He only gave us ninety minutes. You'll stay in the car. Let Burkhart and me handle it.'

Ilona chewed on her knuckle in the backseat. Then she shook her head.

'No. I won't do that. I've spent my life running from him. It's driven me insane on more than one occasion. If I'm going to have any hope of a life, I have to face him, tell him what I think of him, what he did to me, and the others. And then, honestly, I'd like to see him die.'

'New plan then,' Burkhart said as he slowed to a stop about a mile from the orphanage. 'We get suited up, and then five hundred yards shy of the place, you let me out. You two park on the road, go up the drive and in the front. I'll follow through the woods and circle round the back.'

They got out and took the tactical gear from the trunk. Mattie and Ilona Frei put on the bulletproof vests under their jackets.

'You'll be unprotected, Burkhart,' Mattie said.

'But unseen,' Burkhart replied, pulling out the H&K rifle and night-vision scope. 'This guy doesn't know what one invisible man can do to another.'

Mattie clipped the tiny fiber-optic camera through the buttonhole on her lapel. She did the same with Ilona.

'Bury the bud,' Burkhart said. 'The mic, too.'

Mattie pushed the bud deep into her ear and slipped the mic under her wristwatch before climbing in the driver's seat with Ilona as front passenger and Burkhart in the rear.

'We should call Private,' Mattie said.

Burkhart dialed Jack Morgan's number and explained what was happening. Morgan was furious that they had not contacted him or Kripo earlier.

'We're trying to save my son's life, Jack,' Mattie insisted.

'We're heading to the airport,' Morgan said. 'We're renting a helicopter.'

'No,' Burkhart said. 'Not unless you can land a mile away. He's smart. He'll know we've called in backup if he hears a chopper.'

'I'll call Dietrich,' Morgan replied and hung up.

Mattie put the car in gear and drove. A few silent moments later, rain began to spatter the windows. Lightning flashed in the distance, but it was enough to reveal the blades of the huge wind turbines spinning in the breeze.

'It's right up ahead on the left,' she said. 'Five hundred yards.'

'Ready?' Burkhart asked as she slowed to a stop.

'No.'

'Ilona?'

'Yes.' But her response was wrought with doubt and fear.

Mattie twisted in her seat when Burkhart opened the rear door.

'Please tell me Niklas's going to be okay.'

Burkhart put his giant hand on hers as the rain began to pour. 'He's going to be, Mattie. You just have to have faith.'

Chapter 122

Friends, fellow Berliners, I am standing by a big pine tree in the light rain just inside the woods northeast of the rear entrance to the orphanage. I am wet but more than pleased when I hear the crunch of tires as a car pulls off onto the shoulder out on the main road south of Waisenhaus 44.

A moment later I hear a car door open, but no dome light goes on inside. A second door opens. Still no light.

It makes me feel that my suspicions were justified. I slip around the back of the pine tree and press myself tightly to it, chilled to the bone, watching that rear entrance, figuring that this will be how the counterterrorism expert Burkhart will try to outflank me while Ilona Frei and Mattie Engel go through the front door.

They'll be scared shitless, I think, and my heart races.

A mother. A son. A ghost from my past. Their combined fear.

Once Burkhart is dealt with it will be like old times, I decide. One last celebration before I move on.

I stay frozen to the tree, waiting after they've gone. One minute. Two minutes. At three minutes, I'm starting to think I've overthought things and that I should be moving quickly into the orphanage before they can find Nick.

But at three minutes thirty seconds, I become aware of a change in the darkness in front of me. And then I see it, the subtle dim green glow of some sort of night-vision device.

I cling tighter to the tree, my pistol in my right hand, aimed toward the glow. But then I lose it. Gone.

I peer and peer and see nothing. I'm running out of time.

A twig snaps. I slide around the tree, moving the gun toward the sound.

I hear a low voice: 'Go in slow. Let him talk to you first.'

At thirty yards: a rectangular glow, much brighter.

He's looking at his cell phone.

Horrible time to be texting, I think, and shoot twice.

I hear both rounds hit flesh and bone, a gasp, a cough, and then a satisfying crash that's soon drowned by the rain pelting the woods.

Chapter 123

'Burkhart?' Mattie murmured into her mic as they approached the ruins of Waisenhaus 44. She'd heard him gasp and cough. Now all she could make out was static and rain transmitting through the bud.

'What is it?' Ilona whispered. 'What's wrong?'

For a second Mattie didn't know what to do.

That gasp. That cough.

And then it just didn't matter. Niklas was somewhere inside the ruins of the orphanage. She was going to bring him out of there alive.

Alive, she said to herself over and over as she got out her gun, and they climbed up onto the porch of the place. Mattie led Ilona through the busted front door past the entrance to what had been Hariat Ledwig's office.

When they reached the bottom of the staircase, Mattie called out, 'Falk!'

But they heard nothing but the rain and wind. They checked the dining room and the kitchen. Nothing.

They returned to the staircase, and again Mattie cried, 'Falk!'

'Drop the gun,' Falk said from the shadows. 'Toss it behind you.'

Mattie hesitated.

'Drop it if you ever want to see your son again.'

Mattie tossed the pistol back behind her. It clattered away.

'Flashlight too,' Falk said.

She complied, and then she saw her shadow and Ilona's on the risers of the old staircase as Falk shined her light on them.

'Climb,' he said, then made that clicking noise in his throat.

Ilona panicked at the sound and tried to make a run for it. But Falk grabbed her by the hair and yanked her off her feet. She began to shriek.

'Scream all you want,' Falk snarled. 'There's no one who can hear you. We're miles from nowhere and we have unfinished business.' He glared at

Mattie. 'Get upstairs. Your boy's waiting for you.'

Mattie climbed up into the darkness with Ilona moaning behind her. They reached the landing, and Falk directed them down the hall into a room, which faced the rear of the orphanage, looking out over farmland and woods.

His flashlight cut the room, and Mattie thought she saw rope hanging from the exposed beam, before the light focused on the floor.

Falk told them to kneel. When they had, he instructed them to take off their bulletproof vests and clasp their hands behind their heads. He was behind Mattie the entire time, and she never got a good look at his face. He put zip-tie restraints on their wrists and ankles, and then came around the front of them.

In the slanted light of the flashlights brightening the room, Mattie thought that Falk's face and head resembled a wig mannequin's. He was bald, had no eyebrows, and his skin was strangely smooth, with ears tightly pinned back. 'Don't think you're ever getting out of here, hmmm?' Falk said. 'Your friend, Burkhart, the big guy? I put two rounds in his chest. He's not going anywhere ever again.'

Mattie's heart plunged ten stories. Burkhart? Dead? In her mind she saw him making Eggs Burkhart earlier that morning, and laughing at one of Niklas's jokes.

She felt crazed with fear. 'Where's my son?' Mattie demanded.

Falk walked to a door in the corner of the room and pulled out Niklas, who was in restraints. Duct tape sealed his mouth.

'Nicky!' Mattie yelled.

Walleyed, Niklas started whining at his mother.

'Let him go!' Ilona Frei yelled. 'You've got me. You've got what you want!'

Falk laughed. 'And spoil my fun, Ilona? I think not.'

Chapter 124

My friends, fellow Berliners, I light the gas lantern I brought especially for this occasion.

'You remember the lanterns, don't you, Ilona?' I ask. 'The soft wavering light where we used to play in the slaughterhouse?'

Ilona looks hypnotized, staring at the lantern, her mouth stretching against some horror playing in her schizophrenic mind before the light inside her seems to click off. She turns her head and stares at the wall, humming a child's tune.

'You do remember,' I say and click my throat in approval.

Then I haul Mattie Engel to her feet, walk her backward, and tell her to kneel again, hands over her head. I feed a steel hook around the restraints. It's attached to a rope that runs through a pulley I've attached to the beam.

'Stand up,' I say and start pulling out the slack until her arms are stretched tight.

I come around her and smile.

'There,' I say. 'Now that is better, don't you think? Hmmm?'

'Let my son go,' she says. 'Please. He's innocent.'

'You two are like an old record,' I snap. 'If it didn't work for Ilona's mother, or Chris's mother, or any of the others, what makes you think it will work for you? What makes you so special?'

I cross the room to Niklas and tear the tape from his mouth.

Then I return to Mattie, get out a utility knife, and use its razor-sharp blade to slit off her blouse and bra.

When I'm done I display her proudly to her son, Niklas. Then I press the blade to her breast and leer at the boy. 'You love your mommy, don't you?'

Chapter 125

Niklas began to cry in pain and fear for Mattie. 'Why are you doing this?'

Mattie felt more than humiliated, her own shame magnified by Niklas's, and she understood why Falk's methods had garnered confessions. She looked him up and down, spotted the excitement in Falk's face, and the bulge in his slacks, and remembered what Genevieve the sex worker had told her.

Mattie turned livid and shouted, 'Don't show him anything, Niklas. He wants to see your fear. Don't give it to him. No matter what happens. Don't.'

Niklas hesitated, but then clamped his jaw tight and stared back at his mother, nodding with wide and glassy eyes.

My brave, brave little boy, Mattie thought. Falk's joy faded. He twisted his lips at Mattie as if she'd spoiled his fun. Then he shrugged.

'That's okay. I enjoy pain, too.'

He went around behind her and pulled hard on the rope.

The plastic restraints sawed into Mattie's wrists and her shoulders popped as she was lifted off the floor.

The restraints cut her. She felt like her arms were going to dislocate from their sockets.

Mattie had never known such agony. She bit her lip not to scream, doing everything in her power not to show her pain. But finally, as if it were coming from another person, she heard an uncontrolled howl of rage burst from her throat.

When Falk came around in front of her, his eyes were lit up like a kid's at an amusement park.

Mattie refused to look at him. Instead, she focused on Niklas, who was backed up against the wall, shaking and crying but trying to stop. 'Mom.'

Mattie did not reply. Instead she took the rage burning in her and channeled it.

She arched and kicked at Falk. The tips of her shoes just missed his groin but hit him hard in his upper thigh.

He was somewhat shocked before he laughed with delight. 'You're only the second one to ever try that. Didn't work the first time, either.'

Kicking at him had only damaged her wrists

more. The pain was excruciating. She saw black spots dance before her eyes and thought she was going to pass out.

But then Falk went around behind her, released the rope, and lowered her until she stood on the floor, hands snugged up toward the beam.

'Mom, you're bleeding!' Niklas cried.

Dazed, Mattie looked up. Blood trickled and oozed from her wounds.

When Falk came back around to face her, Mattie gasped, 'You did this to the mothers at the slaughterhouse? Hanging them on meat hooks?'

'Got to have some way to move a carcass around.'

'I'm not a carcass.'

'You will be, soon enough.'

He gestured with the knife toward Niklas and then pressed the tip against her rib cage, just below her breast. 'That's how they'll find you, your son, and Ilona. Hanging like carcasses.'

Chapter 126

Dear friends, I must admit I'm enjoying myself, especially because the drumming of rain on the orphanage has become a comfort, deadening everything, focusing everything on the delights of my final interlude: a mother, a son, an old friend, the anticipation of death.

But then I check my watch and say, 'When exactly do you think *they* will be here?'

'Who?' Mattie asks.

I put on one of the bulletproof vests, replying, 'Whoever you called to come and rescue you.'

'We called no one. We did what you told us; now let us go.'

'Liar,' I say. 'You brought big Herr Burkhart when I told you not to. So you must have told someone else what was going on.'

'We didn't,' Mattie says. 'I'm telling you we didn't.'

I stare at her for several long moments.

I suppose it's possible. But highly unlikely. I check my watch again.

She's been out of her car for roughly twenty minutes. I've got at least twenty more to play before clearing the premises.

But I want to be sure, and quickly.

I go to my pack and find a device I picked up just the other day.

I turn around with it in my hand, the tip just showing. I wave it at her.

'What is that?' she says.

'It's too bad we don't have much time,' I say. 'I do so like to let these things unfold at their leisure.'

Mattie starts to squirm and it makes me excited. She has no idea what I've got. Isn't that the big, big fear? The unknown? Human brains can't handle the unknown. Do you know why?

Because their imagination always comes up with something worse.

At last, I open my hand and show her the device.

'It was developed for mountaineers who needed to light fires in high winds,' I say. 'They call it a pocket torch. I bought it last week. Handy.'

I click on the starter. There's a snapping noise and then a thin, intense flame bursts from a tube.

'Twenty-four hundred degrees,' I say, enjoying the terror flaring in Mattie's face. 'The fear of it is primal, isn't it? Fire? You know, I've always found that when all else fails, the fear of having an eye melted usually makes people talk.'

Chapter 127

Thunder broke within several hundred yards of the orphanage, and the lightning flash made the room brighter than day, but all Mattie could see was that evil flame hissing out the nozzle of the pocket torch.

'No!' Niklas screamed. 'Don't! Please!'

Time seemed to slow for Mattie. She was acutely aware of Falk drifting behind her right side where she could not kick at him. She gritted her teeth and twisted her head.

Then, like a delirious whisper coming from another dimension, she heard Burkhart talking in her ear.

'Engel. Mattie. I've been hit twice out behind the orphanage. Left forearm through and through. Tourniqueted. Left thigh. Broken femur. I've got a belt on it too. I can't find my cell phone because I can't move, Mattie. I can't come for you and Ilona and Niklas.'

Burkhart began to choke bitterly. *'I can't save you.'*

331

He got hold of himself. *'If you can hear me, don't give up. Prolong whatever nightmare he's taken you into. Fight. There are people who love you, Mattie. I … I love you. You're beautiful. And brave. And smart. And tough. And your kid is the greatest. Keep fighting until they can get to you. Keep fighting.'*

Falk grabbed Mattie's chin and twisted her head toward him. She saw the flame, orange and red, and shaped like a fine chisel.

It passed her ear, singed her hair, and then stroked her shoulder blade.

The pain was indescribable. Mattie jerked away from it. She screamed, and screamed again.

'Mom!' Niklas was hysterical, up on his knees blubbering. 'Mommy!'

'I'll ask you once more,' Falk said. 'Who's coming? And when?'

Mattie was shaking and on the verge of vomiting from the smell of her own burned flesh, and from the agony she saw painted on her son's face.

She heard Burkhart's voice, telling her to fight.

'We called Berlin police before we came in,' she gasped. 'They're coming. No matter what you do to us, they are going to catch you this time, Falk.'

There was a moment of doubt on Falk's face, but then he grinned. 'Oh, I'll get away. I always do. They'll probably call Halle Kripo, but they're twenty-five minutes away at least. Still, I'll have to move up my time schedule.'

He went to his bag and got out a flathead screwdriver.

Deep in her haze of pain, Mattie still knew what that meant.

'Delay,' Burkhart whispered in her ear. *'Delay.'*

Falk took a step toward Ilona, who was still on her knees and facing the wall and humming like a child.

'How did you do it the first time?' Mattie gasped. 'How did you get your Stasi files and destroy them? How did you get away?'

Chapter 128

My fellow Berliners, at her question, I pause, wanting to ignore her, to finish my business and then leave this place for good.

But a part of me wants someone, anyone, to know of my genius. It's irresistible. And besides. When I set to my work, I am quick and efficient like my father taught me.

'It was relatively easy,' I tell her. 'By the mid-1980s, I could see clearly that the GDR's time was coming to an end. I could also see that my special talents would not be understood if that came to pass. So I set about erasing myself almost three years before the wall fell.'

'How?'

'A bribe to the right people. A threat to the right people. I got hold of my files, which I burned. I knew Mielke was already shredding everything to do with me. So then it was just a matter of waiting until things became destabilized enough. Once I heard about the storming of Stasi headquarters in Leipzig, I knew the time was right. I went out into the streets of

East Berlin like everyone else. And watched while they knocked the wall down with sledgehammers and cranes. When the crowds surged through in both directions, I went west with fake papers, and soon disappeared to Africa.'

I gesture proudly to my face. 'That's where all this was done. Almost a year of work. No one would ever know I was Matthias Falk.'

I grip the screwdriver and half turn toward Ilona.

'And the masks?' Mattie asks.

I can't resist. 'A childhood interest long dormant. I found a mask there, in Africa,' I reply. 'I began collecting them while I was recuperating. A passion turned into a business.'

'How did you fund all this? Where did the money come from?'

I grin. 'That was the first thing that I tortured out of the mothers. I got them to tell me where their family money, jewelry, and silverware were hidden. I had more than enough to do what I had to do. So three years after the wall came down, I flew back to Berlin and started my gallery.'

'And Ilse Frei?'

Ilona Frei stops humming.

'Ahhh, Christoph and Ilse,' I say, truly enjoying the moment. 'In the FKK, Ilse recognized my voice. I saw it in her face the moment it happened. I had to take care of her.'

'And Chris?'

'He managed to track me back to Berlin by going to the FKK clubs in the city, asking about a man with masks. No one talked, except one of my regulars, who told me. I told her to tell Chris

334

about me, and the shop. Once I knew he was on my tail, I led him to the slaughterhouse and ambushed him. I knew he'd be upset being there, not thinking correctly, especially after seeing the rats on Ilse in the subbasement.'

Ilona starts to sob, and my empathetic side understands.

'You didn't know, Ilona?' I say, feeding on her pain. 'Oh, yes, it's true, your dear little sister is gone. And now, so are you.'

I take two steps and grab her by her hair and wrench it upward, revealing the nape of her neck.

Ilona's making these squealing noises like a piglet going to slaughter.

I cock my arm and prepare to drive the screwdriver up into her little piggy brain.

Chapter 129

'Stop right there!' a male voice shouted from behind Mattie. 'Drop it and her or by God I'll blow your head off.'

Falk froze and looked back. Mattie twisted around.

Darek Eberhardt, the farmer who was tilling the fields by Waisenhaus 44 when Mattie first came to the orphanage, was standing in the doorway and looking over the brace of his double-barreled shotgun.

'Drop it!' Eberhardt repeated. 'I know how to use this weapon, mister!'

Falk let go of Ilona and dropped the screw-driver.

'Get on the floor,' Mattie shouted at Falk. 'Face fucking down! Hands where he can see them!'

Falk looked at Mattie in shock, disbelief, and then sullen resentment as he lowered himself to the floor.

Horrified, Eberhardt came around Mattie. 'My God, what's he done to you?'

'He's got a gun,' Mattie said. 'It's over there. And a pocket torch too.'

She was watching Falk, who lay on the floor with his fingers entwined behind his head. His body was tense and alert.

'Got them,' Eberhardt said, and she watched him toss the pistol and the torch out the window.

'Please, Herr Eberhardt,' Mattie said. 'Cut me down. Get us free.'

Eberhardt pulled out a knife and sliced the restraints from Mattie's wrists, the pain almost as bad as fire. Eberhardt set down the shotgun, shrugged off his raincoat, and gave it to her to cover herself.

'Thank you,' she said as Eberhardt went to free Niklas.

She felt dizzy, as if she might faint, then surged with joy at seeing Niklas cut free. He got up and rushed into her arms. 'Mommy,' he sobbed.

Mattie bear-hugged Niklas to her, tears stream-ing down her cheeks as she kissed the top of his head. 'I'm so, so sorry you had to–'

'I thought he was going to kill us.'

'No, no, baby,' Mattie whispered. 'Not today.'

Eberhardt freed Ilona and helped her to her

feet. She moved drunkenly when she asked Mattie, 'Did you see her in the slaughterhouse basement? Ilse?'

Mattie felt gutted. 'I couldn't tell you. I just didn't have the heart to do it.'

'I had hope,' Ilona said in a little-girl voice. 'And now...'

She wheeled around and kicked viciously at Falk, hitting him in the ribs.

'You fucking sick bastard!' she screamed, going into meltdown. 'You killed Ilse and Chris and Greta.' She kicked him again. 'You killed our mothers. You made them confess to things they never did. Why?'

Mattie grabbed her and pulled her away as she continued to shriek.

Chapter 130

Lying there on the floor, I can't help my hard wiring. I'm feeling the kicks Ilona gave me and I'm loving the painful throb.

And I'm hearing the pain in her voice and am loving life all the more.

'Why?' I say with a grin. 'Because I like it, Ilona. I like to be there when the lights go out. And I like making them go out even more. I like to be there when the life drains out of 'em. I like to feel, smell, taste, and hear death. It's as simple as that. Always has been. Cow, pig, mother, child. It's all the same to me.'

The farmer is circling to my left. I can see his rubber boots in my peripheral vision. 'What kind of animal are you?' he demands.

'A predator,' I reply. 'Didn't you know? Killing is in our nature.'

Eberhardt takes a step toward me, as if he is going to kick me too.

But then over the sound of the rain, I hear sirens in the distance. The farmer stops. He hears them too.

He takes several careful steps backward away from me.

Cracking, splintering, the floor beneath his left rubber boot collapses.

He breaks through up to his thigh and is wrenched violently backward.

I'm up and moving even before I realize he's dropped the shotgun.

I take two quick steps and kick him right on the point of the chin.

Eberhardt's head snaps back, out cold. I spin, looking for Mattie.

But she's already on me.

She smashes me in the ribs with a piece of wood. It stuns me. I go to my knees. She steps up to hit me again.

But I drop into a sitting position and lash out with my foot, connecting with her ankle.

She buckles and falls.

I roll to my feet and kick her in the stomach. I hear all the wind go out of her.

The sirens are closer now. I can hear them wailing.

I look at Mattie Engel. 'Time for just one more,

338

I'd say.'

I can see she doesn't understand.

But then I grab little Nicky by the neck.

I lift him, choking, and drag him back toward my screwdriver lying there on the floor. I throw him down. I grab the tool and then headlock the screaming little boy, exposing his neck as if it were a lamb's.

I look at Mattie, who's struggling to get up. She can't even talk.

'Show me your eyes,' I shout. 'I want to see them when Niklas's go dark.'

'Falk!' Ilona screeches behind me and to my left.

I look over my shoulder and see her, a ghost from my past, sweating, hair crazed, holding Eberhardt's shotgun.

Chapter 131

Falk looked at Ilona in amusement.

'My dear old friend Ilona, this isn't in you,' he began, turning toward her as Niklas scrambled away.

'It is in me!' Ilona screamed at him. 'It was in Chris and Ilse and Artur and Greta and Kiefer. And all of them are in me now. They're in me, Falk! I can hear them calling to me. Every one of them.'

'Don't!' Mattie cried.

But Ilona yanked the trigger.

Twelve-gauge buckshot hit Falk and hurled him backward. He slammed off the wall and slid down, bleeding only slightly from his wounds to his face and neck.

Falk looked down at the bulletproof vest, which had taken the brunt of the blast. He started to laugh. 'Don't you know? You can't kill what you can't see?'

He looked up at Ilona, who now stood at point-blank range, aiming at his face. 'What are you going to do?' he asked, his amusement deepening. 'Shoot me in cold blood, become a person like me? Go to jail because of me?'

Ilona appeared on the verge of dissolving. Mattie thought to try to wrestle the gun from her. But then Ilona laughed with bitter delight, and called to Falk the way a mother might to a child.

'I'm insane, remember? No one would ever convict me. Lights-out time, Falk. Lights out for you. Forever.'

'My friend,' Falk began in a begging tone. 'My, my fellow Berliner...'

Sirens came into the orphanage yard. Blue and red lights flashed through the open windows. And Mattie caught a split second of Falk stripped of disguise, a naughty little boy caught red-handed, before Ilona's shotgun roared.

Epilogue

A BEAUTIFUL CITY OF SCARS

Chapter 132

Three months later, just before Christmas, in memory of Chris Schneider and the other victims of Matthias Falk, the employees of Private Berlin and friends gathered at Gethsemane Church in the Prenzlauer Berg neighborhood of East Berlin.

In 1989, the church had been a center of the opposition, and Mattie had felt it appropriate that the last victims of the Stasi be memorialized there.

There were blown-up pictures of Chris and the others arrayed in a semicircle at the front of the church.

Jack Morgan was one of the mourners. He sat with Mattie and Niklas, who held Socrates in his lap. Aunt Cäcilia, who'd been found knocked out and tied up in their apartment, told Niklas to stop fidgeting.

Behind them, Ilona Frei sat with Gerhardt Krainer, who'd testified so courageously on her behalf at the public inquest.

Inspector Weigel and High Commissar Dietrich, who was still serving his suspension, were across the aisle. Behind them, and in the aisle in a wheelchair, Hariat Ledwig dabbed at her eyes, looking at the photographs of the people the children of Waisenhaus 44 had become.

Just before the service began, an older, bent-over man in a dark suit entered the church in a

343

slow shuffle and sat several rows back by himself, his hands resting on a cane.

The minister began the simple ceremony talking of the burdens some are called to endure in life, and spoke of the victims of Matthias Falk as innocent heroes forced to confront the deepest madness of the East German Republic.

Then, one by one mourners rose to talk. Morgan spoke once again about how great and fearless an investigator Christoph Schneider was, one of the best Private had ever seen.

Daniel Brecht talked of Chris's courage and crazy sense of humor. Dr. Gabriel spoke of Chris's professionalism and his refusal to be compromised, calling him the younger brother he never had.

Katharina Doruk recalled Chris's true happiness with Mattie and Niklas.

Ilona Frei stood shakily and said, 'Chris died trying to save my sister and trying to avenge the children of Waisenhaus 44. I'll never forget him. Nor will I forget the other orphans who died at Falk's hands. As horrible as it was, because of them, I feel like I got my sanity back.'

At last it was Mattie's turn to stand and express her feelings.

Chapter 133

For a second, Mattie did not know if she could do it, but then she looked down at Niklas and found renewed strength.

She got up and described the first time she and Chris met. She made the mourners laugh at his awkwardness when he'd asked her out on their first date. She told them about the joy that surrounded her when he asked her to marry him.

Then a somber expression came to her face, and she talked about the emptiness she always felt in him, the dark, hollow part. She also talked about the reaction to the whole story coming out in the press: the slaughterhouse, the bodies, the orphans, the murders, and Falk's Stasi past.

'Over twenty years have passed since the wall fell, and what happened here in East Berlin has not left many of us,' she said. 'People say we should forget what the secret police did to their fellow citizens. They say we should forget the culture of paranoia and brutality it promoted. They say we should forget what happened to people like Chris and Ilse and you, Ilona. We should move on, they say. Move on.'

Tears welled in Mattie's eyes. 'Yes, we should move on. Life is for the living. But we can't forget that people like Matthias Falk existed and thrived in a darker world we only left behind two decades ago. And most of all, we can't forget the good people Falk destroyed. They were real. They laughed and cried and cared for each other. They were children and mothers and fathers, and brothers and sisters and wives and ... lovers.'

For a second, Mattie felt her entire body trembling with loss, but then, with a bittersweet smile, she pointed in the direction of the old man with the cane.

'In that vein, I'd like to introduce August Wolfe,' she said. 'For the past eighteen years, Herr Wolfe has been a professor of literature at the University of Leipzig. For fifteen years before he took that position, he was in and out of Stasi prisons and torture chambers because of positions he took in the mid-1970s regarding the secret police and intellectual freedom.'

Mattie walked down the aisle and extended her hand. The old man took it and struggled to his feet. Mattie patted his arm and told the mourners, 'This is also Chris's father.'

For a moment, there was stunned silence.

Finally, High Commissar Dietrich began to clap. And then everyone was on their feet and clapping.

Chris's father was overcome for several moments.

Then in the sure voice of a professor, he said, 'I thought Chris had died with my wife thirty years ago. It's what I was told happened, and there were no records. I had come to peace with my loss ten years before the wall fell.' He shook his head. 'And then to hear that Chris lived and became a good man?' He shook his head again, tears streaming down his face. 'It's almost too much to bear.

'When Mattie found me last week, and told me, I didn't believe her at first,' he went on. 'And then I became very bitter at the fact that I hadn't just lost an eight-year-old boy, I'd lost the man he'd become.'

He sighed. 'But now, listening to you all describe him.' He choked. 'It was a great, great help to me, an easing of my heartache. I want to thank you for being his friends all these years. Thank you from the bottom of my soul for what you all did to help my son and avenge his death.'

Chapter 134

There wasn't a dry eye in Gethsemane Church when Mattie threw her arms around August Wolfe.

When she broke from his embrace, she looked around and said, 'I know this is a house of God. But those of us who knew Chris well knew that he loved beer. We have it and plenty of his favorite foods at a restaurant down the street. Let's no longer talk of Chris's death or the death of any of Falk's victims. Instead I invite you to raise a glass to them and tell more stories about them and keep them alive in our hearts.'

The minister ended the ceremony and the mourners began to file out.

Morgan went to Chris's father, introduced himself, and offered to help the older man outside. Doruk wheeled Frau Ledwig.

Mattie trailed Brecht and Dr. Gabriel, with one hand on Niklas's shoulder, and the other holding Aunt Cäcilia's hand.

When they reached the rear of the church off the lobby, she told her son and aunt to go on ahead. She'd be right out. They smiled knowingly and left.

Mattie turned and looked at Tom Burkhart, who leaned against the back wall of the church on crutches. His left forearm was wrapped in a bandage. His left leg was casted hip to ankle.

'Did I do good?' she asked. 'Did I do Chris justice?'

'You did better than good,' Burkhart replied. 'You had me bawling back here. Me!'

Mattie smiled. 'You're deeper than you let on, Burkhart.'

'Don't tell anyone. It'll screw up my image.'

She gazed at him for a long moment. 'Did you know you were transmitting that night at Waisenhaus 44?'

Burkhart was genuinely puzzled. 'Transmitting?'

'I could hear you talking to me after Falk shot you.' She paused. 'I heard everything you said to me, Tom.'

Burkhart's eyebrows knitted and he looked away, flushing. 'That right? Everything?'

'Every single word,' Mattie said and smiled again.

Burkhart grinned back at her. 'So?'

Mattie put her hand on his. 'So we move on, Burkhart. But we go slowly. Like so many Berliners, we've still got a lot of healing to do.'

348

Acknowledgments

We would like to thank the Berliners, native and adopted, who patiently took us through the city and helped us to understand its loss, its triumphs, and its living scars. A great thanks goes to Claudia Elitok with the Berlin Kriminalpolizei for her time and candid insight regarding homicide investigations before and after the fall of the Berlin Wall. Guide Philipp Stratmann was a world of information about all things Berlin, from architecture to squatters to slaughterhouses. He also helped us grasp the terror of the divided city, and to appreciate the amazing courage of the people who fought to end that terror. We are grateful to Fulbright Scholar Nicholas Sullivan, who helped us negotiate the labyrinth of the German Federal Archives. Thanks go as well to mountain bike guide Carissa Champlin, who led us along the ruins of the wall and into Treptower Park, dramatically altering the dimensions of this story.

Berlin primitive mask expert Peter Beller was kind enough to let us tour his shop and patiently answered our questions.

Any mistakes or mischaracterizations of time, place, or events are our own.

The publishers hope that this book has given you enjoyable reading. Large Print Books are especially designed to be as easy to see and hold as possible. If you wish a complete list of our books please ask at your local library or write directly to:

Magna Large Print Books
Magna House, Long Preston,
Skipton, North Yorkshire.
BD23 4ND

This Large Print Book for the partially sighted, who cannot read normal print, is published under the auspices of

THE ULVERSCROFT FOUNDATION